THE OTHER SIDE OF MIDNIGHT

GEORGIA LE CARRE

ACKNOWLEDGMENTS

Much love and many thanks to:

Elizabeth Burns
Nichola Rhead
Brittany Urbaniak
Kirstine Moran
Tracy Gray

AUTHOR'S NOTE

Hello dearest reader of mine,

As you probably know I love delivering stories with an unpredictable turn or twist.

This book has an unexpected storyline written specially for those who adore surprises.

If you are that person, then I am honored to welcome you into the extraordinary world of Count Rocco Rossetti.

Love,

Georgia xx

CHAPTER 1

AUTUMN

I t's just struck midnight, but I've no thoughts yet of leaving the backroom in the art shop where I double as Larry's shop assistant and cleaner, and going home. I sneaked back in here after dinner to work on my little painting, but I've become so totally engrossed in it, I could be here for hours more.

I know most artists prefer working in daylight. Not me. I love creating things long after everyone else is tucked up in their beds and the air is shimmering with all their dreams.

I load my brush with the precious oil paints that take up a great proportion of my wages and let it glide effortlessly across the canvass. Almost as if it has a will of its own. I'm still a student with much to learn, but I have to admit my painting is starting to look good. Exceptionally good. Maybe because this painting is special… important.

Well, at least to me, it is.

I take a few steps back to gaze critically at my canvas. It's a strange scene. An old, crumbling, ivy covered castle built into the side of a snow-capped mountain. A road, so narrow only a horse driven carriage could fit, leads up to the fortress. I'm tempted to add a carriage and snorting black horses onto the road, but I'm afraid I'll spoil the painting.

It's important I don't ruin it since I've attempted to paint this scene countless times, but always had to give up after a few strokes. I knew instinctively I can't capture the vivid image in my mind, and something deep inside me demanded I replicate it exactly as it lived in my mind. I can't understand why I had to, I just knew I did.

I start moving forward to add more color to the castle, when I freeze. The skin at the back of my neck is prickling and goose pimples are rising up on my arms. The silence is undisturbed, but the air is different.

My heart slams into my rib cage as I swing my head around and look through the half-open door into the small show-room beyond. All the lamps are turned off, but from the light of the streetlamps I can see right through to the rusty little bells attached to the door. I've been so lost in my work I've not heard them ring, but I know.

Someone has entered the shop!

It can't be a customer at this time of the night, and I know it is not Larry. He would have called out. It is either one of the wild kids in town up to no good, or a robber. Dad sent me for karate classes when I was in high school and I know some good moves. I can definitely handle any kid, and probably even a robber, if he isn't carrying a gun.

But I have an even better idea.

I reach for a stained rag on the wooden trolley next to me and hurriedly wipe off as much paint from my hands so it won't be slippery and tip toe over to the cupboard. I throw the cloth on the floor and pick up the baseball bat next to the cupboard. Gripping the smooth solid wood tightly with both hands, I start to move stealthily towards the door. I'll be damned if I'm going to be cowed by any intruder.

My heart is beating so fast, my blood roars in my ears. I'm ready to swing the bat hard at the slightest provocation… until I trip on the temporary plastic covering Larry placed over some wires he ran across the room just until the electrician came on Monday.

I've bumped my foot against the plastic a few times, but always managed to regain my balance. Not this time. This time the damn thing finally gets me. I feel myself pitch forward. My hands instinctively let go of the bat and fling out to try and grab on to anything that would break my fall, but I only connect with the trolley full of paint tubes and a jar of turpentine filled brushes.

Grasping for the trolley is a big mistake. Not only does it not stop my fall, it accelerates it. The trolley shoots a few feet forward, until it collides with an immovable object, then both the trolley and I crash to the concrete floor in an almighty racket.

The breath is knocked out of me as my back slams onto the floor and paint tubes bounce off me and the jar hits my chest and spills out its contents. I can feel the pungent turpentine seeping into my clothes and reaching my skin.

"Shit," I curse, as I lie there a winded, bruised, stained mess.

Then, I become aware there is someone else in the room with me. I turn my head and see a pair of highly polished black shoes a few feet away from me. My shocked eyes travel upwards and my brain notes how immaculate the creases in

3

his black trousers are. The material is smooth, expensive. He is wearing a long black coat that looks luxuriously soft, the way good cashmere does.

A belt with a custom insignia on the buckle. A two-headed eagle or a phoenix perhaps.

My gaze travels further upwards. Flat stomach. Black turtle-neck sweater. Pale skin, blond hair, sensual mouth, strong jaw, narrow nose and...

Suddenly, my eyes lock with the stranger's, and something shifts inside of me.

I hold my breath without even realizing it. As I stare into those translucent icy blue irises full of mysteries. Time stops. It isn't the way romance books describe it. The rest of the world doesn't drop away. Instead those eyes reach into my soul and whirl me away into another world. It's like a sense of déjà vu as if I've once danced in the snow with this man while a full orchestra played just for us.

I think of steel hardened by fire and feel strong sexual desire for him flower in my belly, but I just can't explain why I would feel that. He is sooooo not my type. I'm contemptuous of arrogant rich men who believe they can buy anything with their money. And there is no doubt he is such a man. I can tell by the curve of his mouth. Nothing has been denied this man. Ever.

For he is like a marvelous piece of art. His pale beauty and gold hair have a strange... darkness to them that immediately makes you wary, but is at the same time so magnetic, so fascinating, you can't look away, you want in. And all you can do is stand there, or in my case, lie there and stare stupidly.

"Are you alright?" he asks. His voice has a hypnotic quality, smooth as honey dripping from a spoon, but laced with a powerful note of authority.

I want to hear him speak again.

He takes another step towards me and bends slightly from his great height to hold a hand out to me. At the moment, I realize something else about him. He is clean. Immaculately clean. Not a blonde hair out of place, not a speck of dust on his expensive clothes, his nails are beautifully manicured, and his skin is so clear and blemish free it is as if he is one of those Gods from Mount Olympus who used to occasionally step down to earth to mate with human women.

I feel my hackles rise.

I do not like this man at all.

I know wholeheartedly, instinctively, definitely.

He is dangerous to me.

CHAPTER 2

AUTUMN

https://www.youtube.com/watch?v=8AHCfZTRGiI
-Hurt-

The smell of turpentine is overpowering, but I can still smell her. She wears no perfume. Just the clean, honest scent of her sweat. I don't let it show on my face, but being this close to her actually makes the blood course through my veins with a deafening force. And the mixture of lust and excitement is almost crippling. All that I thought was dead has come alive again.

I see all kinds of emotions rush across her face. Shock, confusion, surprise, sexual attraction, and finally dislike. Dislike so intense it is closer to hate. I can see she is going to run with that emotion.

Ignoring my outstretched hand, she scrambles to her feet. I retract my hand and watch her put as much space between us as the cluttered area will allow.

"How did you get in here?" she demands aggressively.

I stroll away from her. "You left the door unlocked."

"There's a CLOSED sign on the door," she snaps.

"Is there?" I ask mildly.

"Yes, there is. We're closed. If you want to buy anything you must come back tomorrow. We open again at 10.00 a.m."

She stares at me uneasily. She has convinced herself she hates my guts, but she is trembling, trembling with the same irrational lust I have throbbing in my body. I understand her perfectly. Hate is easy. All the other options terrify her.

"I have to go away in the morning, but I've seen something in the shop I want. Would you be so kind as to put it away for me? Tell Larry to charge it to my account, and I'll send someone around to pick it up on Thursday."

She frowns, immediately suspicious. "Which painting is it?"

"*Miranda Taking a Bath*."

"Oh," she says covering her hand over her mouth. The action serves only to smear more paint on her cheek. My eyes linger on the soft curve.

She drops her hand in confusion. "Of course, I'll put it away for you."

Now that I've established I'm a valuable customer willing to buy the most expensive painting in the premises, I start to walk towards the painting on the easel. But she rushes quickly to stand in front of it and block it from my gaze.

"Ignore this," she mutters uncomfortably. "It's just something I'm working on. Uh, please come out to the shop floor with me. This area is staff only."

"What are you creating?" I ask softly.

"Oh… uh. It's nothing. I'm just a student… playing around."

"Let me see it," I say softly as I stare into her warm hazel eyes. They are full of golden flecks. I let her drown in my gaze until, unable to resist, she moves aside.

The raw beauty of her work takes my breath away. I take in the white squiggles that are supposed to be seagulls flying high over the abandoned castle, the pieces of rock that are falling from the castle rampart. I feel such a sense of loss I want to reach out and touch the wet paint, but I don't. I'm careful to keep my expression neutral and totally veiled, as I drink in her creation. Seconds pass. The air is so quiet I can hear her heart hammering fast and loud in her chest.

I tear my gaze away from the painting and turn to her. "I want it."

Her eyes widen with astonishment. "What?"

"I'd like to buy your painting."

She shakes her head. "It's… it's not for sale."

"I'll give you one hundred thousand for it."

This time her jaw drops with disbelief. "What?"

"Or… name your price."

The shock is replaced by white hot temper. It makes her eyes turn a luminous green. The gold flecks become sparks of bright light. Entranced by her wild beauty, I wait for her passionate outburst eagerly, but she takes a shuddering breath and takes control of herself. I bought the most expensive item in the shop, after all.

"How do I explain this? The paintings for sale are all out on the floor. This piece is not even finished."

I take my wallet out of my coat pocket, count out ten bills, and put it on the old wooden bench. "Here's a thousand. The rest when you finish it."

I can see she is hopelessly poor and cannot help being drawn to the money, but her throat moves as she swallows hard, and stops herself from saying something rude.

"The painting is not for sale," she says through gritted teeth.

"Then take it as the deposit if you change your mind."

Her eyes flash. "I won't change my mind."

I smile slowly. "Keep it, anyway."

She folds her hands in front of her body defiantly. "Why would I want to keep your money?"

"Consider it a tip for fabulous service rendered," I murmur.

She inhales sharply. Even in her great anger she cannot fail to pick up on the sexual tension.

"Tell Larry, Rocco Rossetti called. And don't forget to lock the front door." Then I turn and walk away from her. There is a small smile on my face. You *will* be mine, Autumn DeLaney. Nothing and no one, not even you, will stop me.

CHAPTER 3

AUTUMN

I watch his back disappear into the gloom of the shop, then I hear the sound of the rusty bells twinkle as he pulls the door open. Then the door shuts quietly. Only then, can I jerk out of the trancelike state I am in. I run to the door and lock it. Then I lean my back against it and take deep gasping breaths.

What on earth is the matter with me?

The attraction is not mental. I feel hot and bothered and there is a strange fluttering in my stomach. I place my hand on my belly as I feel the wetness seeping out of me. I cannot believe the visceral reaction my body is displaying. My whole body is craving him. I stand there in the darkness, leaning against the door, breathing in and out until my body calms down.

Then I pull away from the door and walk back to the small back room. I feel strangely restless. Frowning, I pace the floor like a caged animal. Back and forth. Back and forth. I am aware something has happened to me, but I don't know what it is. All I know is I was a different person before the stranger walked into this shop.

I glance at the money lying on the ledge. Then I walk up to it. I pick up one bill and sniff it. The scent of new leather from his wallet fills my nostrils. Then underneath it, another scent floats up… him. Instantly, my heart starts racing. Who is he? Why does my body react to him in this way? I jerk the money away from me and put it back on the pile. I move away from it as if it is tainted or dangerous.

I turn away, walk to my painting, and look at it with new eyes. Yes, it's good. I know that, but it's not worth one hundred thousand dollars. Only a fool would pay that much for an unfinished work by a totally unknown artist, and there is no way in hell he is a fool. I clasp my hands tightly together.

What does he want with me?

Who are you, Rocco Rosetti?

I am no longer able to paint so I clean up the mess and put everything back into its place. Then I switch off the lights, lock up, and go out through the back door. I get on the purple bargain bicycle that I found on Craig's List for thirty five dollars, and ride through the silent town of Hunter's Cross to the trailer park where I live. My caravan faces a field that backs up to the woods. Almost all the caravans are in darkness, except for Mirabella's.

She is a wizened old gypsy and I think she makes her potions late into the night. Once or twice I've run into her selling her good luck charms in the supermarket car park. Once she winked at me and said, "There's a Prince waiting for ya, little one."

Yeah, sure he is, but I was afraid she was going to ask me to buy one of her charms so I just flashed her a polite smile and hurried away in the opposite direction.

I chain my bicycle to the metal railing outside my caravan and unlock my door. I switch on the lamp and everything feels strange. My cozy little home looks shabby and claustrophobic. I go into the bathroom and look in the mirror.

There is paint on my face and hair, and I look a terrible mess, but it is my eyes I am drawn to. I hardly recognize them as mine. They are very bright and my pupils are much larger than I've ever seen them. Shocked and confused, I quickly undress and shower. Under the cascade of warm water my hand strays between my thighs.

I cannot stop myself.

I close my eyes and circle my clit. I think of him, those magnetic blue eyes staring into mine as his fingers slip into me. "Autumn," that commanding voice calls, and I climax quickly with a hoarse grunt.

I pour shampoo on my palm and rub it into my hair. Then I bow my head and let the water pour over me. How strange. The throbbing need for him is still not gone. My body remains as unfulfilled and unsatisfied as it was before I masturbated. I know doing it again will not do the trick either. The only way to quench this… this intense hunger is to allow him into my body.

Something I'm never going to do.

I switch off the tap and get into my toweling robe. I should dry my hair, but I can't be bothered. A few steps later I'm in my tiny kitchen. I have no appetite, but I boil some water and make myself a bowl of ramen noodles. Then I settle on the battered couch and quietly slurp it down.

Afterwards, I pull my crane blanket over me, and think of him. Those eyes. As if he could look right through me and into my soul. I find my hand straying once more between my legs, but I stop myself. I should go to sleep, but I know I won't be able to. Not until I get him out of my mind.

I force myself to think of my painting, of my father, my mother, my brother, my to-do list, my laundry…

Half an hour later, I still cannot stop thinking of him or repeatedly replaying our bizarre encounter in my head. Nothing made sense. His appearance in the shop. His insane offer for my painting. My reaction to him.

I grab my phone and text my best friend, Sam. She is a night-bird like me and is almost certainly awake and surfing the net.

Are you awake?

We grew up together and we were always inseparable, six months ago I came here to paint, and she went on to Atlanta to study something technical to do with computers. What exactly my turpentine soaked brain has never quite been able to grasp.

As soon as my phone rings, I snatch it up and launch into my story. I tell her everything that happened at the store. For a few seconds, after I stop talking, there is only silence from her end.

"Sam?" I call.

"Yeah, yeah, I'm here. I'm just thinking." Sam is the opposite of me. She doesn't rush in where angels fear to tread. She thinks about her every move carefully.

"Okay, have you finished thinking?"

"Maybe you're a better artist than you think," she says.

Sam is a total sweetheart, but I can't help rolling my eyes at her naivety. "Oh please. He offered a hundred thousand bucks for a painting that is not even finished yet."

She laughs. "Perhaps he has so much money he can afford to throw lots of it at anything he fancies." She pauses, then adds dramatically, "Or maybe you're what he fancies."

"What man do you know offers a hundred thousand to sleep with a paint-splattered woman?"

"Maybe he's kinky."

"Can you please be serious?"

"If I was a man with lots of money, I'd pay that for you," she pipes up loyally.

"Thanks, Sam. I feel incredibly valued right now, but can we please step back into the real world for a minute?"

She laughs. "Fine. Have it your way. Personally, I think very rich people are mad. Who knows? Maybe, he really liked your painting, but how could he possibly hang it up next to his Van Gogh and Monet if it was only a thousand dollars? His friends would laugh over their caviar and cocaine when they came over to dinner. This way he can boast that clever him found this unknown artist in a tiny little artist town who is really hot right now and he found her first."

"Hmmm… I wonder if you are in the wrong career path. Don't you think you'd do better as a novelist?"

"Well, if I was a novelist, I would say, be careful. He sounds like a dark one."

"What's that supposed to mean?"

"Just the vibes I get from you. I get the feeling he's disturbed you, and not just about the money. There's something else bothering you, isn't there?"

"Yes," I admitted. "I can't get him out of my mind and I really, really, really want to go to bed with him, but at the same time I'm scared to. There is an air of danger about him, something unknowable about him."

"When you say unknowable, I'm hoping you don't mean rapist/serial killer unknowable."

"No, no, nothing like that. He is too beautiful, mysterious, and magnetic. I can't imagine a woman saying no to him."

"Here's what I would do if I was you. When you see Larry tomorrow ask him all about this guy. Get all the details. If he is legit and he asks you to, then go out with him to a very public place. I'll call you while you're out and you can loudly say you're having dinner with him. That way he will understand that if anything happens to you, the police will be on to him immediately. If he turns out to be dodgy in any way at all just walk away."

My stomach churns as I say the words. "No, I won't go out with him."

"Why not?"

"I cannot explain it in words, but there is something about him that scares me. That I could fall too deep and never recover."

"Wow! I've never heard you talk like this before."

"I've never felt this way before."

"I'm the one who is more reserved and cautious of the two of us, but you know what? If such a man appeared in my life, I would go for it. I would risk a broken heart because otherwise I would spend the rest of my life thinking what if…"

CHAPTER 4

ROCCO

https://www.youtube.com/watch?v=YkADj0TPrJA
-In The Air Tonight-

I put the top down on the custom-built Bugatti, and the cold air rushes through my hair as I press down hard on the clutch and make it fly up the road that winds around the mountain.

The road has been deliberately built in a way to make it impossible for the curious person to come up it. To start with you can't use an ordinary car. It is so narrow in some places an ordinary car will end up with its wheels hanging off the cliff. Other places have potholes so big it becomes downright dangerous to try and maneuver around them. You have to know where they are or you will get stuck.

My privacy is very important to me. I need solitude the way other people need friends. Of course, I have houses in cities all over the world, but I always come back here. To this house high on the mountain top, and shrouded in mist for most of the year. It is my sanctuary.

I pull up to the black cast iron gates, wave my remote, and they part for me. I slow down to a crawl on the cobblestone driveway, and soon arrive at the impressive entrance. It took five years for three craftsmen from Europe to intricately carve the blocks of sandstone imported from Italy.

There is light blazing from most of the downstairs windows.

As I reach the double door, William opens it for me. He is English and has a pale, poker face. He is exactly what one would imagine a butler to look like. Stiff, polite, distant, impossibly efficient. He also speaks only when absolutely necessary. A quality I appreciate greatly. That, and his unceasing loyalty to me. My other staff come and go, but William alone has been with me for longer than anyone else.

He nods gravely. "Good evening, my Lord. Your sister is waiting for you in the music room."

I feel an old fury rush through me like lightning, but I instantly catch myself. There is absolutely no way Isadora can know about Autumn. No way at all. I must calm down, get complete control of myself, and not let her see that anything has changed. I stride towards the music room and find her sitting on the yellow chaise lounge. A furry white dog is curled up in her lap. She has a drink in one hand. She searches my gaze. I know what she is looking for. I feign boredom and head towards the bar.

"Where have you been?" she asks, arching one blonde eyebrow. "I've been waiting for ages."

As I pour myself a drink I hear her petulant voice float towards me.

"You know you're meant to pick up the phone when it rings, especially when it rings... *a thousand times.*"

Instantly, I run out of patience. Throwing the brandy down my throat I start to walk out of the room.

"What if I was hurt or something?" she asks.

"You're not, are you?" I fling, as I carry on walking.

"I might have been," she retorts. "One of these days I just might be in real trouble and because you have chosen to not acknowledge me in your life, I could be hurt or even killed. How would you feel then?"

I stop and turn to look at her. "Who's going to dare drive a stake through your cold heart?"

"Is that supposed to be funny?" she asks, a tinge of irritation coloring her voice.

I sigh. "What do you want, Isadora?'

"When are you going to stop punishing all of us?"

"Never," I say bitterly.

She lifts her dog into her arms and stands. She is tall and willowy and dressed in a skintight dress. There can't be a man alive who can resist my sister. More's the pity because she will drop kick every single one of their hearts into oblivion as soon as she gets bored. She comes forward, her face pleading. "Look, I didn't even do anything."

"But you knew about it." My voice is cold and distant.

"Yes, I knew about it, but I didn't realize how important it was to you."

"It?" I rage, as the black anger returns to fill my chest.

19

She shakes her head in exasperation. "Stop being so fucking sensitive, I was not calling her an it. I was referring to the situation." She takes a deep breath. "I didn't realize how important *she* was to you. I'm sorry. I made a mistake. Have you never made a mistake in your life?"

I stare at her bitterly. "Yes, I have made many, many mistakes in my life. The biggest was trusting my own family."

"For fucks sake we are your family, Rocco. We made a mistake. A big mistake, but you have to understand that they did it because they love you and she was going to destroy you. At some point you're going to have to forgive them... us. We're your blood."

I lift my head. My voice is cold and final. "Perhaps, at some point, but not yet."

Her eyes fill with disappointment.

I turn and leave her.

CHAPTER 5

AUTUMN

After my phone call ends I find it impossible to sleep so I unpack my easel and paints, put out a primed canvas, and start to paint. My strokes are not calm and considered, careful of how much paint I use, but frenzied, rushed, and unusually extravagant. I squeeze out nearly half a jumbo tube of white paint and dash it onto the canvas.

I don't even take a break to step back to consider my next move. The brush seems to move on its own accord. It doesn't even feel as if it is me painting. It is as if I am possessed. This is not even in my usual style. The strokes are short and fat with paint.

I don't know how long I paint, but when I finish my hand feels stiff from holding the brush so long.

I stand back and stare at my painting with some shock. It is hard to believe I painted this scene. It is of two people in the throes of intense passion. The woman's neck is so unnaturally stretched and thrown back it looks as if she must be in terrible agony, but the expression on her face is that of ecstasy. Her legs are wide open. The man's face cannot be seen, but he is blond. His back is broad and powerful, and he dominates her completely as he fucks her hard. Their joining is such that there is no way to tear them apart. Their primitive bodies bled into each other until they seem to be one four-legged feral beast.

I move forward and sign my work. Even my signature has a slightly different flourish to it.

I open the top cupboard, pull out a bottle of Vodka and take a mouthful straight from the bottle. Then I wipe my mouth with the back of my hand. I feel strangely exhilarated. I know without anyone telling me that I turned the corner as an artist. I have painted my best work so far. I take another mouthful. The neat alcohol goes straight to my head. I stick my headphones on and the throb of dance music fills my head. I take another swig of Vodka and start to dance.

I'm behaving totally out of character, but it feels great. It feels amazing to be drinking and dancing on my own while everyone else is asleep. Then, as suddenly as the euphoria had come it is gone. I feel sleepy and utterly exhausted. Dawn is already in the sky.

I fall into bed and do not wake up until the alarm rings at nine.

With a groan, my hand flings out to stop the sound. My head is throbbing slightly. Then I remember. Rocco Rossetti. I shoot out of bed and rush to my painting. Wow! In the bright morning light, it is breathtaking. I approach it with awe. Standing three feet away from it I just stare at it. There is not a stroke on it I'd change. I'm hardly able to believe I created such a complete piece of art in one session.

I take a few photos of it, then I clean up the mess I made last night, dress quickly, and get on my bike. When I get into work, Larry is not in yet, so I open all the doors to remove the lingering smell of turpentine. It is strange that Larry should run an art gallery when he doesn't like the odor of turpentine. Once I've dusted the surfaces in the showroom, and run the vacuum cleaner around the carpet, I change into the white shirt and black knee-length skirt that serves as my work attire.

By the time Larry comes in at half-past ten the air is filled with the aroma of freshly brewed coffee. Larry is a serious, bespectacled man, who looks like a younger version of Bill Gates.

"Good morning," he greets formally, as he takes his leather gloves off.

"Hiya," I greet, as I watch him unwrap the thick scarf from around his neck. He doesn't like the cold much. While he hangs up his thick puffer jacket inside the cupboard, I start to fill his coffee mug. Wearing a yellow sweater, a striped black and white shirt; and a pair of brown slacks he approaches me. I hold the mug out to him.

"Thanks," he says, and starts to turn away.

"Someone called Rocco Rossetti—"

The name is like magic, he whirls around to face me, his eyes shining with anticipation.

"Came into the shop last night while I was working out back," I continue. "He indicated that he wanted to buy *Miranda Taking a Bath*. He says to put it away for him, and someone will come and pick it up on Thursday. Uh… he also left a cash deposit. A thousand dollars."

Larry looks at me in disbelief. "The Count left a deposit! Are you sure that was him?"

I feel my face growing warm. "Um… yeah. He didn't say he was a Count though."

"Describe him."

"Uh, blond, very handsome, beautifully dressed, good—"

He raises his hand to indicate I should stop babbling, and I shut my mouth with a snap.

For a moment he says nothing, then he smiles approvingly. "Well done, Autumn. There should be a nice commission for you in there."

I grin widely. I've never had the chance to sell anything or earn any commission before. I'm just the minion and everybody usually asks to speak directly to Larry before they make a purchase.

"I guess I'll finally be able to pay you back for all the paints," I say.

He frowns. "Ah, no. Don't do that. They were presents. It's not often I see someone so talented and genuinely eager to paint and it gave me pleasure to encourage that passion." He glances at his watch. "I've got to make some phone calls. Take the sold painting out of the window and replace it with…," He pauses as he considers which painting would do best in the shop window. "One of Jerry's, um… how about *The Final Crucifixion?*"

"Great choice," I confirm.

He smiles then starts sprinting up the stairs to his office, only to stop halfway, and turn to me. "I'm catching up with my accounts today so I will have to work right through lunch.

Will you pop out to Franks later and get me a ham sandwich?"

I nod. "Sure."

He disappears out of sight and I hear his footsteps go to his office. I'll have to wait until this evening to ask him about the mysterious Count Rossetti, but for the moment I can do some research of my own.

I reach for my phone and google Count Rocco Rossetti. I noticed last night he wore no wedding ring, so he must at least be in the list of 'Most Eligible' bachelors that magazines like to compile. I expect to find a trove of info, but after trying various spellings of his name, I come up with nothing.

Not one single entry, which is really, really odd considering he is titled, rich, and breathtakingly handsome.

CHAPTER 6

AUTUMN

Turns out Larry doesn't know much about the Count either. He has come in a few times and bought some of Larry's best pieces. The payment is sent from a numbered account in Switzerland, and there is no delivery address because he always gets someone to pick up the paintings.

Thursday comes by and a tall, thin man in a black suit comes to pick up the painting. He waits politely as I bring the securely wrapped painting out from the back. Then he thanks me and exits the shop. I stand at the door and watch curiously as he carefully puts it into the trunk of one of those narrow three wheel vehicles. Larry comes to stand behind me.

"Strange, isn't it?" he murmurs.

"Yes, very strange," I reply.

"I think the Count lives up the mountain, don't you?"

I turn to look at Larry. "Really? Someone lives up there?"

"Well, that's the rumor I heard when I moved here five years ago. Apparently, there's a huge sandstone mansion up there."

"Have you never wanted to check it out?"

"Are you kidding? There are 'No Trespassing' signs all over the place, and the road leading up to it is treacherous to say the least. So narrow, I've heard of people getting stuck and having to abandon their cars because recovery trucks cannot go up. No way I'm taking my lovely BMW on that dirt path."

I frown. "If the road is so narrow how did all the building equipment go up... the lorries, the cranes, the sandstones."

"No idea," he confesses.

"So... he just lives up there alone?"

"Staff. Lots of them. I've seen a few around town shopping, but they are not a friendly lot. I've heard they will give you a blank stare and walk away if you try to engage them in any kind of chit chat or conversation."

"Why do you think he lives up there?"

Larry shrugs. "Your guess is as good as mine."

"Do you think he might be a fugitive from the law or something?"

Larry smiles. "Don't be so dramatic, Autumn. I imagine he is just an eccentric European aristocrat, one of those recluses who jealously guard their privacy."

"He doesn't have a European accent though," I note.

"No, he doesn't. I must admit I've never given it much thought. Perhaps he was born in this country. Anyway, I better go do some work. Marion wants me home early today."

He goes upstairs and spends a bit of time filing away some invoices. Thirty minutes later Larry leaves. At five I put the closed sign on, change out of my work clothes and into my jeans and sweatshirt.

Then, I pull my painting out from the cupboard, put it back on the easel, and study it. It does not have the fire and raw passion of the painting I did last night, but it is haunting. There is something about this painting that feels real. As if there were once real people living in that gray castle until terrible things happened to them and they abandoned it and left it to rot away.

I paint for a couple of hours, but my thoughts keep returning to Rocco Rossetti. My research has revealed that the etymology of the surname Rossetti links back to the word red. It was a name given to people with red hair. Rocco is pure blond though. The kind of blond that shines like spun gold. Extraordinary, really. In fact, everything about him is extraordinary. Living in isolation up on an inaccessible mountain. Offering me all that money for an unfinished painting. His looks. His piercing eyes. Even his unexpected appearance at the shop.

It's close to eight when I put all my paints and brushes away. Tonight, I'm tired. I cycle home, warm up a can of macaroni and cheese, then curl up on the couch to eat it. It's not great, but tomorrow I get paid and I will treat myself to a feast, a massive Chinese take-out. The whole works. There will even be leftovers which I will leave for the raccoons.

Once the food is gone, I feel so exhausted I go to bed without even bothering with a shower. But I don't sleep soundly. I keep dreaming of him. Strange, confusing dreams. In them, I am afraid of something as I keep looking behind me as I run through unending, twisting, dark forests. Something is chasing me, but I do not know what. It feels as if I am running towards him for safety and refuge, but I never get to him.

I wake up suddenly.

It is three in the morning. Feeling restless and ravenous I go to the freezer and take out a tub of ice cream and remove the plastic lid. I put it into the microwave. I grab a spoon from the washing rack and ten seconds later the microwave pings. With one hand clutching my duvet around myself and the other holding the ice cream and spoon, I pull open the door and go outside into the night. There is a half-moon in the sky and it paints the field in front of me silver. A deer walks quietly across the field and I watch the way it picks its delicate legs over the long grasses until it disappears into the dark of the woods.

All the other caravans are in darkness. Only the old gypsy woman's windows glow with yellow light.

It is so cold my breath mists as I sit on the plastic chair under my window and begin to eat my ice cream. The ice cream tastes and feels incredible as it melts in my hot mouth. With the Count in my heart like a delicious secret, I close my eyes and relish the sensation of the cold liquid sliding down my throat. It's so great to be alive. So damn great.

Right at that moment I wouldn't have changed places with anybody else on earth.

CHAPTER 7

AUTUMN

Two days pass. Soon it will be time to close, but Rocco Rossetti doesn't come to the shop. He must know by now that I transferred the deposit he left for my painting to *Miranda Taking a Bath*.

I know my body is waiting for him, because I jump every time the rusty doorbells ring. My painting of the crumbling castle is nearly finished. It is intricate and detailed. Yesterday, after Larry had gone out of the door I pulled it out and put it on the easel, but Larry had forgotten to turn off the lights in his office upstairs and he came back into the shop. To my surprise he came and stood next to me.

I was nervous to have him look at my painting. Of his verdict. It was my baby so of course I loved it, and Rocco Rossetti had wanted to buy it unfinished, but Larry was a connoisseur. He knew about great art and could recognize a winner at a glance. I could hear my heart beating like a mad thing and I hardly dared to breathe.

Finally, unable to bear the tension anymore I turned and looked at his profile. "Well, what do you think?"

"Hmmm… it's very good."

"But…" I prompted softly.

He met my gaze. "It's not you."

"What do you mean?"

He shrugged. "Remember when you told me you used to climb the tallest trees and go higher than any boy in your neighborhood, and how a branch you were standing on gave way and you fell and broke your arm so badly the bone was sticking out of your flesh?"

"Yeah?"

"And how you climbed straight back up that tree while your arm was still in a sling."

"Yeah?"

"Do you remember the sensation you felt as you were climbing that tree with one arm in a sling? The crazy exhilaration of knowing how dangerous what you were doing was and the memory of the pain of breaking your bones still fresh in your mind, but conquering and mastering your fears, anyway."

And suddenly I knew what he was talking about. He was talking about the kind of painting I had done alone in my caravan the night I met Rocco Rossetti. That painting of me and Rocco having dirty, animalistic sex together.

"You're a daredevil, Autumn," Larry added passionately. "This kind of painting is pleasing to the eye and is fine for people who want something pretty to hang in their living room, but you are capable of something far, far greater. Do you understand what I'm saying?"

I nodded slowly.

He smiled suddenly at me. "Until you find that spark in you, you won't be all you can be, but don't be disheartened. I'm still happy for you to hang this piece in the showroom when it is finished. For sure someone will buy it."

"It's not for sale," I say quickly.

"Okay," he says easily, and walks away.

Since that illuminating encounter with Larry, I haven't painted anything. I know he is right. I will only paint again when that same irresistible urge to create that had come upon me that night when I painted in the caravan strikes me again.

I turn to look at the clock. Half-an-hour before closing time. Maybe I should order a large pepperoni pizza and take it home. I can certainly afford it, I found an extra two thousand dollars in my paycheck this month. Larry said it is my commission for selling the painting. I felt bad and told him honestly that I'd done nothing to encourage the sale. In fact, I'd been a bit startled by his appearance and so had been quite rude to him, but Larry waved away my objections with the final words, "If you hadn't been in the shop in the first place the Count would not have been able to come in and buy the painting."

Upstairs, I hear Larry start to move around. He is getting ready to leave.

The rusty bells ring and my head whirls around. The air is knocked out of my lungs as my gaze collides with a pair of translucent blue eyes. Wearing all black and looking as impossibly immaculate as he did the other night, he locks his gaze on me... and suddenly I can't look away. The air becomes thick with lust, mine. What is it about him? The moment I see him I start thinking about climbing him. Impaling myself on him.

It is only when Larry's footsteps on the wooden stairs penetrate my crazed state that I manage to drag my gaze away. I can feel myself trembling as Larry arrives in the showroom. He sees our customer and immediately his face splits into a beaming smile. He appears genuinely happy to see the Count.

"Ah, Count Rossetti. How wonderful to see you again," he gushes expansively.

The Count smiles, and I stare at him, mesmerized. His whole face transforms and he appears utterly, indescribably, and unbelievably handsome. I know I sound like a silly teenager with a crush on a pop star, but without warning that wild feeling fills me again. I *need* to paint his face.

"Autumn," Larry calls.

I turn my head dazedly towards him.

He raises his eyebrows, and I realize he must have been speaking, but I've not heard a word.

Hot color rushes up my throat. "Sorry?" I mumble, totally embarrassed.

He inclines his head so slightly towards the backroom. It would have been imperceptible to anyone else watching, but it finally clicks in my cotton-wool head. What the hell was I doing? I shouldn't be standing here staring with open-mouthed awe at the Count. I should have scuttled off to the backroom ages ago, and let the two men talk business.

"Please excuse me," I mutter without meeting the eyes of the Count, and quickly start walking away.

I've not even gone two steps, when I hear his voice say, "Don't go. I've come to invite you both to dinner."

CHAPTER 8

AUTUMN

I freeze. I'm not sure if I've heard correctly, but when I turn around Larry's stunned expression is enough to know I have. My knees feel wobbly and my mind is blank. Dinner? Me? Why? My gaze swings past Larry's comical face towards the Count. He is staring at me with those brilliantly blue eyes.

I open my mouth, but no words come out.

Thank God, Larry fills the strange silence in the room. "We'd love to accept."

The Count's eyes never leave me. "Are you free tonight?"

"Of course we are," Larry answers for me.

"Good. Shall we say eight at the Four Seasons?"

"Great. We'll meet you there," Larry accepts without consulting me.

"Until then…" The Count bows his head formally at us, then withdraws. The rusty bells chime in the silence he leaves behind.

I exhale the breath I'm holding and I turn to look at Larry. "What was that all about?" I croak.

"You don't have anything to do tonight, do you?" Larry asks belatedly.

"I was actually going to paint," I reply tartly.

"Look, I'm sorry. I should have asked you first, but it would have been churlish to refuse his invitation. He is my best customer," Larry apologizes.

"I think you should go without me."

"Please come, Autumn. I'll pay you overtime," Larry says persuasively.

"It's not the money. I just wouldn't feel comfortable. To start with I don't know him. What will I do while you guys talk business?"

"Have you had dinner at the Four Seasons before?"

It's the best restaurant for miles around. A famous New York Chef opened it many years ago. In the beginning people wondered why anyone, let alone such a bigwig in the culinary world, would open such a fine restaurant in such a rural place. Who would come and pay his inflated prices, but it turned out he made a wise decision. People will always come and pay for extraordinary service and food. I've even heard that it's hard to get a table there.

"No," I admit. "My wages don't reach to meals that costs hundreds of dollars per head."

"Well," Larry says, slipping seamlessly into sales mode, "this is your opportunity to eat there. I should tell you that their rib-eye steak is indescribably wonderful. The best I've ever had. They use only grass-fed beef, and it literally melts in your mouth. It is served with a creamy French peppercorn sauce. I have no idea how it is made, but it's like silk on your tongue."

My mouth drops with a mixture of disbelief and amusement. "Are you trying to bribe me with food, Larry?"

"Is it working?" he asks hopefully.

"Actually, it is… a bit. That creamy sauce did catch my attention."

Larry sees that he has drawn blood and really goes for it. "Yeah? Well, let me tell you about the dessert. They have this rich chocolate fudge cake, which they serve warm with the most luxurious Cornish ice cream from England you've ever tasted. As if that was not enough a waiter actually comes around and pours melted warm gooey chocolate from a tiny jar onto your slice. It's absolutely to die for."

I start laughing.

We both know he has won, but he is not finished. Larry likes to be sure of his victories. "And for the starter you have their signature dish. Smoked duck served with the freshest, most delicious pomegranate, walnut and rocket salad you have ever tasted."

"Stop," I plead, my empty stomach rumbling.

"Will you come, Autumn? As a favor to me."

"To be honest I would come just for that chocolate cake and gooey sauce, but I honestly have nothing to wear to a place like that, Larry. My wardrobe consists of t-shirts, sweatshirts and jeans. And all the shops are already shut by now."

He frowns and is silent for a moment and I can almost hear the gears in his brain working. When he finds the solution to his predicament, his whole face glows like a light bulb. "You are the same size as my wife's niece, Jenna. I'll get her to bring a few dresses for you to try on. Would that be all right?"

My eyes widen. Wow! He really, really doesn't want to let the Count down. I've met Jenna once when she dropped some-thing off, and she is the same size as me. What harm can it do to go to dinner with them? It's not like I'll ever be alone with the Count. I shrug. "Sure."

"Great. Thank you for this, Autumn," he says, relief all over his face, as he pulls his phone out of his pocket. "By the way what size shoes do you wear?"

CHAPTER 9

AUTUMN

Jenna has smaller feet than me, but Larry calls his wife and finds out she is the same size as me. He gets her to drop off two boxes of shoes. I gasp when I open the boxes. Two almost new, totally gorgeous pair of Louboutins. One red one black. Twenty minutes later Jenna comes around carrying three dresses and a red coat on hangers. I wonder if Marion and Jenna discussed what they would be bringing over, because the red coat is almost exactly the same color as one of the pairs of shoes.

I go into the backroom and try on the slinky black dress first. It is more sophisticated than anything I've ever owned. I put it on and immediately know I don't have to try the others. It fits beautifully, with slim-fitting three quarter sleeves, a scoop neckline, and a fairly tight skirt that ends just under my knee. There is a slit on the right thigh that turns the dress from elegant to sexy.

Gingerly, I step into the pair of red shoes. It's been a long while since I wore high heels, but after a few steps around the backroom I realize that the shoes are very comfortable and easy to walk in. I find a tube of lipstick at the bottom of my purse and use it on my lips and cheeks. Then I let my hair down and secure the side with a couple of clips I find inside my drawer. To my surprise, I also find an old tube of mascara in there. The wand is a bit dried up, but I manage to get some onto my eyelashes. I pull on the red coat and I'm ready.

I feel like Cinderella as I walk out of the backroom into the shop. Larry is sitting on the leather sofa. He has opened a bottle of champagne and is sipping from a flute. He looks up when I enter, and whistles.

"Whoa, Autumn. It's a good thing I'm head over heels in love with my wife, because you look positively edible," he says with a smile.

I feel myself blush at the compliment.

"Come and have a drink with me before we leave. We still have fifteen minutes to kill." He fills a glass with champagne and holds it out to me.

I go over and take it from him. I take a sip and deliciously cold bubbles run down my throat and hit my empty stomach. "Why do you think the Count wants to take us to dinner?"

He takes a sip of his drink before answering. "I'm not sure, but I have my suspicions."

Before I can ask him to elaborate, his phone rings and he apologizes and says he has to take the call. He wanders away with his phone held to his ear and I lean back on the sofa and decide to enjoy my glass of expensive French champagne. Five minutes later, I can feel myself start to get slightly tipsy. It's a good feeling.

By the time Larry comes back I'm positively merry, and it's nearly time to leave. I stand and Larry laughs when he sees me wobble on his wife's shoes.

"What has become of youth these days?" he teases. "One glass of champagne and they're tripping."

"I didn't realize bubbles could be so potent," I murmur.

He smiles at me with fatherly affection. "Yeah, champagne goes to your head fast."

"Now he tells me."

"Don't drink anything else until you get some food in you," he advises as he opens the door for me.

Outside it's cold and I'm glad for the warmth of Jenna's thick coat. We get into Larry's car and he starts the engine. I lean my head back on the headrest. The nervousness I felt at the thought of meeting Rocco Rossetti is gone. Instead, I listen to Larry's voice telling me a story about what his youngest kid, Briana did last night, and feel pleasantly tipsy and benevolent towards the whole world.

Thirty minutes later we arrive at the Four Seasons. Confidently, I get out of the car. This is going to be a good night. I love chocolate fudge cake, and I've never had anyone come and pour gooey melted chocolate onto it just before I tuck in. And that grass-fed beef steak and smoked duck salad sounded very good too. I've never had smoked duck so that will be another experience I can tick off.

We walk together to the entrance and the doorman greets us and pulls the restaurant door. The hostess takes my coat and leads us into the restaurant. All the tables are full of customers, but we pass them all and end up in another section of the restaurant which is completely empty, except for one table.

As soon as my eyes meet his, all thoughts of food flee. And that other hunger comes back with a vengeance. I feel my knees turn into jelly. He stands as we approach. As we get nearer I feel an intense desire to pee. Before we can reach the table I turn to the hostess. "Where's the Ladies?"

She indicates with her hand as she speaks, "Turn right out of here, and the first door on your left."

"Thanks," I reply, then turning to Larry, and say, "Won't be long."

The first door on the left opens into a vast luxurious area tiled with pink marble. My father used to say, you can tell the quality of a restaurant purely by the state of their restrooms. If this restroom was any indication, the food must be heaven.

I use the toilet quickly and gaze at my reflection with some surprise as I wash my hands. In the small mirror inside the backroom bathroom of the store I can't see myself properly, but I can now. Jenna's dress has completely transformed me. I look elegant and sophisticated.

After wiping my hands on a luxuriously thick white hand towel, I take a deep breath and head back out to join the men. As soon as the Count sees me, he stands, which forces Larry to stand as well. The idea of Larry standing at my arrival is amusing and I have to force myself not to break out into laughter, but as I arrive at the table I know instantly that something is wrong.

Larry is looking at me with a pleading expression, the pleasant feeling from the glass of champagne evaporates into nothing, and my stomach clenches with nerves.

CHAPTER 10

AUTUMN

I take my seat and both men sit down. I turn to Larry. "What's wrong?"

He glances quickly at the Count, then back to me. "Something urgent has come up, Autumn, and I've got to leave, but please do stay and have dinner with the Count."

My eyes widen with astonishment. "What?"

"It would be a shame for you to miss a lovely dinner because of me, so please do stay. I'll arrange for a taxi to take you home." Once again, he pleads with his eyes.

My gaze darts to the Count and my breath catches. He is watching me with a strange intensity, but there is no expression on his face to indicate whether he is agreeable to this new development. I turn back to Larry. "It's okay, Larry. We'll have dinner together another day."

"No, no, please stay and have some food, Autumn. I'd hate it if you went hungry. I feel bad enough as it is."

My stomach is in knots. "I won't exactly go hungry, Larry. I was planning to order a large pizza and eat most of it."

Larry starts to look desperate. "Autumn, you're already here. You might as well stay and eat here."

I stare at Larry curiously. He has never begged me to do something before and it's clear he desperately wants me to stay and have dinner here. Why? Does he think it's something I could never afford otherwise? Or is it because he doesn't want to upset the Count? I'm going with the latter. I turn towards the Count. "What do you think?"

His eyes are mesmerizing. For a few seconds, he does not speak and I am lost in his blue gaze. Then he opens his mouth and quietly says just one word. "Stay."

The word is like a stone thrown into a lake. It causes ripples inside me. I feel the power and authority in that word and the need to obey the command. Even though I'm not comfortable with the idea of having dinner with him alone, I feel unable to disobey him. Next to me I sense Larry shifting uncomfortably, but I cannot tear my eyes away from Rocco Rossetti. My limbs feel frozen and I feel entranced. Then my mouth opens and I whisper, "Okay."

His mouth twists slightly into a smile. Then Larry speaks, and I am suddenly freed from the hypnotic spell of his intense gaze. I turn blindly towards him. He smiles gratefully at me. "Thank you, Autumn. The restaurant owns a fleet of taxis so I'll book one for you now."

I nod speechlessly.

He stands and looks at Rocco Rossetti. "Dinner's on me next time, Count."

The Count nods. His demeanor is that of an important man dismissing a servant.

Larry looks at me. "Please text me when you get home, Autumn, so I know you got home safely."

I nod.

"Well, goodnight to both of you then."

"Goodnight, Larry," I say.

The Count only nods.

Then Larry almost sprints out of the room.

Once he is gone, I turn slowly back towards the Count. "Do you have something to do with Larry's emergency?"

One eyebrow rises. "What do you think?"

"I think… yes."

"Well done," he murmurs.

I feel my heart begin to pound. "Why do you want to have dinner with me?"

He leans forward and his eyes sparkle like sapphires under a spotlight. "Why do you think?"

"Because you want to sleep with me?" My voice is hoarse, barely a whisper.

He looks amused. "Obviously, but I am also intrigued by you."

My eyes widen with disbelief. "*You* are intrigued by *me*?"

"You wouldn't be here, otherwise," he replies, reaching for the wine menu. "White or red?"

"White," I say automatically. Just then a waiter, a painfully thin man with sandy brown hair, responds to his action of reaching for the menu by arriving by his side.

"The usual," he tells the waiter as he hands the menu to him without having looked at it, or even opened it.

"Thank you, Count Rossetti," the waiter says, and with a courteous nod he withdraws.

The Count turns his piercing, intense attention back to me.

I swallow hard. "I suppose you come here often."

"When I am around," he says simply.

I look around me at all the empty tables around us. "Strange, all these tables are unoccupied while the other dining area is completely booked out?"

"I don't like crowds. When I dine here, I always book the whole area."

"They let you do that?" I ask, surprised.

A flash of amusement passes over his eyes, probably at the thought of anyone 'letting' him do something. "I own this restaurant. I needed somewhere good to eat out."

Of course he did, but before I can reply the waiter comes back with the wine. I can tell just by looking at the label that it is an old wine. A special wine. Silently, the waiter uncorks the bottle and quarter-fills our glasses with the straw-colored liquid. The glasses immediately mist. Then he places the bottle into a silver ice bucket and withdraws.

The Count lifts his glass towards me in a silent toast. Gripping the stem of my wine glass I take a sip. The wine is cold on my tongue, but as it starts to warm to the temperature in my mouth, it tastes like no wine I have ever tasted before. I used to laugh at the wine connoisseurs who would claim they could taste cappuccino with a hint of charcoal, or elderberry with pencil shavings. I always thought they were just being pretentious, but now…

Now, I feel as if I have become one of them.

For I can taste and smell not just the grapes, but the oak barrels the wine has been kept in, and even the earth they have been grown in. It is as if all my senses have been sharpened. As the aromatic, velvety wine swirls in my mouth the sensation is one of sheer opulence and decadence. I know I am not imagining it, so it must be him. I am so attuned and aware of him that all my perceptions have become more sensitive and sharper.

"Like it?" he asks softly.

"I have never tasted anything so delicious," I reply truthfully.

He smiles, but strangely, his beautiful face seems almost sad. "You must take a bottle back with you."

"I'm pretty certain I can't afford to do any such thing," I reply.

"It's a gift from me to you."

"Why?"

He shrugs. "Why not? I have more than I can ever spend."

I put the glass down and lean back. There is so much I want to know about him. "So… what is a Count doing in a sleepy place like Hunter's Cross when the most glamorous cities beckon?"

"I enjoy living on mountains away from prying eyes, and when this mountain and surrounding land came up for sale… it suited me perfectly so I bought it."

"The whole mountain belongs to you?" I ask, astonished. He seems to belong to a different world than me. A mysterious world where money is no object and beautiful people flittered around the world, owning fine restaurants because they needed somewhere good to eat, offered ludicrous sums of money for unknown artists, and owned whole mountains because they liked seclusion.

He nods and I think of my painting, of the crumbling castle built into the mountain, and as if he can read my mind he asks, "Have you finished your painting?"

"Yes, but I'm afraid it's still not for sale."

A strange expression crosses his eyes, but he doesn't push further. "Perhaps you'd like to look at the menu."

CHAPTER 11

AUTUMN

I pull the menu towards me, but find that I can't concentrate at all. The words swim as if I am inside the magical world of Harry Potter. I look up and he is watching me. His eyes are like crushed gems. At that moment, the desire to go to him and kiss him is so strong that it actually shocks me. I stare at him. I lick my bottom lip and instantly his gaze makes an excursion to my mouth… and lingers there.

The sexual attraction is incredible. I can feel my body trembling with desire for him. I have never ever in my life wanted someone as much as I want him. I want to climb into his lap and suck his tongue and let him take me. Right now. Right here on this table.

"Ready to order?" he asks smoothly.

Unable to speak, I nod.

He lifts a long, elegant finger and a waiter materializes at his side. "Are you ready to order, Ma'am?" he asks politely.

"I'll have the smoked duck and pomegranate salad to start, and the rib-eye steak as my main," I mumble, hoping the menu has not changed.

"Very good. Rare, medium, or well done?" the waiter asks.

"Well done." To make sure he gets it, I add, "almost burnt."

He flinches slightly. Obviously, he doesn't approve of over-done meat, but he nods politely, then angles his body towards the Count.

"The usual," the Count says quietly, never taking his eyes off me.

The waiter thanks him and slinks away, and I am left alone with him again. Something shimmers between us and I feel myself being helplessly drawn to him. Unmet desire throbs inside my body. My brain searches for something to say, something that will break the spell of his eyes, his person.

"Larry tells me the road leading up to your mountain is very narrow and dangerous, how did you get the cranes, trucks full of equipment and building materials up there?" I whisper hoarsely.

"The road was originally built to accommodate them."

"And you narrowed it afterwards?" I ask incredulously.

"Yes."

I look at him in amazement. "Why not just build big gates?"

"The higher the gates the more curiosity they evoke. A pot-holed, dangerous road suits me better."

"You're strange, you know that?"

He laughs suddenly, and I stare at him with astonishment. In laughter, he is indescribably beautiful. His teeth are an orthodontist's wet dream, straight and white and his whole face seems to glow with ethereal beauty. The longer I spend in his company the more I feel as if I am a moth and he is a flame. I can't stop myself from flying towards him, but he is going to incinerate me. All that will be left will be the ashes of my desire for this sensuously beautiful, mysterious, and I am certain, dangerous man.

I reach blindly for my wine glass and take another sip. The wine touches my tongue and another explosion of tastes and smells overwhelms me. *Go easy, Autumn. Go easy*, I tell myself. It is hard for me to believe I'm not in reality trapped inside a dream because everything feels so fantastical and exaggerated. The desire for him, his beauty, the way all the colors around me seem more vivid, the way I am reacting to the wine in my mouth, the heightened sensations I feel, or the way my fingertips are tingling.

"Tell me about you," he coaxes, charm oozing out of every pore.

I normally don't like talking about myself, but to my surprise, I immediately start blabbing out my whole history. Like a quickly running brook, I tell him about my parents, how they were both killed in a car crash while I was in college, my utter devastation when I rushed back and saw those two coffins. He stares at me avidly. There's no murmur of condolence, but it's not necessary. No one has paid me such rapt attention before. His focus is laser like. As if I am the most important person in the world. No scratch that, as if I am the only person in the world.

I tell him about my art, about Sam, about how I moved here so I could paint. Once when I'm talking about Larry, his eyes flash. I cannot tell what that fleeting, but intense expression is. It looked like rage or possessiveness, but surely it can't have been either emotion. His relationship with Larry is one of buyer and seller, and what can he possibly be possessive about? He does not interrupt me and I continue talking.

When the waiter arrives, it is as if I am shaken out of a hypnotic trance. I stop abruptly mid-sentence and look around at him in a daze. He puts our starters in front of us. I stare at it. It is like a mini work of art. The blush of the smoked duck's flesh against the green on one of the leaves and the pomegranates gleaming like little rubies in between.

"*Buon appetito*," I hear the Count say softly.

I look up curiously. "Are you Italian?"

"No, I'm actually descended from an ancient German lineage."

"Why do you have an Italian name?"

"My ancestors moved to Italy in the fifteenth century, and because they were pale with red hair, they were given the name Rossetti."

My eyes move to his shining blond hair. It is unusual to see a man who is blond, let alone one who is so blond he looks almost unreal. The strange thing about him is his eyelashes and eyebrows are not fair, but dark brown, which almost makes it look as if he is wearing mascara, but I can see he is not. Even the suggestion he might be is laughable. There is nothing remotely feminine about him. In fact, he bristles with danger. Simmering just under his skin is something dark and unknowable. Something lethal... and something that lures me to him. The attraction is fatal, but I cannot resist it.

"I'd like to paint you," I blurt out.

A secretive look comes into his face, then he lifts his fork and smiles. "I'd like nothing better."

A wild joy rushes through my veins, as I follow suit and lift my fork. Larry did not exaggerate. The salad is absolutely, totally, and utterly delicious. My heart throbs so loudly I can hear it, my fingertips tingle, and my tongue is in heaven as I eat my food. It is a strange and exhilarating experience.

CHAPTER 12

AUTUMN

I have never seen a man eat in such a dignified way. He loads small amounts of the almost transparent layer of his beef carpaccio onto the back of his fork and slips the meat between his lips. Once inside his mouth, his chewing is almost imperceptible.

Time flies. We speak, but I'm in such a state of anticipation and desire, I can't even remember what we talk about. The second course arrives, with it comes a different bottle of wine. Red this time, and the label is yellowed with age. Dark-red liquid splashes into my glass. The waiters withdraw and the Count makes a gesture with his open palm to indicate I should try the wine. The first taste is aromatic, seductive, and rich.

It appears the Count has ordered the same dish as me, but his is rare. As he cuts into the meat, thin blood seeps through and pools on his plate. Normally, I would shudder to see it, but tonight everything seems vividly beautiful. Even the blood on his plate.

When I cut into the meat on my plate I realize it is not actually well-done at all, but what I would normally call medium. There is still some pink in the middle, but to my surprise, I am not repulsed by it. I have no inclination to send it back for a little while longer in the pan. I cut a small piece and put it into my mouth. The meat is full of flavor and so tender it almost melts in my mouth. It mixes with the lingering taste of tannin from the wine.

"How's your steak?" the Count asks.

"Delicious."

"Good," he says simply.

I cut into a buttered whole carrot. It is not the normal variety. It is small and almost maroon. I chew on the perfectly cooked vegetable. It seems to be richer and more flavorsome than any other carrot I have ever eaten. "This carrot is really delicious too."

"It should be. It's a wild South American variety that is grown organically inside a greenhouse. Not a drop of pesticide has been used in its production."

My eyebrows rise. "Really? Wow, they're really serious about food here, aren't they?"

"Yes, Francois, the Chef, is meticulous and uncompromising when it comes to the quality of his food."

I stare into his cold, luminous eyes and feel that spell swirl around me like a mist. Again, my body fills with desire for him, but he drops his eyelids over his eyes and says, "Eat your food, Autumn."

I feel myself blush as I bend my head towards my food. I am behaving like a gawky, silly, infatuated teenager. My irritation with myself makes me say the stupidest, most unsophisticated thing I could possibly have said. I want to kick myself even as the dumb words are pouring out of my mouth. "I'm not going to sleep with you."

His eyes glitter as he gazes at me. "You might want to wait until you're asked."

My face burns. "Well, it's just good to get it out there."

"Thanks for the warning," he says gravely, but I can tell he is amused by my gaucheness.

I dig myself deeper into the ground. "Good. As long as both of us understand where we stand."

"Of course."

I search for a different topic. "Tell me about you."

"What would you like to know?"

"What do you do for a living?"

"I have no need to *do* anything for a living. I have investment portfolios that are handled by capable managers. My time is my own. I read, I hunt, I swim, I climb mountains, I take long walks, I travel a bit, and I have my own charity."

"It sounds very solitary?"

"It is," he agrees quietly.

"Don't you like people then?" I ask curiously.

"Not usually."

"Why not?"

"One day I will tell you."

"That sounds very mysterious, Count Rossetti," I whisper, staring into his hypnotic eyes.

"Call me, Rocco," he instructs softly, mesmerizingly.

"Rocco," I breathe.

The air around us changes. His pupils grow so large his eyes appear almost black.

I press my lips together as I try to control the insane reactions inside my body. The way this man looks at me is just crazy. It turns my insides to jelly. No one has ever had this power over me. I literally melt under his gaze.

He picks up his glass of wine and considers me over the rim. "Where would you like to paint me?"

When I gave into the overwhelming need to paint him and blurted it out to him I hadn't properly thought about a plan of how I would accomplish that. I swallow and try to marshal my wayward thoughts. Obviously, I can't ask him to come to my tiny caravan and there isn't enough space in the backroom of the shop.

"Perhaps you can come up to my house," he suggests silkily.

I stare at him. Why do I feel as if I have stepped into a trap that he set for me? After all, painting him was my idea.

He smiles. "I'm not a spider, Autumn. And you're not a hapless fly I want to eat. Well, not in the traditional sense, anyway."

My eyes widen with shock, and between my legs I become wet. Did he just allude to wanting to eat me out?

CHAPTER 13

ROCCO

Even from here, I can scent her arousal. It is so strong and sweet it takes all my control not to lay her on the table, open her legs, and suck her sweet cleave. I pick up the wine glass and inhale the scent of old grapes to distract me from her tantalizing scent.

I watch the twin spots of color appear in her cheeks. She lays her knife and fork down with trembling fingers. It is as impossible for her to eat as it is for me. I am starving, but not for food, for her. For a taste of her.

"What do you really want from me, Count Rosse... Rocco?"

"When someone asks you out to dinner what do they usually want from you?" I parry.

"It's usually one of two things. A) They want to go to bed with me. B) They want to go to bed with me."

If she only knew. I lean back. "I want more."

She leans forward. "You want more than sex? Why do I find that hard to believe?"

"Why is it so hard to believe?"

"You are a man of the world. A Count. A man who thinks nothing of spending $100,000 on a painting by an unknown painter. You bought a mountain, then narrowed the roads to stop people going up it, for God's sake. You must have access to the most beautiful women in the world. What could you possibly want with me? I'm totally unglamorous. Everything I'm wearing today is borrowed because my whole wardrobe is old sweatshirts and jeans. I live in a trailer park, and I'm boring. I spend every moment I'm not working painting."

"Perhaps you intrigue me as much as I intrigue you."

"You only intrigue me so much as I want to paint you."

"Since you are immune to… my charms you have nothing to worry about. Come up to my house and paint me."

Her teeth sink into her bottom lip. The delicate skin around it turns white. My stomach clenches and coils with thick need.

"What are you scared of little Autumn? Me or yourself?"

She takes the bait beautifully. "I'm not scared of myself," she denies hotly.

"Then it is settled. You will come to my house to paint."

"How will I get there?" Her acceptance is grudging.

I smile with satisfaction. "I will send Raoul to pick you up. Just let me know when and where."

She licks her lips, her face uncertain. "The thing is I like to paint late into the night… when everyone is asleep."

I lift my glass and inhale the fumes of the wine deeply, in the hope it will distract me from the rich scent of her arousal. It's so strong now, it's starting to affect me. It's actually getting hard for me to stay calm and seated.

"I'm an insomniac so that would be no problem," I tell her.

"Uh… tomorrow night Larry is hosting a cheese and wine affair at the gallery for some of his artists and I have to clean up after them, so it'll be a late night for me, how about the day after? Your man can pick me up from the shop at 8.00 p.m."

"8.00 pm Tuesday, it is," I confirm softly.

She nods and looks down at her unfinished plate of food. Like me she is unable to eat and the food has gone cold.

"Would you like some dessert?"

Keeping her eyes on her plate she shakes her head regretfully. "It is a crime to waste such great food, but I simply don't seem to have the appetite today."

"Would you like the chocolate fudge cake to go?"

Her body tenses and her head jerks up, her eyes are wide. "How did you know I wanted to have that?"

I smile at the suspicion in her eyes. "I thought all girls like chocolate. It is our bestseller."

"I'm not a girl," she snaps defiantly. Her eyes are brilliant with emotion. It makes her even more beautiful. The image of her lying amongst tubes of paint and brushes on the floor, a baseball bat rolling next to her, comes back. She's a fighter. I like that.

I would have liked to have goaded her further, see her fly into a magnificent rage, and then take her while she is kicking and screaming, and turn her into putty in my arms, but there will be time for that later.

"My apologies. I should have said young ladies," I concede softly.

I gesture to the waiter loitering by the door. He jumps to attention and comes out.

"One chocolate cake to go."

"Yes, my Lord," he says politely and hurries away.

"Thank you for the cake... and dinner. It really was delicious," she mumbles awkwardly into the tense silence.

"The pleasure was all mine."

She chews her bottom lip. "I guess I should call for my taxi now."

"It's already taken care of."

She nods. "Oh, okay."

The waiter comes back carrying a black carrier bag tied with a red ribbon and puts it on the table in front of her.

"There is a small tub of ice cream so if you are not going to eat it as you get home you should put it in the freezer. Your dessert will be best if you warm up the chocolate sauce first. Seven seconds in a microwave oven will give it the perfect consistency and heat," he tells her.

She looks up at him, bestows a sweet smile, and thanks him. He smiles back at her. The smile is tentative and tinged with sexual attraction. He wants her!

Black fury explodes in my guts. It surges into my veins like poison and curls my hands into fists. She is mine. How dare he even look at her? An animal-like growl spews from deep within me.

Startled, both of them turn to look at me. With a fearful look at me, he hurries away.

She opens her mouth, no doubt to question me about the primitive sound, but I stare at her with such intensity that she is sucked into my world and held transfixed by the naked craving for her she sees in my eyes. She forgets her question.

"Shall we go?" I murmur, standing up.

Before she can get her senses together, I am around to her side. Confused, she grabs the bag and stands. Her knees wobble slightly. We walk together to the entrance. Not touching, but I am so aware of her, my skin tingles. The hostess comes out with her coat and I take it from her. My hands itch to touch her skin, but I resist the urge. She is so close I can hear her heart beating. Her scent of apricots and rain on freshly mown grass fills my nostrils. As she thrusts her hands through the sleeves, I am so close to the white curve of her neck I feel almost dizzy with the need to dip my head and kiss that smooth skin.

I slip her coat over her shoulders and take a step back. She turns around to face me. The overhead light falls on her upturned face, turning her eyes into enormous pools of liquid desire.

"Well, goodnight then," she whispers.

CHAPTER 14

AUTUMN

He doesn't wish me goodnight. Instead, he moves forward and goes down the steps towards the taxi. Something about the way he moves reminds me of a stalking animal. It is quiet, sleek, and designed not to alarm. But there is hidden power there. A shocking amount of it. Of that I am certain. He walks over to the driver's side and looks down at him, his aristocratic face stern and proud.

"Drive carefully," he instructs.

The man says something I cannot hear, and he nods and hands him what looks like some folded fifty dollar notes. Then he comes around and opens the back door for me. I'm not used to men opening doors for me. The feminist in me wants to reject the idea, equality and everything, but the romantic in me cannot help but appreciate the gesture. Women should always have doors opened for them. It's actually a lovely thing.

"Thank you," I murmur.

"Until Tuesday," he says, and there is something almost courtly about the slight inclination of his head.

"Until Tuesday," I repeat and slip into the cab.

The driver puts the car into motion. I turn back to look at him. He is standing there very tall and straight just looking at the departing car. I have another weird sensation of déjà vu. As if I have already watched him standing alone in the cold night air. Something very cold slithers through me.

I shiver and the coldness is gone, but it leaves behind its shadow, the feeling that something dark and ominous is waiting to take over my life. As if I'm approaching an end, but strangely, it terrifies and beckons me in equal measure.

I ask the driver to drop me off at the entrance of the trailer park. As I walk to my caravan, I meet Joe on his way to the bar. He smells of cheap aftershave.

"Whoa, is that you, Autumn?" he asks, coming to a stop a few feet in front of me.

"Hi, Joe," I greet without slowing my steps.

"You're looking hot, babe."

"Thanks, Joe. Have a nice night."

"Sure thing, babe. Sure thing," he calls as I pass him by.

For a few seconds, I don't hear his feet moving on and I can feel his eyes boring into my back, but then gravel under his feet crunch as he heads away from me. I exhale the breath I'm holding. As I get closer to his caravan, I hear his wife sobbing.

She is a pitiful creature. When I first came to live in this park, I used to try and give her the courage to leave him, but I quickly realized it was no use. She was and presumably still is hopelessly ensnared by him. No matter how many times he betrays her, or beats her up, all he has to do is buy a bunch of flowers and grovel, and she will instantly forget the malice and hurt, and melt into his arms again.

Once I get into my caravan, I text Larry to say I've arrived back safely. Then I get out of my borrowed plumes and into my comfortable clothes. Then put my headphones in and call Sam.

"About time you called," she says. "I've been waiting to hear the latest about Rocco Whatshisname."

"Well, Rocco Whatshisname is actually a Count and he took me out to dinner tonight."

"What?" she screams in my ear.

I wince. "Will you not do that please. I've got my headphones on."

"Sorry," she says, not sounding sorry at all. "Come on, give me all the gory deets.

"Well, he took me to the Four Seasons—"

"Wow!" she breathes, impressed. "Was the food amazing?"

"Absolutely. I even brought home dessert," I say as I pull the red ribbon from the handle of the black carrier bag. Inside is another black box.

"What kind of dessert?"

"Chocolate fudge cake," I reply as I open the box. It's almost like a kit inside. There is the chocolate sauce in a little plastic container, a smaller container of cream, a small bag of chocolate shavings, a thinly sliced strawberry, and a small container of ice cream.

"Good for you. Now tell me what happened? What was the date like?"

"Well, it's hard to say." I place the chocolate sauce in the microwave oven, snap it closed, turn the dial to seven, and switch it on.

"Well, the hell kind of answer is that?" she demands impatiently.

"I mean, I've never had a date like that. It's like surreal. Almost like I dreamed it all."

"Have you been drinking, Autumn?"

I carefully put the slice of cake on a plate. "A little bit. Maybe it's the alcohol. Larry opened a bottle of champagne this evening and I drank a glass on an empty stomach. Perhaps it's just that. Yeah, that must be it."

"Listen, I'm going to hang up if you don't tell me what happened. I can't make heads or tails here."

The microwave pings. As I lay the strawberry slices next to the cake, pour the warm chocolate sauce over the cake, sprinkle the chocolate shavings over the cake, and scoop the ice cream on to the side. I try to tell her about my date, but she is right even now I sound jumbled, confused, and incoherent. I take a photo of my cake and send it to her.

"You sent me a photo," she says.

"Yup, my cake."

"Very nice," she comments.

I take a fork and scoop up one end of the cake.

"So you like this guy then?" Sam asks, and my fork freezes in the air.

The question is like a whisper in my head. It makes me see the truth. No, I don't 'like' him. I want him. No, even that is too tame. I crave him… desperately.

"Yes, I like him," I tell Sam. "A lot."

I put the morsel of cake in my mouth. It crumbles then melts on my tongue. I close my eyes and I see him. His eyes.

"Look, I gotta go, I'm supposed to meet Bianca for late night coffee and I'm already late, but I'll call you tomorrow."

"Have fun," I say.

I pull my headphones off my ears and go outside. It is cold and still. I sit on the chair and eat my dessert. It is delicious and utterly decadent. The chocolate is so dark and pure it leaves a bitter aftertaste in my mouth. There is no one around, but the creatures of the night scurrying around quietly, so I lift the plate and lick the last remnants off.

Like a feral animal.

CHAPTER 15

ROCCO

I stand in the shadows of the trees across the field from her caravan and watch her lick the plate. She is so unspoiled it is almost unbelievable. She puts the plate back on her lap and stares directly in my direction. I know she cannot see me, but it makes the blood in my veins pound harder. I don't move a muscle. A small raccoon appears in the underbrush close to me. I am so still it walks right past me.

She stands and goes back into the caravan, and I feel the muscles in my body relax.

Suddenly I become aware there is someone else in the woods with me. It is the old witch. She is moving slowly in my direction. Usually, when I hear her moving around looking for herbs, roots, and fruit on my mountain I move away.

I turn towards her and wait. She is carrying a small lamp and I see her light moving slowly through the trees. Finally, she appears.

"Are you ready to take her?" she asks.

"No, guard her for me for a little while longer," I say.

"I can't watch her for much longer. Soon they will come." Then she bends her head and mutters something in Greek about her magic not being able to keep them away.

"It won't be much longer," I promise.

She lifts her head, and focuses her old eyes on me. "I will do everything in my power to help you, my Prince. Everything."

I incline my head. "Thank you, Zelena."

She bows low. "Good night, my Prince."

"Goodnight," I reply, with a nod.

She takes a respectful step backwards, blows out her lamp, and begins to walk slowly towards the clearing. I watch as she crosses the field on her short, thick legs. As she reaches Autumn's caravan she turns and glances in my direction, before disappearing behind it.

There is so much adrenaline in my body, my hands are shaking. I start to run. I run as fast as I can. Freezing wind rushes into my face and hair as I streak through the woods all the way to the highway. Then I run along the deserted road for almost an hour. When I finally come to a stop, my hands are no longer shaking with excess adrenaline, but the craving for her has not abated. Not one bit.

I turn around and begin to run back the way I came, towards my car. I take off my light jacket, throw it into the car, and slide into my seat. I turn on the ignition and slam my foot on the gas. My car hurtles through the night as I travel up the narrow, pot-holed, dangerous road at breakneck speed.

As I get to the gates, I see that I have guests.

William greets me at the door, his face impassive. "Your mother and sister are waiting in the music room, my Lord. May I get you some refreshments?"

I don't allow my expression to change. "No, thank you, William."

When I arrive at the entrance of the music room I see they are both already on their feet, guarded and waiting. My gaze instantly fixates on my mother. Her hair is worn differently, but the years haven't touched her at all. Her auburn hair, ruler straight, extends down her back to her waist, but she is slender and as imposing as ever. Like me, her face is carefully expressionless, but her eyes are watchful and calculating as she gazes at me. She is as familiar to me as the hairs on my head, but even after all these years, I still can't look at her without my stomach turning with hate.

Isadora immediately steps forward, her eyes filled with warning, but I ignore her and address the woman who gave birth to me.

"What are you doing here?" My voice is icy.

She smiles at me, a soft and endearing smile that aggravates me even more. Does she think such manipulations will work on me? I glare back at her.

"It's been so long, Rocco," she murmurs. "You still haven't forgiven me?"

The fury that sears through me is impossible to resist. Forgive her? How dare she? "If you don't leave right now, I will rip you apart."

"Rocco," Isadora breathes. "She's your mother. She just wants to make up. She loves you. And no matter what she thought she was acting in your best interests."

A lifetime ago Isadora could have made me believe the fairy tale that because this woman bore me she has my best interest at hand. But no longer. Even an animal will fight to the death to protect its child, but for this shallow, vain creature it is her own best interest that she places above all else.

I turn and begin to walk away.

"Isn't it high time that you appreciated what I did?" she dares to ask. "That… that woman was a disease. She was going to ruin you and, just like I predicted, she did. Look at you now. It's been so long and you're still not over her."

"Mother!" Isadora warns, beginning to move in front of my mother.

Neither could move fast enough to avoid me.

In a flash, I'm on my mother, my hand is curled around her neck. The smell of her perfume sickens me. "You keep testing me, Junia," I snarl.

"What are you going to do?" she taunts. "Kill your own mother? Go ahead."

With an agonized roar, I fling her away, and she crashes into the sofa.

"Is that the best you can do, my son?" she asks, without moving from her prone position.

"Get out of my house. And the same goes for you too, Isadora. I never want to lay eyes on either of you again."

After I hear them leave, I go to the library and pour myself a drink. I am so furious I can feel a muscle ticking in my jaw. As the fiery drink runs down my throat I know. They didn't come here to ask for forgiveness or to make up. The old witch was right. There is very little time left.

They have come for Autumn.

CHAPTER 16

AUTUMN

The next day Larry comes in earlier than usual. I'm still vacuuming the carpet. I switch it off and face him.

"Everything alright?" he asks, looking at me intently through his glasses.

"Yes, everything is fine."

He looks relieved. "Good. Sorry, I had to run out on you last night."

I force a smile. "No problems. You missed a great dinner. What was the emergency?"

"Burst pipe," he lies uncomfortably, a sheepish look on his face.

I'm not going to call him out on his lie. He has been too good to me. As it happens I enjoyed my time with Rocco so no harm done. "Oh, right. Is it all sorted now?"

Now he looks distinctively guilty. "Yeah. It's all good."

"I'll drop Jenna's dress off at the cleaners at lunchtime and return it once it's clean with her coat, but I've brought Marion's shoes back and she can pick them up anytime she wants."

"Yes, okay, I'll let them know," he says, obviously disinterested in the turn the conversation has taken. He pauses then adds. "So... it was a good dinner, then? Everything went well?"

"Yes, everything went well."

"Good. That's good." He stands awkwardly in the middle of the room for a few seconds.

I say nothing.

"Well, I guess you're busy. You have to get ready for tonight's party."

"Mmm..."

"Right. I'll be upstairs if you need me."

After he goes upstairs I carry on with vacuuming the showroom and wonder what the Count told him to make him leave the restaurant last night, but as I put away the vacuum cleaner the day pounces on me and there is no more time to think.

The florist arrives with the flowers for tonight and I get busy with arranging them around the room. The wine gets delivered and after a while the chairs arrive. I take them out of their stacks and arrange them around the gallery. Afterwards I take the wine glasses out of their boxes, wash and polish them until they shine.

At lunchtime, I drop off the dress at the dry cleaners, then pop into the deli to pick up the trays of finger food I ordered.

It's only five doors away from the gallery, so Ella, the girl who works there, and I walk back carrying the trays of food.

I file away the receipts into the accounts file. A tourist wanders in. Usually, Larry will come down when a customer comes in, but he is on the phone so I deal with the man. To my surprise, I manage to sell him a small sculpture. Feeling proud of myself I run upstairs to tell Larry about the sale.

"This is your second sale. I'll have to give you a rise," he says beaming with pleasure.

I clatter back down the stairs and start to open the bottles of red wine. They are good wines and need to breathe. Larry comes down at five thirty and starts spraying the room with his bottles of room fragrances. I retreat to the backroom to allow the aerosols to settle. I use the time to run a brush through my hair and slap on some lipstick.

When the first of the artists and their partners begin to arrive, I remove the coverings from the silver trays of food and start to serve the wine. It is a good night. Most of the artists are too proud to talk to the woman serving the drinks, but I get to hear snippets of their lives, their thoughts about their work, and once I even overheard an artist talking about his secret method of mixing colors. They are great drinkers and after the last dregs of wine are all gone just after eleven o'clock, Larry manages to get them out of the door.

"Want a lift home?" Larry asks.

"Nah, I want to do some cleaning before I leave."

"Do it in the morning."

I shake my head. "I have a different routine in the morning."

He must still be feeling guilty about running out on me last night because he says, "Well, shall I at least help to clear away the bottles?"

"If you stay any longer Marion will start to think we're having an affair."

Larry visibly starts and I laugh at the startled expression on his face. It's obvious the thought has never crossed his mind.

"Will she?" he asks nervously.

"Just go," I say, taking out a roll of black trash bags. I promise you, I'll be done in no time. Half an hour tops."

He frowns. "Are you sure? It's so late."

I grin at him. "I usually leave here in the early hours of the morning."

"Do you?"

"Yup."

"All right, if you're sure."

Once he's gone I bag all the rubbish and wash all the wine glasses. Leaving them overnight only makes the red wine dry and much harder to clean. Then I lock up and go out back. I notice immediately that I have a flat tire.

"Oh damn," I mutter, crouching next to it.

I consider calling a taxi, then decide to just walk back. It is a beautiful night, and will just take me an extra twenty or so minutes to get home. I start off down the road. Ten minutes later it starts to rain. I run to the bus stop with the intention of waiting the downpour out, but even before I can sit down a long black car with tinted windows comes to a stop next to me.

I have never seen a car like that in town before. The window of the back seat rolls down and the most beautiful woman I have ever seen in my life smiles at me. Her eyes are ocean-blue, her skin is pale, and her hair is platinum blonde, but I am certain the color is not from a bottle. She is mesmerizingly beautiful, almost angelic, but I am afraid of her. I glance around me. The street is completely deserted.

"Do you need a lift?" she asks, her voice silky and hypnotic.

Every cell in my body screams at me to beware. I take an instinctive step backwards. "I'm fine, thank you." Even my voice sounds shrill and panicked.

"Well, at least have an umbrella, then," she says, and holds out an umbrella in her outstretched hand.

"Thanks, but I'll just wait the rain out," I reply warily.

"Go on, take it. I promise, I won't bite." She laughs, a tinkling, sweet sound. When she laughs she is even more beautiful.

I stare at her. Something about her flawless beauty reminds me of Rocco, but where he attracts me, hers has a strange deadly quality that repels.

"Go on," she coaxes softly, her beautiful lips hardly moving.

As if I have been hypnotized, my hand, against my will, reaches out for the umbrella.

"Good night," she murmurs, once the umbrella is in my grasp.

The electric window rises up smoothly, and the car pulls away, but the encounter is so bizarre for a few seconds I am frozen and staring at the empty spot where the car and the woman had been. Then, as if released from the grip of invisible hands, I find I can move again. I shake my head as if to dislodge the fog in it, unfurl the umbrella, and start walking home. The raindrops fall on the umbrella in a relentless staccato beat.

But my heart is racing even faster. I feel fear, but I do not know why.

CHAPTER 17

AUTUMN

I have strange dreams of running and being chased, but they are confused and jumbled and I wake up with a sense of dread. And then I remember, today is the day I paint Rocco and suddenly my body becomes alive with a strange excitement.

The day passes with incredible slowness. During my lunch break I get my bicycle tire replaced then it's back to more hours that never seem to pass. Finally, Larry goes home and thirty minutes later I start to close the store. As I come out of the backroom holding my knapsack full of my painting gear and a prepared canvas, the rusty doorbells chime.

A man in a dark suit wearing a hat comes in. I know instantly he is Raoul. He has swarthy skin, dark eyes, and the look of a loyal servant.

"Miss Delaney?" he says, bowing his head courteously.

I never told Rocco my last name, but I suppose he could have asked Larry. "Yes, that's me."

He gives an old-fashioned bow. "I'm Raoul. Are you ready to leave?"

For a split second, it feels as if I am standing at a crossroad. Making an important decision that will alter my life forever, but then the feeling passes and I say, "Yeah, I'm ready."

He offers to carry my knapsack for me, but I tell him it is not heavy. Instead he picks up the easel that I had already brought into the showroom. He drops into silence as he waits for me to lock up. We get into a grey and yellow mini, and old French songs stream out of the music system. It's not my thing, obviously, but it's not exactly unpleasant either. In fact, it kind of suits the man and his lost-in-time vibe.

Soon we leave the town. As every sign of human habitation begins to fade we start on the winding road up the mountain. I look around me curiously. The road is dangerously narrow and full of loose stones. Sometimes it feels as if we are an inch away from falling right off the road and careening down the mountain, but Raoul is an excellent driver, and after a while I start to relax and notice that the higher we climb the more beautiful the scenery becomes.

The different types of trees give way to tall, looming pines. Dark has already fallen, but I can still make out the vibrant wildflowers that grow between the rocks at the side of the road. I roll down the window and breathe in the fresh mountain air. It is crisp and cold and smells of the pine trees.

As we turn the last bend, the house comes into view and I gasp with surprise. Enormous, Gothic, and utterly majestic, it's dark jutting peaks soar up into the sky and tower over everything with a stern, forbidding beauty. It seems impossible that such a massive mansion is home to one man. I stare with amazement as a big set of black gates open as if by magic and the car drives through them.

To withstand the elements, it has been built like a fortress, with thick walls; numberless, narrow Gothic windows set deep into them, and jutting corners that give the impression of an abode that harbors dark and sinister secrets... perhaps even foul truths. It won't surprise me to hear there is an unlit dungeon underneath the house guarded by ferocious dogs.

"Welcome to *Ze Dem Adelar.*"

I feel a shiver go through me. My voice is hushed and awed. I taste the foreign words quietly on my tongue. "*Ze Dem Adelar.* Is that German?"

"Yes."

"What do the words mean?"

"It means at the Eagle in German."

It is an apt name for a house so high on a mountain, but I remember the insignia I saw on the buckle of his belt. That two-headed bird must be an eagle and it must be the emblem of his family or something.

Suddenly, it starts to lash with rain and the smell of wild-flowers and pine needles fills my nostrils. The car stops directly in front of the flight of shallow stone steps. As I get out the great wooden door opens and a tall, erect man in a black suit stands in the entrance. His face is in darkness, but his silent, stillness seems to belong in an old-fashioned movie. I have the weird sensation of going back in time. As if the house is suspended somewhere in the past.

I hesitate at the foot of the steps. A fierce gust of wind slaps cold rain into my face.

"Go on. A storm will be upon us soon. I'll take your easel into the house," Raoul encourages from behind me.

I walk up the steps and see the face of the man. It is long and carefully expressionless, but because his eyebrows droop down he appears sad. He is wearing white gloves and holding a small silver platter with a white towel folded neatly on it. He bows his head, then repeats Raoul's words, but in a more formal, distant way.

"Welcome to *Ze Dem Adelar*, Miss Delaney." His accent reveals him to be English. "I am William, the butler. May I take your coat?"

"No, I'll keep it on for a while longer."

"Of course," he murmurs, as he holds the silver platter out to me. "A towel, if you need it."

"Thank you." I take the towel and hurriedly run it on my face and hands while he politely glances away.

When I put it back on the silver tray, he says, "The Count awaits you in the drawing room. This way, please."

I turn around and note that Raoul has disappeared. There must be another entrance for the staff and no doubt he will bring my easel in through there. Silently, I follow William through the house. The ceiling soars above us like a church, and the stone walls give the place a very still and silent air. When we are walking on flagstones, our footsteps echo through the vast spaces, but when we walk on runner carpets, it feels as if we are walking in a mausoleum or museum.

One thing for sure, it doesn't feel like a home. The mixture of gothic architecture and grey stones is forbidding. Here and there, I see beautiful figures and creatures carved into the stone, famous scenes from the past, mostly Greek, but the coldly precise lines repel rather than invite.

Finally, William gives a knock and opens a door.

"Miss Delaney," he announces, and stands back.

CHAPTER 18

AUTUMN

I walk into the lofty room, tastefully decorated in shades of duck-egg blue. Rocco is standing next to a massive fireplace with a fire crackling inside it. The flames add an orange glow to the side of his face and I realize that this house is the perfect setting for him. This house may not look like home to me, but I see now that it is perfect for him. Here, for the first time, he doesn't stand out as an object of awe and curiosity. Dressed in a fine-knit, black, turtle-neck sweater and perfectly-tailored, black trousers, he looks every inch the aloof master of his cold and aloof surroundings. He is the rightful owner of the rugged, isolated eagle's perch.

"Hello, Autumn," he greets softly.

"Hi." That was meant to be casual and nonchalant, but it comes out like a squawk.

"Would you like something to drink, or some refreshments, perhaps?"

I would have loved a strong drink, a double vodka, but I grasp my knapsack harder, and shake my head.

"Thank you, William."

Behind me, the door closes with a soft click. We are alone. A blind panic hits me and I blurt out the first thing that comes into my head. "It must have been very difficult to build a house like this on a mountain."

"Yes, I'm sure the architect and builders had their share of difficulties, but I wouldn't know."

I couldn't help myself. "You just paid for it."

His mouth twists. "Ah, you don't approve of money."

I dig in. "The kind of riches it takes to build a house like this is usually ill-gotten."

"I'm afraid I have to agree with you," he concedes.

I stare at him with surprise. "Did you just admit your money is ill-gotten?"

He shrugs. "I built my fortune on the considerable pile my ancestors left behind. No doubt much of it must have been acquired on the backs of the oppressed and dispossessed."

"And you don't feel bad about it?"

I see a flash of some emotion in his eyes, but I do not know him well enough to know what it is. "A clean slate was denied to me."

I wanted to ask him what he meant, but he changes the subject smoothly.

"Have you dined?"

"Uh, I had a very heavy lunch, Mrs. Appleby's lasagna from the deli, so I'll be good until I get home later tonight. If you need to eat, I'm quite happy to hang around and to set up my gear."

"In that case, we'll have a late supper after you've finished painting for the night."

"No, that's okay," I reply immediately.

"It will save you the trouble of cooking when you get back," he adds suavely.

Ramen noodles is not exactly cooking and I really don't want to spend more time in his company than is strictly necessary, but it seems churlish to refuse his hospitality. "All right."

He nods. "Good. Let me show you the house and you can pick out a suitable room for you to paint in. Leave your things here until we find the right location for you."

He starts moving towards the door and as he passes me I get a whiff of his fragrance and the hairs on my skin rise. He smells like those stormy nights when the air is alive with electrons and excitement. When he gets to the door he turns back to look at me, one eyebrow raised.

"Coming?"

I pull myself out of my stupor, hurriedly place my knapsack on the floor, lean my stretched canvas on the floor against a chair, and go to him.

As he shows me around the house, I listen to his melodious voice call out the names of the rooms, each one a beautiful work of art in itself. The whole house is a treasure trove. There are Greek and Roman marble statues, ancient tapestries from Persia, intricate stone friezes, and marvelous paintings, some of which I recognize as masterpieces worth millions. And yet there is no part of the house which is not cold and unwelcoming. The whole house is awe-inspiring and beautiful… and strangely dead.

I spot a painting in one of the grand rooms that makes me do a double take. It can't, it… but the style is so similar. "Is that?" I whisper.

"Yes, it is."

"But I have never seen a picture of this painting anywhere."

"That's because it's never been photographed. It's been in my family ever since it was acquired directly from the painter."

I walk towards the painting in a daze. Wow! An original, one of a kind, Van Gogh masterpiece, the world has never seen. It seems almost unbelievable. And his family bought the painting directly from Van Gogh! What a story! I stare at the painting of a vase of what looks like red dahlias on a wooden table. It is similar to his painting of sunflowers, but somehow so much richer.

"It's so, so, so beautiful," I say in an awed whisper.

"Have it if you want," he offers from behind me.

I whirl around in shock. "What?"

He shrugs one shoulder. "If you like it so much, have it."

I stare at him incredulously. "This is the *only* painting of red flowers that Van Gogh has ever done. It must be worth hundreds of millions."

His mouth twists into a bitter smile, and he makes a dismissive waving gesture. "All these things are worthless to me. Nothing gives me joy. Take it. "

I shake my head. "I can't. It's too much."

His eyes never leave mine. "How about an exchange? Your painting of the castle for this one."

My jaw actually drops with disbelief. The first thought that flashes into my head is: is he serious? Yes, he looks serious. Next: is he a madman? If indeed he is, he gives a very good impression of being sane. After that: What cat and mouse game is he playing? Because nobody in their right mind would exchange a Van Gogh for my amateurish painting. My chest fills with suspicion and distrust.

"Why do you want my painting?" I ask softly.

He doesn't hesitate and he seems utterly sincere as he says simply, "It gives me joy."

I exhale the breath I'm holding. "All right. You can have it, but I won't take your Van Gogh." I turn to look at the painting inside its heavy gilded frame. "To start with I have nowhere to hang it and I would be terrified of it getting stolen. Let it remain here. It is enough that I have seen it."

He bows his head formally. "Thank you, Autumn. You do me a great honor."

After that the tour of the ground floor of the mansion continues, but something is different inside me. I no longer see him as an insanely rich Count who has more money than sense. He is too beautiful and privileged to be pitied, but I can see now his great wealth and all his wonderful material possessions have not brought him any happiness at all. In fact, he seems to be desperately lonely on a level I cannot even begin to comprehend. Of course, I felt sad and mourned for my parents when they died, but that was a natural process of grieving for my terrible loss. But even then, I never felt as deeply alone as he seems to be. I would even go so far as to say, he is somehow damaged. Something very bad has happened to him in the past, and he has never gotten over it.

"And this is the library," he announces, as he stands back to allow me to precede him.

Of course, it's absolutely beautiful. Like something from a magical movie. There must be thousands upon thousands of leather-bound books here. I breathe in the cool, dry air, scented with the fragrance of leather and old paper. It is full of history and ancient secrets. All those authors long gone who have left a little bit of their souls on those aged, yellowed pages. There is no fireplace here, presumably to protect the books from smoke and soot, but the cold doesn't really bother me. Through the many narrow windows I see a storm is starting outside. Wild streaks of white lightning fill the window panes, as I turn to face him.

He is watching me silently, expressionlessly. The flashes of light make him appear like a supernatural being. Exactly the way I want to depict him on canvas.

"Here. I will paint you here," I say decisively.

He smiles. "Good. It is my favorite room."

CHAPTER 19

ROCCO

The wind howls outside and rain lashes at the windows. The storm has been raging for more than an hour now. I am positioned slightly turned away from her, but I can see her from the corner of my eye. And I have done nothing but watch her. Every expression that crosses her face, every movement she makes, every pause, every backward journey. I cannot stop watching her. The craving for her is so visceral it is an ache in my gut.

I see her: naked, defenseless, and begging me to take her... I can almost taste her sweetness.

I take deep, even breaths and force myself to calm down. To match her state of composure and tranquility. Painting has given her Zen-like peace of mind. Her concentration and focus are so absolute I'm certain she can carry on working for many more hours, but reluctantly, she stops and addresses me.

"Do you need... like a bathroom break or something?" she asks, her brush still.

"Not a bathroom break, but dinner would be nice."

Her eyes dart to her painting then back to me. She bites her bottom lip. While she was painting, she lost the usual nervousness she shows when she is around me. Her hands had moved quickly and without hesitation, but now the nervousness is back. "Yes, of course, we can stop for dinner."

"Would you like to wash up first?"

She drops her brush into the jar of turpentine. "Yes, I'll use the restroom first and join you afterwards. Will dinner be in the dining room?"

I nod. "Yes."

She stands awkwardly next to her easel for a second, then she begins to move towards the door. "See you in the dining room."

As she walks out, William enters. "Shall I serve dinner now?"

I nod, he leaves, his shoes hardly making a sound on the hardwood. I walk to the small table where there is a decanter of whiskey and a crystal glass next to it. I pour myself a generous amount of the amber liquid. It is Irish whiskey from the time of the prohibition. It is rare and even my own stocks are dwindling. I savor it on my tongue, then let the fiery liquor run down my throat.

I walk towards the window. I see my ghostly reflection in the windowpane. I reach out my hand and touch the face on the cold glass. It feels as if I have been standing here waiting and looking at my own pale echo for centuries.

I close my eyes and think of Autumn.

Of the way she lifted her arms and gathered her hair into a ponytail so it would not disturb her while she worked. How the action had left her ears and white neck so exposed I could see the little pulse beating at the hollow of her throat. I hungered for her then. The desire was blind and ancient. Like a strongly beating heart it had a life and a will of its own. The need was too terrible, too terrible to bear.

I forgot where I was, who I was.

I stood and had already taken two steps towards her, when her sweet voice asking, "Is everything okay?" somehow penetrated my monstrous hunger. I apologized, made some excuse, and sat back down, shocked. Finally. Finally, I understood what I'd never comprehended before, the agony of desire.

I had come so close to almost losing control. So close it was frightening.

My eyes snap open. In the glass my eyes look haunted and desperate. What if I can't do this? What if I can't control myself? What if I am just like my family? Principles are all good… until they are put to the test.

An image of my father's face, cold and forbidding, comes into my head and a low growl rattles dangerously in my throat. I can and I will do this. I will do it if it kills me. I have not spent all these years watching her, protecting her, and guiding her towards me, to fail now.

She is mine.

A white flash of light is followed by a roar of thunder. I already know the road down the mountain will be unusable tonight. I will ask William to get one of the maids to prepare the suite next to mine for her.

I put the empty glass back on the table and leave the room without looking at her unfinished portrait of me.

CHAPTER 20

AUTUMN

As I wash my hands I stare at my own reflection. I don't look at myself. My skin looks feverish and my eyes seem to glitter strangely. I tell myself it is just the excitement of being in this vast mansion on a mountain. A place no one in the village has ever been inside.

My eyes slide away at the lie. I wipe my hands on a fluffy hand towel and start to make my way to the dining room. Halfway there I pause. Then I turn around and go back to the library. I want to just look at my painting again. There is no one in the library and I walk quickly towards my painting.

I stand a few feet away and look at it. I have made a good start. The outline and the base coat are done, but I have left his eyes completely blank. Later, when everything else is done I will paint them. They are the doorways to his tortured soul.

I close my eyes and remember them.

Immediately they float into view. Translucent and haunted with pain. As blue as the ocean on a sunny day, but in their midst, I detect fiery glints. Glints, I know will change with his emotions. They are so vivid I know I can paint them when I am at home.

I open my eyes and am about to turn away from my canvas when there is a sudden loud clap of thunder, and all the lights go out. A small cry of surprise escapes out of my mouth. As there is no fireplace in this room, the room is now in complete blackness. I freeze with a strange and unnamable fear. Without the lights this place seems sinister. I can hear my heart beating loudly in my chest. Firmly, I tell myself not to be a dramatic coward. All I have to do is wait for another flash of lightning and I will be able to see a path to the door.

I take a deep breath. The darkness seems velvet. Seems almost to touch my skin. I feel my hands tremble. Then suddenly, there is a light at the doorway. I turn towards it like a newborn baby turning towards it's mother's nipple. Instinctively, without thought, purely from muscle memory.

Rocco is holding a candlestick. And in the flickering yellow light he seems bulkier, deadlier, and scarier. A predator! The light in his eyes that I had naively thought was torment, glowed like the pitiless fire in a falcon's eyes. My whole body freezes.

I open my mouth to speak and to my amazement no words will come out. My mind is blank. I can't even think of his name. It's not that I forgot, but I'm so astonished by my discovery it won't come to mind. My mouth trembles in shock.

"I'm afraid the storm has caused a power cut," he says, moving further into the room. "Let me escort you to the dining room."

I can feel the blood roaring in my ears as I stare at him blankly.

He stops about six feet away from me. "Don't be afraid, Autumn. The generator will kick in soon."

A little voice in my head says, run. I take shallow breaths. "I'm not afraid," I lie. "I was just startled."

"Good. Let us eat." His voice is calm.

In a strange daze, I follow him. The fear makes me hypersensitive. I can smell the beeswax from the candle and I can smell him. Like rain-soaked grass, or the woods early in the morning in spring. Hidden under the sweetness, the smell of earth. I can feel his strength, his power, and his will.

The tall doors of the dining room are open, and when we get to the entrance I gasp at the extraordinary sight. The long dining table is covered in a snow-white table cloth and set for two, and the massive room is illuminated by hundreds and hundreds of candles. The grand mirrors are full of the candles reflections. There are five servants silently lighting even more. I have dreamed this before. Even the perfume of flowers that fills the air. It is like a scene from a wedding night.

"But they must have started lighting these candles ages ago," I breathe.

"They have. Power cuts during storms are one of the drawbacks of living on a mountain top."

Silently, the servants troop out of the room.

"Come," he says, as William magically appears and pulls out a chair that is next to the head of the table for me.

As I slip between the table and chair, I feel him push the velvet chair forward slightly. Rocco sits at the head. I stare at him in awe. In the bright, warm light given off by the numerous candles, his skin is radiantly flawless. I want to reach out and touch his skin. My fingers tingle with the need. A strange sense of panic overwhelms me. What is happening to me? Why does he have this effect on me?

William pours wine into a glass on my right as waiters arrive with plates of food.

As one of them places the food in front of me, he murmurs, "Lobster meat on tender green leaves with orange dressing." I look at the plate's contents as if they are totally foreign to me. Then I lift my eyes and meet the Count's cold gaze.

He starts to smile, but his smile dies, and his eyes narrow. "What's the matter?"

I shake my head and turn away from him. How can I tell him that his beauty has put a spell on me? That I am unable to eat even a mouthful, because my stomach is churning with desire for him. "I have to return," I whisper hoarsely, then I push the heavy chair back and stand restlessly.

He reacts so swiftly, I do not actually see him move, but suddenly he is by my side. "The road is dangerous. There would have been landslides during the storm. It will not be safe until the morning."

"Are you keeping me prisoner here?" I rage, taking a step further away from his intoxicating presence, and staring at him with accusing eyes. My breath comes in great gasps. I want to run out of that luxuriously warm, wonderland candles, away from his allure and his beauty that burns into my soul, but his eyes lock with mine, and suddenly I can't move a single muscle.

His eyes are fierce and blazing, but when he speaks his voice is hypnotically calm and shockingly persuasive. "You are not my prisoner, Autumn."

"Then I want to leave," I cry wildly, but the horror is completely gone. I don't want to leave him! I never really wanted to. It was just the fear of giving in to my dark desires. Of letting them take control. I am not afraid of him. I am afraid of myself.

His lips part and a small sigh escapes him.

Automatically, my gaze slithers towards his mouth, the fragile, thin skin of his lips. I want that silky mouth on my body. I want us entangled and mindless with desire. I don't know if he can read my thoughts, but his eyes darken.

His body is very still, only those sensuous lips move. "Are you afraid of me, Autumn?"

"A little bit," I whisper, staring into the depths of those luminous eyes.

"Don't be. I will never hurt you."

At that moment, in the flickering light from all those candles, I know that is the truth. He may be dangerous to others, but I am absolutely and utterly safe with him. I can trust him with my life. "Yes, I believe you."

He smiles. "Good. You must be hungry. Shall we eat?"

I nod. I am hungry, but not for food. I move towards the chair and sit down. I slip a cherry tomato into my mouth and let it break between my teeth. Its juice, sharp and sweet, explodes on my tongue. I have never tasted a more delicious tomato in my life. It is the strangest thing, but every time I am around this man, all my senses become more alive and alert, and everything tastes, smells, looks, and feels like nothing I have experienced before.

I chew and swallow. Then I look sideways and catch the Count looking at me. The beautiful man is cradling his goblet of red wine in his hand, the stem of the glass is between his third and fourth finger.

And I remember something. Something that has been troubling me ever since it happened.

CHAPTER 21

AUTUMN

"I met a lady the other day," I tell him. "An incredibly beautiful, blonde lady in a long black car."

He goes incredibly still, like a statue. "What?"

"Yeah, it was raining and I was waiting at the bus stop. She stopped the car and gave me an umbrella. Do you know—"

The question is cut away by the scream that erupts from my mouth. The goblet he was holding has smashed in his hand. Blood and wine mix and spill on the white table cloth. For a split second, I see a jagged piece of glass sticking from his flesh. In the candle light his blood appears tinged with blue. Before I can even begin to react, he has already pulled the broken glass from his palm, and wrapped his hand in a napkin.

"Oh, my God. That looks like a really deep wound," I cry belatedly.

"It's nothing," he says quietly. "Please excuse me, while I get a bandage on the cut." He makes an old-fashioned bow and exits the room.

I'm still staring at the spilled wine and blood on the immaculate tablecloth, when William comes in with two servants. One of them is carrying a table cloth and another is carrying a goblet wine glass. Silently, I stand and watch as they expertly change the tablecloth and put everything back on the table. William pours wine into the glass. Then he nods at me, and they leave.

I look around the room and my eye is caught by a painting inside a glass case at the far end of the room. I walk towards it in sheer disbelief. Surely, not, but it is unmistakably, *The Storm on the Sea of Galilee*! Painted by Rembrandt in 1633, and stolen in 1990. No one has seen it since then. I have only seen photos of it, and it is more of a legend to me than an actual piece, but from the first moment I laid eyes on it, the energy and beauty of it struck and inspired me. And here it is now. As I stand staring at its incredible magic, I know without a doubt it is no replica I am looking at. It is the original, the real thing.

I am in front of Rembrandt Van Rijn's stolen masterpiece.

His approach has been soundless, but I know he is standing behind me without turning around. The hairs on my neck are standing, my fingertips are tingling.

"Where did you get the painting from?" I whisper.

"Paris."

I turn to face him. "You knew it was stolen, of course."

"Of course."

"But you wanted it."

He seems unrepentant. "Yes, I wanted it."

"So you reached out and took it?"

"Yes."

I think of that library crammed with thousands of old books. He is a collector of things. But not an ordinary thing, rare and precious things. "I suppose you have other houses in other parts of the world full of beautiful stolen artworks?"

He nods, and again I see that flash of despair in his eyes.

"But none of it gives you joy?"

"Nothing I own gives me joy... anymore." There is a bitter twist to his lips. The air becomes thick and slow with the smell of candle wax, exotic flowers, wet grasses, and him. I breathe in the scent. It is intoxicating.

I take a step towards him and reach for his hand. His fingers are long and thick, but his skin is cool and as smooth as a woman's. Certainly, smoother than mine. No doubt he has never done a day's work in his life. We are so close I can smell him. That sweet smell of grass, rain, and earth.

My skin tingles as I turn his palm upwards. There is a bandage across it. A vague sensation of relief washes over me. I thought the wound was more serious than that. As the relief fades I feel a strong urge to run my hand up to his wrist and feel his heartbeat. Resisting the compulsion, I drop his hand.

"Who is the blonde lady?" I ask, looking up into his mesmerizing eyes.

"My sister."

I nod slowly as I digest this fact. Even though she was beautiful and blonde like him she did not share any similar features with him or have a similar energy signature so it never crossed my mind they could be brother and sister. The only reason I thought they were somehow connected was because they were both so obviously different from all the other folk in the town.

"What does she want with me?"

His face is still and unreadable. "I don't know."

"So why were you so shocked that she approached me?"

"Because I didn't know she knew about you," he answers quietly.

I chew my bottom lip as an image of his beautiful sister rises into my mind. Something about her, I don't exactly know what, makes me feel very wary. "I don't want to be dragged into any family feud."

He smiles tightly. "Of course. I will tell her to keep away from you."

"Good."

"Shall we resume our meal?"

I nod and we move towards the table.

As soon as we are seated again, two waiters carrying plates come into the room. As they put the plates down in front of us, I see that it is exactly the same dish as before.

"What a waste. Our food was almost untouched and perfectly good to eat," I remark.

"From the moment a living being dies, the fungus that has lived inside it all its life, begins the rotting process. If one must eat dead things then they must be freshly killed and consumed immediately."

I take a deep breath. I have never given the food I eat much thought. Everything I put into my mouth has been bought in a supermarket, café, or restaurant and I have never pondered where it has come from, let alone how freshly killed it is. In fact, I hate the idea that it was alive and happily living its little life only a little while ago, and it was killed just to feed me. I look down at the lobster flesh nestled amongst the green leaves. Oh dear!

"*Buon appetito*," Rocco murmurs.

"I don't think I can eat this," I mutter.

"Why not?"

I look at him and he appears genuinely puzzled. "I know this is really hypocritical of me," I begin, "but it makes me feel terrible to connect my food to living, breathing creatures. I've always bought my raw meat, poultry, or fish cut, cleaned and laid out on a polystyrene tray and wrapped in see-through plastic."

"And unrecognizable as an animal," he finished.

"Exactly"

He leans back. "It is the nature of this world, Autumn. All living things are food to something else."

"If you don't eat your lobster, one of the dogs will eat it, if dogs don't, some wild creature searching the dustbins will, if they don't get it, the maggots will. In the end, we are all maggot food anyway."

"Now, you're really putting me off," I mumble.

"Have you ever seen a pride of lions bringing down a buffalo on TV?"

"Yes, once. And I didn't like it."

"I have seen it unfold in real life."

My eyes widen. "You have? What was it like"

"More than once. It's always a fierce battle, the very air fizzes with their adrenaline. The enormous buffalo in the prime of his life does not want to die. He fights back valiantly. He snorts and bucks when he feels the sharp claws of one of the lionesses tears into his rump. He shakes her off as blood pours down his hide. In desperation, he turns and gores one of the male lions in the face. The lion falls to the dust with a thump, but with a growl of fury he springs back. Blood pouring from his wound, he grabs the bull by the neck, and sinks his teeth into his prey's windpipe. The weight of the fully grown adult male lion forces the two-thousand-pound beast to his knees.

"The other three lionesses circle the choking buffalo. The buffalo's eyes are enormous and wild with terror. He already knows he does not stand a chance, but even then, the majestic beast does not go quietly. He kicks hard and tries his best to throw off the lion. The other younger lions start pouncing on him. Their combined weight brings him completely down.

"The felled beast screams for its long dead mother, but his windpipe is obstructed and only a dull, sad moan comes out. The heartbreaking sound carries in the still night of the savannah. The other buffalo hear the awful gouts of sound from one of their own, but they can do nothing. They don't see well in the dark. The herd moves restlessly away from the smell of the lions and the blood.

"It takes at least ten minutes for the great beast to die. His eyes fill with an incoherent, mad appeal. As it dies the crazy animal tries to reason with its hungry enemy, to beg silently for mercy. But there is no pity. No, no pity at all. The last minutes of his life sees the lions begin to feast on him while he is still alive.

"They always start with the belly. Tearing it open and eating its smoking innards. The buffalo surrenders and dies, but his death is not a gift to the lions, but to his own kind and the land itself. It is the chase and the battle that breaks open the hard earth so when the rains come they absorb into the soil and allow the grasses to grow so his sons and grandsons can feed on it. In the distance, hyenas are already beginning to gather. Their teeth are big and very white because they are used for crunching bones."

Rocco stops and takes a sip of his wine.

"If the big cats, the hyena, the wild dogs, and the crocodiles do not eat because like you, they pity their prey, not only will they perish, but the whole Savannah will become a dustbowl, and all those wonderful iconic animals will die of starvation.

"That lobster on your plate lived in a hydroponic pond as part of a natural system. It led as happy a life as any lobster can. It died swiftly to feed you."

For a moment I hesitate, then I push my fork into a piece of lobster meat and put it on my tongue. There is no revulsion because it is buttery and delicious.

CHAPTER 22

ROCCO

https://www.youtube.com/watch?v=swq_X9VQ744
-Stairway To Heaven-

I watch her as she speaks of her art. Bright, vital, boiling with life, and utterly secure of her place in the world. There is no mourning or regret in her. She lives in the present only. Like fire. No care for the past or the future. No holding back for fear of what will happen when all the wood has been consumed. Just burning brightly.

And that wild freedom is indescribably beautiful to me.

Fiercely, I note her every tiny corporeal detail. The sweep of her silky eyelashes, the way the flickering light hits the curve of her cheek, the strands of hair that have come loose from their moorings and sway gently when she turns her head.

At the edges of fascination, a thought gnaws. I push it away. This moment is too precious to ruin. Later. Later, I will deal with the fact that the enemy knows. Isadora knows about Autumn. Do my parents know too? Isadora is greedy… but not stupid. She would have told them. That is the reason my mother turned up here a few days ago. They are gathering, as elusive as shadows. Just as she represents life and innocence, they represent death, but I cannot give them what they want. If she dies I die with her.

"What about you?" Autumn breaks into my dark thoughts. "What do you think about modern art?"

I lift my glass and swirl the old wine in it. In the candlelight, it looks like blood. "I'm afraid I'm not a fan."

"We sell a lot of it at the gallery. What is it that you don't approve of?"

"I find it hard to be a fan of a red dot pointed on a white canvas, or a calf cut in half and displayed in a glass case filled with brine, or the display of a particularly slutty, unmade bed."

"Ah, that. It's moved on since then"

I take a sip of wine. "Glad to hear of it."

She leans forward, and the light makes her appear like an angel. A conjuring trick. "I'm going to change your mind. What do you look for in a piece of art?"

"Show me something that I can lose myself in."

She is as tense as a catapult on full stretch. Then she nods. "You're on."

"Hmmm."

She's about to say something else, when she stops herself, and looks down at her plate. The peach flavored crepe is gone, and all that's left is a bit of chocolate sauce. I have stood in the woods and watched her lick her plate when she didn't know I was there. She wants to do it now. It is only my presence that stops her.

I want her to forget I am next to her. I stay very still and clear my mind of all thoughts. I allow precisely nothing to be in my head. I don't move a muscle. I don't even allow myself to breathe. I become as unthreatening as a piece of crushed flower, or a flat black and white photo. It is something I have done all my life. Watching, without being seen.

Then... I will her to do what she wants.

She presses her finger on her plate, collects some sauce on it and puts her finger in her mouth. As suddenly as she forgot my presence, she realizes where she is, and pulls her finger quickly out of her mouth. Hot color rushes up her neck and into her cheeks.

I stare at her.

Yes, for a moment, for a fraction of a moment, she forgot her natural wariness of me. She forgot I was even there. It was only a moment, but it's enough. It is the first time she has crossed that vast, vast gulf between us, and began to accept me.

The thrill is savage and dark. My cock throbs and lengthens. The desire for her is more than I can bear.

"What is it?" she whispers. Her innocence is child-like. She doesn't even understand a man's desire for her. The need to taste her is incredible.

I stand. "William will show you to your room, and tomorrow morning Raoul will take you back down the mountain. Perhaps I will see you tomorrow evening in the library?"

She looks up at me, her eyes are confused. "Yes, I'll see you tomorrow evening."

"Goodnight, Autumn."

"Goodnight, Rocco."

I turn and as I reach the doorway, I see William walking towards me.

"Goodnight, My Lord," he murmurs.

I walk towards my office. I pick up the phone and dial.

"Hello, Rocco," Isadora purrs.

"Stay away from her," I growl.

"She doesn't just belong to you. She belongs to all of us," she replies sweetly.

My hands clench with frustration and anger. "How did you find her?"

"Ah, that. You did it the old-fashioned way. We hit pay dirt with ancestry.com."

"Don't make me choose between her and you," I warn.

She laughs, a careless, mirthless, soulless laughter. "Don't be a spoilsport, little brother. May the best man... or woman win."

The severed connection whirls in my ear. I lay the receiver back into its cradle, and walk towards the front door. I open it and a gust of cold wet wind rushes into my face. I walk out into the relentless rain. It soaks my clothes and steams my breath. I pass through the gates and follow the little path into the forest. Under the canopy of the trees I pause. The storm rages on and rain drips from the leaves.

I need to think.

And I think best when I'm hunting.

CHAPTER 23

AUTUMN

"You will find everything you need on the bed and in the bathroom, but should you require anything else please do not hesitate to ring that bell over there." He points towards a bell next to a massive dark wood, four poster bed.

"Thanks," I say, gripping my candlestick.

"Will you be having breakfast in the morning?"

"Er… no. I have to get to work."

"Ah. What time would you like to leave tomorrow?"

"Well, I have to be at work by nine o'clock."

"In that case please come down by eight o'clock and Raoul will take you down the mountain."

"That would be wonderful, thank you."

"Good night, Miss Delaney."

"Good night, William."

After he leaves, I look around the large room. There are three candelabras placed around it, but the edges of the room are full shadows. There is a vague sensation I have gone back in time. A large tapestry hangs on one wall and the curtains, which are all drawn shut, look thick and costly. An open door leads off the en-suite bathroom.

I walk over to the bed where one end has been turned. There is a small silver tray with two silver foil wrapped chocolates on it. The linen looks very white and crisp and smells of lavender. I touch it, and am surprised by how smooth and opulent it feels. Almost silky. I think of my cheap, scratchy sheets back in my caravan. How wonderful it must be to sleep in a bed like this every day.

I sit on the bed. The mattress is luxuriously thick and bouncy. Unwrapping the chocolate, I pop it into my mouth. As it melts on my tongue, I run my fingers down the intricately patterned silver and dusky-green, brocade canopy hanging from the four posters of the bed.

Truly, a bed fit for a Princess.

I eat the second chocolate before I venture out into the bathroom. I find some neatly folded clothes laid out on a cream and blue armchair. When I whisk the first one open, I find, to my delight, it is an old-fashioned, full sleeved, nightgown made of cotton and lace. Underneath it is a fluffy towel. A magnificent bath with gold taps and clawed feet stands on a pink marble plinth. The idea of having a bath in such sumptuous surroundings is alluring. Especially, since I haven't had a bath in years. It's always a quick shower in my tiny plastic cubicle.

I run a bath and pour sweet smelling salts into it. Then I lock the bedroom door, and step into the steaming water.

It feels wonderfully sensuous to slip into the silky, scented water. The sensation of decadence is magnified by the candlelight. I luxuriate in the warm water for a long time, thinking of Rocco. I replay everything that happened tonight in my head. He is a mystery. A beautiful mystery. I'd have stayed longer, if my phone had not started to ring. Knowing it can only be Sam, I run to it, leaving wet patches on the floor.

"Hey Sam," I say, as I put her on speaker, and wrap myself inside a fluffy towel.

"OMG, you won't believe what has just happened," she screams excitedly.

"What?" I ask, immediately getting caught up in her exhilaration.

"Remember that app contest I entered?"

"Vaguely," I murmur.

"I've won it. I got the first prize. They sent me an email this morning, but I never saw it until now."

"Oh, wow! Congratulations, Sam. That's amazing."

"I can hardly believe it."

"There were three thousand entries and I beat all of them."

I feel almost choked with happiness for her. "Oh, Sam. I am so proud of you," I whisper.

"Ask me what I won then?"

I grin. "What did you win?"

"I won a scholarship for the rest of my studies."

"Oh, WOW!" I scream. "That is truly amazing."

"That's not all. I also won ten thousand dollars and I've won the chance to meet Leon Joseph Chernyshevsky."

"Sorry, that name doesn't ring a bell for me."

"What? I've told you about him before."

"Uh, you know, whenever you start talking about computers I switch off, right?"

"Leon Joseph Chernyshevsky is almost like God," she says in an awed voice. "He's a mathematical genius."

I giggle softly. "A computer God. Right, okay."

"You better not have that attitude when you meet him."

I stop laughing. "What?"

"Well, the meeting is going to be at a black-tie dinner party in New York, and I'm allowed to bring a guest. You're that guest."

"Back up, back up a second. New York?"

"Yes, New York, but don't worry. It's all paid for. Here's the plan. I'm coming down to you and we'll travel together to New York." She stops to take a breath. "We'll be travelling first class, Autumn. We'll be picked up at the airport, drop our bags off in our suite at the Four Seasons Hotel. Afterwards we can spend the whole day in the Big Apple just sightseeing and shopping. And, and, get this: we're allowed to order anything we like from room service. Even champagne!"

"Hang on, hang on. When is all this supposed to happen?"

"I'm coming the day after tomorrow and we'll be flying out on Friday. The dinner is on Saturday."

"Sam, I have to work on Saturday."

"Oh, come on. Larry can give you one day off. You haven't had a day off since you started work there. It's just one damn day. You'll be back on Sunday night."

I sit on the bed. "You sure you want me to come with you?"

"Are you kidding me? Who else would I ask? You're the only one who would be truly happy for me. Everyone else I know would be jealous as hell and try to ruin it for me."

"How do you know I'm not jealous as hell?"

"Because you'd rather die than get a scholarship in my field, and I'm gonna stick my neck out and say you'll almost certainly find Leon Joseph Chernyshevsky the most boring person you've ever met in your life."

I laugh. "I have to say, I think you're right." Then I take off the towel and quickly pull the Victorian nightgown over my head. Snapping a selfie of myself, I send it to her.

"What on earth are you wearing?" she asks with a laugh.

I laugh too. "This is the nightgown I've been given for the night. Sexy, huh?"

"Where the hell are you?"

"I am in Rocco's house."

"Whoa! What?"

"It's not what you're thinking, I came here to paint his portrait and I was supposed to go back after that, but there was a big storm. Actually, it's still raining outside. Apparently, the roads are too dangerous to use so I'm staying the night. I have my own room, and the door is locked."

"What's the house like?" she asks curiously.

"Like something out of a period movie. Very beautiful, but somehow cold and dead," I whisper, as I slip between the covers. The sheets are silky and cold and I move around to warm them up before huddling onto my side.

"Like the owner?"

"Yes, like the owner," I echo quietly.

"But you really like him, don't you?"

Somewhere in my mind, thoughts uncoil like wool on a spool. I think of Rocco's blue eyes, how calm and meditative they can get, even though I've seen them blaze dangerously when provoked. "Like is too mild a term," I tell her softly. "This man makes my blood race. He frightens me, Sam. No, strike that. He doesn't scare me. I scare me. When I am near him, I feel almost like a feral animal, without the veneer of civilization. I want him. Even that is not right. I crave him. Every cell in my body wakes up and cries out for him, and my skin tingles as if it *knows* him."

"Jesus, Autumn. That's so freaking crazy," she mutters, shocked.

"I know it's fucked up, but that's how I feel."

"Wow! I haven't heard you swear in a very long time."

"I know, but it's like I'm changing inside. When I am with him, I feel different. There are no limits. There are no rights or wrongs."

"I hate to say this, but I don't have a good feeling about this," she admits reluctantly.

"Yeah, I don't have a good feeling about it either, but the force pulling me towards him is beyond my control. I've tried to resist it, but it's like an event or thing from which all else must follow. It sounds so crazy, and I can't even believe I'm saying it, but it is as if our mating is pre-ordained."

There is stunned silence while she digests what I said. Finally, she speaks. "Maybe I can meet him when I come down to see you?"

"Maybe," I whisper.

After that we stop talking about him and make our plans, our voices hushed with excitement. It's been a long time since I last saw Sam, and the thought of travelling with her to New York is thrilling, an adventure. Neither of us has been to the Big Apple. We speak in hushed tones for more than an hour.

Outside the wind howls like a banshee.

CHAPTER 24

AUTUMN

It is another hour before Sam and I finally manage to say goodbye. There is something about the unknowable about the house that makes me feel wary so I leave the candles to burn down as I drift off to sleep. William said they would last at least eight hours, so I reckon, by the time they burn out dawn will already be in the sky.

I am awakened suddenly by a strange scratching sound at the window. The room is in total darkness. The storm is still raging outside and in the flashes of light from the lightning I can see the candles are all only half burnt, but someone has extinguished them.

My heart is thudding in my chest. The room is like the inside of a fridge. My breath mists in the icy air. I hear someone call my name. The sound is coming from the window. Full of fear, I turn my head and see a young woman. She couldn't have been more than sixteen. Her hair is long and black, and her skin is deathly pale. Her lips are blue from the cold, her pale blue eyes are enormous with distress, and her white dress is soaked and sticking to her thin, child-like body. She is scratching desperately on the window pane.

"Open the window, please," she begs pitifully in a hoarse whisper. "I have something very important to tell you."

I know I shouldn't. I don't even want to, but I can't stop myself. I get out of bed and walk to the window. My God, she is standing on the ledge of the first-floor window. Shivering, I open the window, and the waif quickly pushes it open. Her head snakes forward, and it is only then I notice her pale eyes have black slits, like cats or reptilians. They glare murderously at me as if she is demon possessed. Without warning, she reaches a skinny hand out and clamps it on my wrist. Her hand is icy and my skin crawls with terror.

I freeze.

I'm too shocked to do anything even when she yanks my hand towards her. The strength in that tiny body is so extraordinary she hauls me right out of the room, and through the open window. Too late, I try to grab the edges of the window, but they slip away from me, like moving rope. For a split-second I am suspended out of the window. In sheer terror, I see nothing but darkness all around me.

Good God, Rocco's house is floating in a black abyss!

The waif lets go of my wrist, and cries out, "Now fly away. Quick. Before it's too late."

But of course, I can't fly. My arms flail helplessly in the empty air before I begin to fall, the cold wind rushes into my face. I open my mouth and begin to scream. I scream and scream and scream in the blackness. Something velvety, like a bat's wing, brushes against my cheek, and I lose it. With a howl of fury and horror I begin to fight and struggle with the evil in the darkness.

"Autumn, wake up. Wake up," a voice calls urgently.

My eyes snap open and I see Rocco bending over me. I throw my hands around his neck with sheer relief. Taking great gasping breaths, I sob, "I was falling. I was falling into a dark abyss."

"It was just a nightmare," he soothes.

In those few seconds I'm buried in his chest, time slows down to frames. Frame one, I hear his heart. A beat so steady it is hypnotic. Frame two, I breathe in his scent. He smells of rain and pine trees. Frame three, I feel his body. It is hard, lean, and filled with a wild animal's power. I feel it throbbing in his veins. Frame four, it makes my brain do cartwheels and my body come alive with pure lust.

I let go of his neck and move away from his body.

"Are you all right?" he asks.

"Yes, I'm fine," I reply, but the dream was so astonishingly real, my eyes rush towards the window. It is closed. The candles are all still lit and the room is not freezing cold. I hug myself.

"It was just a nightmare," he repeats, as he straightens.

I meet his eyes. They are as calm as an ocean on a bright day. I swallow. Up this close, his skin appears radiant, his cheeks rosy. As if he has been drinking or running. He can't have been drinking because there is no scent of alcohol on his breath. His hair is damp. Maybe he just got out of the shower. The heat from the water has warmed his skin.

Another thought occurs to me. "How did you get in here? I locked the door."

"I kicked it open. You were screaming."

"I see." I cover my mouth and try to think. "I'm sorry if I woke you up."

"You didn't."

I search his face. "I'm sorry about the door. I can pay for it if you give me the bill."

"Thank you for the offer, but that won't be necessary," he says stiffly.

I paste a smile on my face. "Thanks for coming to my rescue."

"It was nothing. Would you like a glass of hot milk or something?"

"Uh, no. I'm fine."

He stands, as if to leave.

I frown. "Is this house haunted?"

Amusement flickers in his eyes. "Not to my knowledge."

"I dreamed of a waif with blazing eyes who pushed me out of the window and told me to fly away before it was too late. It was a very, very vivid dream."

His expression doesn't change and yet I feel as if my dream means something to him. "Have you never had such a dream then?"

"No, never."

He nods and takes another step away from the bed. "Hmm... I was just going to have a drink. Would you like to join me?"

I don't hesitate. It will be impossible for me to go back to sleep. Not with the dream still so fresh and horrible in my mind. I push the covers back and put my bare feet onto the carpet. "Yes, I'd love to."

CHAPTER 25

AUTUMN

We walk down the corridor together. Me, barefoot, my virginal, voluminous nightgown fluttering around my shins, and him silent and brooding. I steal a glance sideways when we walk past the grand staircase. "Where are we going?"

"To the tower."

"You don't behead people up there or something, do you?" I ask, as we turn a corner and arrive at a narrow winding staircase.

"Go up and see for yourself," he invites smoothly.

I put a foot on the cold granite step. Then up on another and another. My feet are silent. Five steps up and I hear his shoes behind me. Soon I arrive at the top of the stairs and a small sigh of wonder escapes me. The room is massive and round with a platform in the middle. The entire ceiling is made of domed glass. The rain has stopped and there are stars in the clear sky.

"Wow, an observatory. How neat," I exclaim, walking towards a big telescope pointed upwards.

I hear a sound behind me, a flick of a switch, a whirling sound, and then the ceiling begins to part silently. The storm has washed away all the clouds and the night is full of bright stars shining like diamonds. It is truly beautiful.

"Oh, my God!" I gasp.

"Breathtaking, isn't it?" he whispers close to me.

My heart starts fluttering. I turn to look at him. In the moonlight his flawless skin looks like it is made of the finest white marble. My hands itch to touch his face and I feel in my heart a burning, wicked craving to taste his sensuous lips. Confused by the intensity of my desire for him, I turn away from him and lift my eyes towards the gorgeous night sky. But I see nothing. My heart is hammering in my chest. It is pure agony.

"You're really lucky, you know?" I mumble awkwardly.

He doesn't answer me. Instead, he asks, "What would you like to drink?"

I don't take my eyes away from the spectacular night sky. "Whatever you're having will be fine."

It must have only been seconds, and my skin starts tingling again. He is close by. I turn to look at him. He is holding two tall glasses with rounded sides, and a bottle of champagne, but the bottle has barnacles stuck to it.

"What is that?" I ask curiously.

"Shipwreck champagne," he says simply.

My eyes widen. "You mean this is a bottle from an actual shipwreck."

"Veuve Clicquot from 1841."

My mouth opens with amazement. "Did you just say 1841?"

He nods.

I stare at the bottle. "No way! I didn't even know champagne could last that long."

"This is one of the world's oldest bottles."

"How much is it?" I whisper.

"No idea. I don't usually buy my own wines."

I shake my head in wonder. How utterly different his life is from anyone I know. "You have an agent who buys your wines for you?"

"I have several."

"And you're going to open this rare champagne now?"

He shrugs. "There is no one else in the world I know who would appreciate this more than you."

"Are you sure you're not confusing me with someone else? I'm a total philistine. I've been known to drink cheap Vodka straight from the bottle."

"You drink cheap Vodka because you cannot afford better, but it doesn't mean you do not have a very keen sense of smell and taste."

I grin at him. "I'm not what you think I am, but if you want to open a bottle that I'm assuming costs thousands of dollars, then go for it."

He pops the cork with a quiet hiss. "Come," he says, and leads me to the platform. He presses a button and a circular seat rises from its base. It is almost like a bed. You could lie there and watch the stars for hours.

"Oh, how decadent," I murmur as I climb onto it and arrange my nightdress around my legs.

"Would you like some blankets?"

"No, I'm not one of those hothouse flowers that wither away in the cold. Even in the winter I'll sleep without heating and with the bathroom window open."

He sits next to me. Not too close. There is at least six inches between us. Then he fills a glass and hands it to me before filling his. I watch his hands. Hairless, the skin pale, but the sinews underneath make them appear powerful and muscular. He lifts his glass.

"To the stars."

"To the stars," I echo softly.

The champagne fizzles on my tongue. There is something magic about drinking it under the night stars with Rocco. I close my eyes. 1841. Wow! And then a strange thing happens. I smell the warm grapes. I realize I have never tasted anything so rich and wonderful. I open my eyes and stare at him. "This is astonishing."

He looks at me eagerly. "What does it taste of?"

I close my eyes. "It tastes of sunshine, earth, wooden barrels, and the skin of women who have pressed the grapes." I open my eyes suddenly, embarrassed. What's wrong with me? Of course, I can't taste the skin of the women who have touched the grapes.

His eyes are full of secrets, as his lips curve into a mysterious smile. "See. You are not a philistine."

"How would you describe it?"

"It has a rare complexity. Perfectly balanced accents of game, mushrooms, and dried fruit."

His description makes me feel unsophisticated. Why didn't I say that? "Yes that is what I was trying to say without much success... there is an authenticity, richness, and purity about it."

"What you are trying to describe is the fact it is grown without chemical fertilizers."

I nod and take another sip of the delicious champagne. He is right. It has no chemical aftertaste. I have noticed that he is very particular that the food and drinks he consumes are of the highest quality, and also grown and stored in the most natural way possible. "Purity is important to you, isn't it?"

"Yes," he admits softly.

I smile impishly. "You must be the purest person I know."

"No, I'm not pure."

"Well, you certainly are the most majestic," I counter.

His eyes dim. "Once we were majestic. No more."

"What happened?"

Mentally, he withdraws from me. "It's a long story. Perhaps one day I'll tell you."

I take a sip of the delicious champagne and drop my head backwards to stare at the blanket of twinkling stars. "When I was about two years old I was convinced I could fly. My mother said she had to watch me like a hawk, or I would have climbed up on the dining table and launched myself into the air. I only finally gave up when I fell on my head one day. My mother always said I've been soft in the head ever since."

He chuckles. A low, hypnotic sound that makes me turn my head to watch him. In light from the moon and stars he is like something from a dream. Unreal. Impossible to ever possess, or call my own.

"Here, let me make it more comfortable for you," he says, pressing another button on the console. The seat of the chairs start to move downwards until the space becomes a platform again. I lie back and he joins me.

Not close enough to touch, of course, but close enough that I can feel his presence.

CHAPTER 26

AUTUMN

I can feel the champagne fizzing in my veins, making me feel light-headed. I turn my face to look at his profile and he immediately does the same. Our eyes lock, and intense desire like I have never known throbs between us. It is wild and dangerous.

My throat becomes dry and my heart thumps so loud in my chest I am certain he can hear it.

I let my gaze drop to his lips. They look so red and inviting my thighs clench. There is only about a foot separating us, and every cell in my body is screaming at me to close the distance and taste those red lips with my tongue, but I am frozen. I cannot move a muscle. It is as if I am under a spell.

"It would be borderline cruel if you didn't kiss me now," I whisper.

He exhales as if he has been waiting for a very, very long time to hear me say that. His irises become molten, the pupils growing. All the world falls away and time stands still. He is so beautiful my breath catches. Then he begins to inch closer and closer toward me, until I feel his warm breath tickle my face. I smell the rain.

I close my eyes.

I wait for the touch of his lips and it soon comes, soft and cool, but the mere contact sets the fire that has already been burning inside of me, ablaze. He tastes me, slowly and lightly. I feel my hands lift into the air, trembling, as my hands try to find his body.

The pang of desire that hits my core is so strong it is almost painful and sends a gasp straight into his mouth. He pulls away, and my eyes flutter mindlessly open at the loss of contact. I look into his eyes and they are languid with passion. The pupils have grown so large his eyes are almost black.

Desire blazes through me, scorching me beyond anything I could dream of, and waking every nerve in my body. As if all of me has been asleep until this moment. I'm unleashed, unbridled, and on the quest for more. I throw my hands around his shoulders and slip my tongue experimentally into his mouth.

Molten ecstasy pools between my thighs. As my tongue teases and strokes his, I feel my awareness of everything else beyond his touch, begin to slip away.

I've kissed a few guys in my lifetime and a couple of them were actually quite good kissers and they did make me go 'mmmm… that's nice', but compared to what Rocco is doing to me their efforts can't even be called a kiss. This is so intense.

He sucks on my lips with a fervency that convinces me I could be brought to orgasm in this way. If we went on for just a few more minutes, I will embarrass myself by climaxing right here and now.

The groans that sound from my mouth are cries of the sweet, crippling anguish my body can't contain. I feel myself tremble, as I sink even deeper into him, my hands moving to his belt.

As I tug on it desperately he freezes suddenly, then pulls away.

One moment he was in my arms, and in the next, he's already on his feet and pushing his hand through his hair.

I feel the loss like a betrayal.

He uses the back of his hand to wipe his mouth, and I feel it in my soul. With a searing gaze, he turns around from me. His shoulders are tense and stiff. It feels as though I've been ripped into pieces and scattered in a thousand directions.

"What's the matter?" I croak, rising up on my elbows.

"We're not ready for this."

For a second I am stunned. Then I become furious. He led me on. He led me on. "Fuck you," I yell as I crawl off the platform. I run to the stairs and descend quickly. My heart feels hurt. He was playing with me. Maybe it was funny for him to play with the poor little artist. Tears blur my eyes as I hasten down the circular stairs. Suddenly, my foot hits the step at the wrong angle and my ankle twists. My hands rush to catch the banister to stop me from tumbling down the flight of stairs, but before I can grasp it, he is behind me, his strong hand sliding around my waist. His scent, rain and grass and earth overwhelms my senses.

It happens so fast I don't even fully register what happens. All I know is I am in his arms and being carried down the rest of the steps.

"Put me down," I gasp, startled by how quickly he responded.

But he ignores me and carries me down the dark corridor we came through earlier. There is no light to guide him, but he must be so used to the dimensions of his home, he never stops, hesitates, or shows any kind of doubt about exactly where to put his next step. We travel in the pitch-black darkness.

He stops to open my bedroom door, then carries me to bed. Silently, he puts me down and pulls the covers over my body. His hair shines like spun gold.

I catch his wrist. "Don't you want me?"

He peels my fingers from around his wrist, lifts my hand up to his lips, and kisses my palm gently. My heart feels as if it could jump out of my chest.

"You've never been with a man, have you?" His voice is soft and kind.

I feel the hot blood of shame rush into my cheeks. "How did you know? Did I do something wrong?"

He shakes his head. "No, you did nothing wrong. On the contrary. It's just… true innocence cannot be faked."

"Is that the reason you stopped?"

"I stopped because you are not ready."

"What does that mean?" I ask, confused.

He releases my hand. "There are things you need to know about me."

I frown up at him. The ripple of worry in my mind is like a stone thrown into a still lake. It disturbs, spreads, cannot be stopped. "What kind of things?"

He forces a tight smile. "It is late. Let's talk when you come around tomorrow night."

I think about forcing the issue then change my mind and nod. I need time to compose my jumbled thoughts too. Tomorrow will be better. "All right… is it something very bad."

He takes a deep breath. "It depends on you." Then he stands. "Sleep well, Autumn. I'll see you tomorrow night."

"Good night, Rocco."

After the door closes I pick up my cell phone and see that it is now almost 3 a.m. I turn my head towards the window and instantly see in my head an image of the waif crying out, "Now fly away. Quick. Before it's too late."

CHAPTER 27

AUTUMN

I t takes a long time for me to go to sleep, and when I do, my slumber is fitful and disturbed. At the agreed time, I go downstairs and find Raoul already loitering around the stairs waiting for me. He returns my greeting and immediately lapses into silence. There is a thick fog, but as we go down the mountain I note two landslides last night that must have been cleared away earlier in the morning. There is fresh mud and stones by the roadside.

He drops me off at the shop and I start my routine of cleaning then changing into my work clothes. Larry comes in earlier than usual and from the back door. "Come on," he says, "I've got something to show you."

"What is it?" I ask following him.

When I get outside, I see him standing in front of an old, blue station wagon.

"What do you think?" he asks.

"You bought a station wagon?" I ask bemused. Quite frankly, I can't picture Larry behind the wheel of such a car. Ever since I've known him, he's always driven glossy BMWs.

He nods and dangles a set of keys. "Yeah, for you."

My eyes widen with surprise. "For me?"

"Well, it was Marion's idea really. She was horrified when I told her you had to walk home in the rain that night because of a tire puncture. You can still use your bike, but if the weather is bad, or you get a problem with your bike, you'll have this old girl to fall back on. Besides, you can also start making some local deliveries."

I take the key from him and walk around the car in disbelief.

Larry pounds on the hood of the wagon. "She's quite solid, but the AC is broken, and it'll be an expensive repair job, so you'll just have to roll down the windows if it gets too hot in the summer."

"I still can't quite believe it," I mumble.

"You know how to drive, right?"

"Yes, but I haven't driven in ages."

"That's all right. We'll take her for a quick run at lunchtime, and I'll show you how everything works then."

I turn to look at him. "Thanks, Larry. It's really kind of you and Marion, and I'm really, really grateful, but I desperately need to ask another favor from you."

"What is it?"

I suck in my breath nervously. "I know it's very short notice, but I need to have this Friday and Saturday off. My best friend is coming to town and we're going to fly to New York for the weekend. She won a prize and she wants me to go with her. It's an all paid for trip. An opportunity of a lifetime and we'll—"

He holds his palm up to indicate I should stop talking and I immediately snap my mouth shut, conscious I was babbling.

"Of course, you can have the time off," he says with a kind smile.

I clasp my hands together and laugh with relief. "Thank you so much, Larry. You're the best boss any girl can have."

He shrugs and starts to walk towards the back door. "It's no problem. You've never had a day off since you came to work here, and between me and Marion we'll manage."

I take one last look at my new car before following him into the gallery.

At lunchtime, Larry and I take the car out for a run. For the first five minutes it's awkward, then it all comes back. After dropping him off at the gallery I drive back to my caravan and do a bit of spring cleaning. I open windows, I change the sheets, I clean out the cupboard. Before I leave for work again, I stick a change of clothing into my knapsack.

The day crawls slowly without a single sale. It's normal for the middle of the week, but boring as hell, and it is a great relief when I can start to close the shop.

Exactly, at the agreed time, Raoul comes to collect me. As his tall thin frame walks through the door, the nervousness I'd managed to somehow ignore all day, comes back in full force. Tonight, Rocco will tell me something, which I might consider too horrible to allow myself to be with him. Even the thought of walking away from him makes me feel quite ill.

In silence, we drive up the mountain.

The higher we get up the mountain, the more uneasy and troubled I become. In fact, I feel so horrible, my stomach feels queasy. I press the button on the door, and the window goes down. I hang my head out of the window and breathe in the clean scent of the pine trees. I hate to admit it, but a big part of me doesn't want to know, because I don't want to walk away.

I want to be with him.

The car comes to a stop and I get out and begin to walk to the house. As I get to the bottom of the steps leading to the entrance, the massive doors open, and William appears at the doorway. His face is in shadow, but his voice rings out clear and loud in the still night.

"I'm sorry, Miss Delaney, but the Count has suddenly taken ill and cannot sit for your painting tonight. You must go back and make new arrangements directly with him."

For a second I freeze with shock. Then I run up the stone steps and stand a foot away from him.

"I want to see him," I state confidently.

"No one can see him today," he answers, his eyes, his stance, and his voice, utterly implacable.

CHAPTER 28

AUTUMN

I glance back and see Raoul standing by the car, his eyes on me. He is waiting for me to return so he can drive me back. I turn back to William. His face is completely expressionless. I weigh my chances.

He is tall, but not broad, and the entrance is very wide.

For a split second, I hesitate, then I dash past him into the tall foyer. I can hear him call me, his voice stern, but I run as quickly as I can towards the stairs. When I hear both their footsteps behind me I start sprinting up the stairs. Cycling gives me the advantage. When I get to the top of the staircase, they are only half-way up. Good.

I turn into the corridor on the left and begin running down it.

I know from listening to a door close after Rocco left me in the early hours of the morning that his bedroom must be next to the one I was in. I dash down the corridor past my room and open the first door after it. It is dark and empty. I turn and quickly open the door opposite… and I am standing in a massive room. It is decorated in a completely different way to the one I was in last night.

There is a vast bed with a tall, intricately carved, breathtakingly beautiful, silver headboard. Never in my life have I seen such an unusual headboard.

But my eyes move to the still body on the bed. I run and drop to my knees next to him in disbelief. He is shivering and his face is ghastly pale, as white as a sheet, actually. There is a sheen of sweat on his forehead and his breathing is shallow. He seems to be gasping for breath. I can tell he is in terrible pain by the way his eyes are squeezed shut. I touch his hand and it is ice cold. I recoil in shock. He opens his eyes and the pupils are like tiny pinpricks. He is so delirious he does not even see me.

William arrives at the doorway and I turn towards him in a panic and scream. "What's wrong with him?"

"It is some sort of parasite he picked up in the tropics. These relapses occur from time to time, but the bouts never last more than a day."

"What are you talking about? He looks like shit. He needs to see a doctor *now*."

"The doctor is aware of his condition," William replies calmly. "He has medicine." He waves his hand in the direction of the bedside table where there is a water glass and a small bottle with a green liquid in it.

"Autumn," Rocco whispers deliriously.

I turn back towards him. "Yes, I'm here."

"You should go home. I'll be fine in a few hours. Come back tomorrow," he gasps, barely able to keep his eyes open.

I take his icy hand in mine and rub it vigorously to lend it some warmth. "I'm not going anywhere, not while you're like this. I'm staying right here."

He groans, but is too weak to object. I look at William. "Can I have some hot water bottles and more blankets for him please, William? He is freezing."

William nods and silently withdraws.

Alone with Rocco, I tenderly stroke his golden hair. He looks so vulnerable, so alone, and so utterly abandoned by the world. I can see now that he was telling the truth, all the money in the world has not brought him any joy. At that moment, I make the decision that no matter what confessions he has to reveal to me, I will not forsake him.

He is so cold, I lay my body on top of him. "Are you in pain?"

He opens his eyes and looks at me. "Oh, Autumn. Oh, my little Autumn. It is nothing. Just a back ache," he gasps.

"Wait a moment," I say and go to the en-suite bathroom. I find a towel which I use to wipe away the cold sweat on his forehead.

When William comes back with blankets and two hot water bottles I put them on his chest and stomach and cover him in the blankets. Then I lie next to him and listen to the faint beat of his heart.

"You should go home, Autumn," he mutters feverishly. "It's not safe here for you while I am like this. I cannot protect you."

"Nothing is going to happen to me. I promise I will leave when you go to sleep."

His hand finds mine, and it is just as cold and clammy as it had been before the hot water bottles and extra blankets. I wrap my hands around it, bury my nose in his neck, and breathe in the scent of him. A feral, yes entirely feral, sensation fills my chest. I feel the way I imagine a mother would feel about her newborn child. As if she alone is solely responsible for the helpless thing. As if she has been sent to earth to protect, guard, and save it from any who would seek to harm the vulnerable thing in her arms. And God help anyone who tries to hurt it.

He mumbles something restlessly.

"Shhh… it's okay. Sleep, Rocco. Sleep," I try to soothe.

"You must leave," he growls, but there is no power in his voice.

"I'll go home when you go to sleep."

He draws a shuddering breath. "Promise?"

"Promise."

Minutes pass, and his breathing slowly becomes less fraught, less frightening. Where his skin touches mine or the hot water bottles it is warm, but everywhere else it remains scarily cold.

Sometimes moans of pain escape out of his mouth, and it hurts my heart to hear it, but finally, he falls into a light sleep. I dare not even breathe because I do not want to wake him up. So it irritates me when I hear a noise from the doorway. William is standing there.

Quickly, I put my finger to my lips. He motions for me to come to him. As gently as I can I slide off the bed. Rocco makes a sound in his throat, but his eyes remain closed. I tip toe towards William.

"The Count's sister is here. She wishes to speak to you," he says quietly.

I feel a cold shiver go through me, and I glance back uneasily at the sleeping figure on the bed. I don't want to, but I know I must face her. Clearly, she's part of Rocco's life and therefore mine too.

Squaring my shoulders, I follow William out of the room.

CHAPTER 29

AUTUMN

She is even more beautiful in the bright lights of the chandelier. Her hips are as slender as a snake and her legs are long and slim. There is a smile on her lips. "Please, sit down," she invites, gesturing towards a sofa patterned with soft-blue birds on a white background.

There is an open bottle of wine and two glasses on the low table next to it. I walk stiffly towards the sofa and perch uncomfortably on the edge of it.

"How is the poor lamb?" she asks, taking a seat on the sofa opposite. She seems supremely confident.

"William says he will be better tomorrow," I say carefully.

She twists her mouth downwards, a curiously flirtatious gesture. "Yes, these horrible bouts come, but thankfully they do go away pretty quickly."

"What are they?" I ask curiously.

She shrugs. "You must ask my brother."

I nod. I do not know what it is about her, but my skin is actually crawling with revulsion.

"We haven't been formally introduced. I'm Isadora."

"Nice to meet you," I reply automatically.

"So you're an artist."

"I work at an art gallery, but you already know that."

She smiles. "Yes. It's a small town and I've seen you there."

"You don't live around here, do you?"

"No, I don't."

She doesn't elaborate further and I realize I don't want to make small talk with her. "Why did you want to see me?"

"Well, to start with I know my brother really likes you, and I wanted to welcome you into our family. We are a family with many problems, but we all love Rocco and want what's best for him."

At that point, I have a strange impression. She is being kind, but what she really wants to be is cruel. I push the impression away, but it stays at the fringes of my mind not as something I imagined, but something real. There is something risky, dangerous even about her. If I'm being unkind then, the word I would use is repulsive.

"Thank you. That's very kind of you," I say, even though I am mentally putting distance between us.

"Let's have a glass of wine," she drawls.

My whole body rejects the offer. I shake my head politely. "Thank you, but I'm not in the mood today. I should go up and be with Rocco. Perhaps another day."

"Oh, please say yes," she pleads, suddenly leaning forward eagerly. "Rocco is asleep. He won't mind you having a drink with me."

There is something desperate about her invitation. As if me agreeing to have a drink with her is very important to her.

"It's from our family's vineyard in France," she adds anxiously.

I'm about to refuse again, when something crazy happens. I look into her beautiful, dreadful blue eyes and can't look away. To my surprise, I find myself saying, "All right."

"Wonderful," she gushes.

Her eyes are shining with an unholy light. It is as if I have not just assented to a glass of wine together, but something far, far more important. In a daze, I watch as she picks up the bottle and pours the red liquid into the two glasses. Part of me regrets agreeing, but I tell myself what harm can one glass do?

She holds out a glass to me and I take it from her. I am careful not to touch her skin. She lifts the glass jubilantly for a toast.

"To you and Rocco," she sings.

I find it impossible to repeat her words. There is something false about her toast. Instead, I simply lift the glass to my lips. It happens so swiftly, everything is a blur. One moment I'm about to take a sip and the next the glass has been knocked out of my hand and is on the ground. The red liquid seeping into the pale carpet.

In total shock, I whirl my head around and see Rocco standing behind me.

Even though he is holding onto the back of the sofa, he is swaying with the effort of being upright. His face appears even more bloodless than it was before, sweat gleams on his forehead, and his face drawn and pinched as if he is in intense pain, but his eyes blaze with terrible fury. I turn my head to look at his sister. There is absolutely no expression on her face. She is sitting on the sofa as still as a statue.

"Sorry, if I startled you. That wine is corked," Rocco mutters, as he drags his gaze to me.

I can't say a word. I'm too shocked. I just stare at him stupidly.

"William," he calls, wincing with pain.

William appears almost immediately.

"Please arrange a ride for Miss Delaney immediately."

"Yes, my Lord," William says, and nods towards me. "If you'd like to follow me, Miss. Delaney."

For a second, I think about refusing, but one look at Rocco's tight, pain-filled face tells me not to argue. Wordlessly, I follow William out of the room. Raoul is already waiting for me in the foyer. We go out into the night silently. There is a cold wind blowing outside and the moon is very full. As I get into the car, I look back at the house. Through one of the windows I can see Rocco and his sister. She is standing opposite him, facing him.

And it is clear she is just as furious as he is.

CHAPTER 30

ROCCO

"What the fuck are you doing here?" I snarl.

"Believe it or not, I was in the area and William told me you were poorly."

I ignore the blatant lie. "What were you trying to do?"

Her eyes flash. "For heaven's sake. Anybody would think I was trying to poison her or something. I just wanted to get to know her. She seems… nice."

My back hurts so much I feel dizzy, but I know I have to have it out with her. I have to somehow stop her from doing something stupid. "Don't be a bitch, Isadora."

She smiles condescendingly. "You must have it really bad for her, little brother."

"Back off, Isadora," I growl.

"Back off? I haven't done anything."

"I know exactly what you were trying to do. If you make her do anything she doesn't want, all of us will lose."

"Then stop wasting time and do what you are supposed to do. It's not only you who is suffering you know." She tugs at her hair and it comes off. Her thick lustrous hair is a wig!

I stare at her in horror. On her almost bald head are patches of red skin and several thin strands of hair.

"That's right. You're not the only one. Something is happening to mother too. She is losing her teeth. They are just dropping out of her mouth for no reason and her breath is putrid as if she is rotting inside. As for father, you should see what he looks like now. Old beyond his years."

I take a step back from her. The pain in my back is now so strong, I feel faint.

"We all need her, Rocco. It's for the common good of all of us," she cries.

I shake my head. "The rights of a group shouldn't be more important than the right of the individual. I will not allow it. Not now not ever. I have enough demons to contend with."

"Why are you so against it? How do you know she won't want it? As far as I can tell most of them will give up everything to be one of us."

"One of us? Look at us? What is so fucking great about us?" I ask bitterly.

She fits her wig over her diseased head. "It's not your choice to make. It's hers. Time is running out and if you won't do it I will," she snaps.

"It won't work without me," I mumble through the pain.

"I'm desperate. I'll try it."

"Pour me a whiskey," I mutter. The hurt has got into my head and it is so intense, I feel myself sinking to my knees.

I don't hear her moving around, but a few seconds later, I see her hold half a glass of amber liquid close to my face. I take the glass and pour the whiskey down my throat. The burn has little effect on me. I give the glass back to her. "Another one," I gasp.

She gives me another half-full glass and I throw it back. My head bobs with the goddamn agony in my neck and back.

She kneels next to me. "Why do you want to carry on suffering like this, Rocco? Just tell her. Give her the choice. Who knows our thing might be her thing," she says.

An image of Autumn flashes into my mind. The innocence in her eyes... Isadora will never understand such a thing. I reach out a hand and catch Isadora's wrist roughly. "Don't hurt her, Isadora."

"Why would I do that? I don't want to hurt her. I just want my family to be whole again."

I let go of her and try to focus on her face, but it swims before my eyes. "What if she says no, will you hurt her then?"

She smiles, a cruel smile. "She'll never say no. Not when she's already more than half in love with you. Now, let's get you back to bed. You look like shit."

I know she is my enemy. I know she can be deadly. I know she will take pleasure in hurting Autumn... so I offer my hand out as if in friendship. Her slender hand curls round mine, then tightens like a vice, and effortlessly she pulls me to my feet.

Yes, she will be a formidable opponent.

CHAPTER 31

AUTUMN

As we journey back down the mountain I stare blindly out of the window. I'm shocked and in a state of utter confusion. What had just happened back there? There is no way Rocco knocked the glass out of my hand because he believed the wine was corked.

Was the wine poisoned?

Why on earth would Isadora want to poison me? I'm nothing to her. I nibble on the nail of my thumb. Thank God, Sam is coming tomorrow. I feel as if I have fallen into a rabbit hole. It will be good to be with someone normal. I'll tell her everything. I need to know I'm not going mad.

When Raoul drops me outside the shop, I decide to cycle home. The fresh air and exercise will do me good. By the time I get back it's a quarter to midnight. As I'm chaining my bike to the metal pipe of my caravan, I notice the light in the old gypsy's windows.

For a few seconds I hesitate, then I start walking towards her caravan. I knock on her door and immediately hear some movements inside. She opens the door and peers at me.

I swallow and suddenly feel ridiculous. "I know it's very late, but how much do you charge to read someone's fortune?"

"Ah, you are the child who lives in the caravan yonder," she states, her voice is low and gruff.

"Yes."

She smiles. "Well, since we are neighbors, I'll be happy to read your fortune for ten dollars?"

That seems too cheap, and I'm immediately filled with pity for her. She is so old and yet she has to read fortunes for such a pittance. "Could you read it now?"

"Now?"

I nod. "Yes, I'm in a bit of a mess, and I… er… just wondered if you could maybe see something in my future in your crystal ball or tarot cards." I can't believe I just said crystal ball.

A gleam of amusement shines momentarily in her eyes, then it is gone. "Come in, little one. Let's see what the tea leaves have to say to you."

The inside of her caravan is a surprise. I'd imagined it would be crammed with dusty ornaments, bohemian crystal table-ware, lace curtains, chintz cushions and old furniture, but instead it is incredibly clean and surprisingly bare. It's hard to imagine a human being lives here. There is a small, square wooden table, two plain chairs tucked under it, and a neatly made narrow bed. There is nothing on the table or any of the shelves. On the kitchen counter sits an electric kettle, a ceramic container, and two fine bone china teacups and their saucers decorated with roses.

She closes the door behind me and I reach into my back pocket and pull out a ten dollar bill. When I hand it to her, she nods and carelessly puts it on the counter. She switches on the kettle and asks me to take a seat.

I pull out one of the chairs and sit down. She opens the ceramic container and pours loose tea into one of the teacups. When the kettle begins to whistle, she pours the boiling water into the teacup, and brings the cup to me. She puts it in front of me and goes to sit opposite me.

"When it cools, drink it," she says.

I look down at the cup of tea, and to my surprise find there is a lot happening inside the cup. I watch the brown essence from the tea leaves start to stain the water. The clouds of brown fascinate me. I could have stared at the process for hours and maybe I do. It's strange, but it's as if I've been hypnotized by the movements in the teacup.

"You can drink it now," she murmurs softly.

I drink the bitter brew and put the cup back on the saucer. She takes the cup and looks into it. For a while she says nothing as she studies the patterns the tea leaves make, then she raises her head and looks directly into my eyes.

I am surprised by how bright her eyes are. They shine like stars in her wrinkled old face.

"You have come about a man. You have come to ask if you can trust him?"

"Yes," I whisper.

"First I must tell you there is danger. Danger lurks around you." She looks away from me. "And there is loss. Terrible loss for you."

My stomach clenches with dread. "What do you mean?"

"I cannot say more than that. All I can see is the loss of something very important to you."

"You mean him?" I ask anxiously.

"No, not him. Something else."

"Can I trust him?"

"Yes, you can trust him, but he is also in danger. Secrets. Many terrible secrets." She gazes at the tea leaves, then frowns. "His family. They want something from you."

"What?" I cry. "What do they want?"

She shakes her head. "Stay away from them. They mean you harm."

She puts the cup down. "Show me your hand."

I put out my right hand and she takes it in hers and looks at it. Then she uses her other hand to stroke my palm gently, as if she is so starved of human contact that she needs to touch another human being. My chest fills with pity for the lonely old woman, and I push to the back of my mind all the dire predictions and warnings she has made. I reach out my other hand and grasp her hand tightly. She looks up and I see her eyes are filled with tears.

"In five minutes, it will be my birthday," she says, and her voice breaks.

"Really?"

She nods sadly, and extricates her hand from mine.

"Hang on. Just wait for me. I'll only be five minutes," I say and jump to my feet. I run back to my caravan. I bought a little congratulatory cake for Sam. It came with those joke candles that never go off so I quickly light the candles on it, and carefully carry it back to the gypsy's caravan. I push open the door and shout, "Happy Birthday."

As long as I live I will never forget that sweet and innocent time I spend with her. How I sing to her and how she beams at me. She has never seen a candle that splutters back to life before and she cackles with delight and surprise. I cut the small cake and she finds two small plates in one of the kitchen cupboards. I find out her name is Zelena.

"I should go," I say, licking a bit of icing from my fingers.

"Wait. I have something for you."

I watch in surprise as she gets up and pulls a battered black suitcase from under the bed. From it she extracts a small jeweled box. I can tell just by looking at it that it is terribly ancient. She puts the box on the table in front of me.

I open the box and find a lovely locket shaped in a strange symbol. It seems to be made of precious stones. A round ruby, and around it a mix of white and purple stones, but the craftsmanship is of a particularly excellent quality, and it is clearly very valuable. In fact, it looks like something that should be under glass in a museum.

"I can't take this," I gasp, but when I look up at her, I see her silently taking off a thin gold chain from around her neck.

"I have no need for it. It is an amulet," she explains. "For protection."

I stare at her in surprise. It feels wrong to take it from her and yet she seems utterly fixed in her intention to give it to me. She fixes the amulet onto her chain and comes towards me. "It belonged to my grandmother. My daughter died so I have no one to give it to."

She comes close to me, and the scent of herbs and fresh flowers fills my nostrils. Bizarrely, the smell is familiar to me. I inhale deeply and feel certain I recognize it from somewhere. She fastens the chain around my neck, and it is still warm from her flesh.

Then her gnarled, roughened hand strokes my cheek tenderly.

I want to ask her for the name of the perfume she is wearing, but the words are stuck in my throat. Then she withdraws her hand and says, "Go now, my child. Never forget, love will conquer everything. Everything."

CHAPTER 32

AUTUMN

I have strange dreams all night long. Of tall, beautiful people I've never met before, but they gather around me protectively and touch my face the way Zelena did. Tenderly, as if they love me. Some of them whisper, "Courage, Autumn. Courage. Love will conquer everything."

When my alarm rings in the morning, I feel groggy and unprepared for the world. The first thing I do is cradle the amulet Zelena gave me. I don't exactly understand what happened last night. I paid her ten dollars for a fortune telling session, and came away with an obviously valuable and ancient piece of jewelry. I feel slightly guilty, as if I have taken advantage of a very lonely old woman, but she was so totally sure she wanted me to have it. If anything, it felt as if she had been waiting to give it to me. Which of course, is nonsense. I'm a complete stranger to her.

Still, I resolve to visit her more often and take her little presents of food. Her kitchen had nothing in it. I'll be the granddaughter she never had.

As I get out of bed, I wonder how Rocco is feeling, if his bout of pain and sickness is over yet. I decide to call when I get to the gallery and find out, but just as I'm unlocking the back door of the gallery, the phone starts ringing inside. I rush to it and it is William.

"Miss Delaney," he says formally. "The Count is much better this morning. He has finally fallen asleep. He asked me to inform you that he will see you tonight."

I explain to him that my best friend is coming to visit and we will be going away together for the weekend. Could he also please tell Rocco that I will see him on Monday night, if that is all right with him.

I put down the phone and feel happier. Rocco is fine and Sam is coming today. The day passes easily. Some customers come in, and one even buys a small painting by my favorite South African artist. He paints using mud and chalk and minerals he finds in the earth.

At nearly three in the afternoon the rusty bell above the door rings and Sam walks through. We laugh and scream so much Larry comes down to see what the commotion is about. When I tell him about Sam's achievement he insists on opening a bottle of champagne. We toast to her success. It is a good afternoon, the sun slants in through the big glass windows, Sam's hair is like fire, Larry seems relaxed and untroubled, and I feel happy. Sam asks me if I have something to wear for the black-tie event and I say, 'Kind of."

Immediately Larry chases us out of the gallery. "Go on. Get out of here. Go buy something before all the shops shut."

We spill out of the gallery laughing. The champagne is fizzing in my veins, as I link arms with Sam. There is only one boutique worth going to in town, not that I've even been in it, but judging purely from the dresses they display in their window, so we head towards it. Even from across the street, I see the most beautiful dress I have ever seen in my life in their window.

"Wow, look at that," Sam exclaims.

We cross the street and stand on the pavement staring at the dress. "Beautiful, isn't it?"

She turns towards me. "That's the dress we're getting for you."

I shake my head. "No way I'm paying that much for a dress I will never wear more than once."

"You're not paying for it. I am. Remember I won ten thousand."

I frown. "No, I don't want you to spend that kind of money on a dress for me. The prize is for you."

"Come on. Let's go in and see how much it is first."

The sales assistant comes forward with a smile. "Hello."

"Hiya. How much is the green dress in the window?" Sam asks.

"Ah, the pure silk evening dress. You have excellent taste. It will look wonderful with your red hair."

"It's not me. It's for her."

The woman doesn't blink an eyelid. "It would look amazing with your chocolate hair too."

"So how much is it?" I ask.

"It's a steal at two thousand dollars."

Sam and I look at each other. It is well out of both our budgets. "I'll find something else."

"Okay," she agrees and we start to look at the racks. Sam finds a red dress with a plunging neckline. I try it on, and both Sam and the shop assistant assure me it is 'the one'. Sam comes close to me. "What's that?" she asks, touching the amulet.

"A gypsy gave it to me," I explain.

"Really? Wow! For a moment there, I thought it was precious. It looks freaking real."

"It is real," I whisper.

Her eyes widen with surprise. "Whoa! Okay, you need to tell me more, my girl."

I nod. "Yeah, there is a lot I want to talk to you about."

The dress is carefully packed for me, then I reject all attempts by Sam to pay for my new dress, and put it on my credit card. Then we go back to the gallery, get into my station wagon and drive back to the caravan.

CHAPTER 33

AUTUMN

"Living in a caravan is actually pretty cool," Sam declares as she deposits her luggage on the floor and walks around the place.

"Make yourself at home," I invite, and go off to use the toilet. I can hear her opening cupboard doors and closing them.

When I pull the door open, she is standing outside the door with a spatula in her hand.

"You don't have any food in your fridge and there are only packets of ramen noodles in your cupboards," she points out.

"I know," I reply, my eyes going to the utensil. "Why are you holding a spatula?"

She brings it down and smacks me on my head.

"Hey!" I shriek, but before I can catch her, she evades me and with a cheeky laugh sprints away. She takes refuge behind the table. I make a few tries to catch her, but we end up going round and round the table. I give up and toss an empty box of oats at her. She ducks easily and it sails past.

She grins at me. "Missed."

"Don't be so smug. You're sleeping in my bed," I warn.

She stands with her hands on her hips and huffs, "How many times do I have to tell you to stop eating that poison?"

"But I like them and they're so easy to make," I say in my defense.

"They taste like freaking plastic."

"No, they don't."

She sighs elaborately. "Look, I plan to live a very long life and I want us both to be two old ladies together. If you keep eating this shit I'm going to be burying your sorry ass way before your time."

"You'll get on like a house on fire with Rocco. He's fastidious about eating pure food too."

Her eyebrows rise. "Really? I'm starting to like the man more and more."

"I bought a cake for you, but I gave it away to the gypsy last night."

"Mmm... yes, the mysterious gypsy. You'll need to tell me all about that too, but first, let's go to the grocery store and get you some food. My treat."

It's always been like this with Sam since I was fourteen, when I walked into my third-grade class to find my seat partner was a girl with a riot of flame-colored curly locks. She has refused to let me go since then. Always mothering me, worrying about me, protecting me.

Thirty minutes later, we're strolling through the aisles of the store. I watch bemused as Sam dumps into the cart packs of whole wheat cereal, organic rice, the good orange juice. Then she drops a bag of frozen spicy chicken wings in.

"Surely that's not healthy?" I ask surprised.

"Nope, but this is for tonight. We're celebrating, remember?"

I try to hide my smile as I roll the cart behind her and watch her pick a large bag of nachos, sour cream, microwaveable popcorn, chocolate cake, and two bottles of champagne.

Soon we're done, and return to my car in the lot. We dump everything in the back, and I start my car and reverse out of the lot and drive home."

"So what's new between you and Mr. Ghost?"

I glance at her. "That's what we're calling him now?"

"Do you have a better name for him?"

"Rocco." I answer dryly.

"And how exactly are you sure that's his real name as he doesn't seem to exist online?"

I roll my eyes. "Not everyone alive right now exists online, Sam."

"Only those that are alive and have something to hide don't exist online."

I turn to see her lips twitching from barely held back amusement. "You're having a blast, aren't you?"

"He's some kind of venture capitalist, right."

"That's what he said."

"Did you ask him for any notable companies he's involved with that you and I might have heard about?"

"I didn't think to ask him mundane things like that. I'm an artist. Besides, when I am with him I become almost hypnotized by him."

"Autumn?" she calls, in a horrified voice. "That's what gullible prey do."

"I know, but I just can't help it. There's something about him. It's like we're meant to be together. I can't explain it."

When we get back to the caravan, we put everything away, open our feast and lay it all on the table. Then we open the champagne, I have no flutes or wine glasses, so we pour it into mugs, and toast to both of us.

"May we always be sisters in crime," Sam says cheekily.

"May we always be sisters in crime," I echo, even though the last time we committed a crime was many years ago, when we went into a shop during the school vacation and stole two pencil cases. Our parents made us return them, which was embarrassing, but having our phones taken away and not being allowed to speak to each other for the rest of the vacation permanently cured us of ever wanting to steal or commit any kind of crime again.

As the evening passes into night, I tell her everything. About what happened at the observatory, about last night, how sick he was, his sister arriving, and him knocking the wine out of my hand, even my trip to Zelena's caravan and what she told me.

Sam puts her glass down on the table. "I want to see his house."

"What?"

"I want us to drive up the mountain and I want to see his house."

"Now?"

"Yes."

"But we've been drinking."

"You've been drinking. I've only had two glasses so far, so I'm well under the limit." She stands. "Come on, I'll drive. When we get back we can finish this feast, drink the other bottle and curl up with a movie until we fall asleep."

"We should wait until the morning. It's a really narrow, dangerous road up the mountain," I object doubtfully.

"Nonsense. I've eyesight like a cat, and I'm a fantastic driver. Get your coat on."

As I stand reluctantly, Sam has already snatched the keys of the station wagon off the kitchen counter and is shrugging into her coat. She turns to me with a big grin. "What're you waiting for? Chop. Chop."

CHAPTER 34

AUTUMN

We have the music on loud as we drive up the winding mountain road. Sam is bobbing her head and singing along.

"You just want to see the house, then we're going back, right?" I ask.

She looks at me and giggles. "Of course not. We're going to ring the bell, and I'm going to meet the guy you're literally melting over."

I'm staring at her, so I don't see the disaster unfolding in front of us. Only her shocked expression and sudden screech of horror causes my head to whirl around to face the front.

"Hit the brakes, Sam. Hit the brakes!" I scream, my hands slamming instinctively on the dashboard, as I take in the incredible sight of a huge boulder rolling down the mountain!

The rock hits the road a few meters away in front of us and disintegrates into fragments like pieces of a smashed toy, and those pieces are now hurling straight at us.

"Autumn!" Sam screams, and shields her arms over her head protectively, but I can't look away. My heart is pounding in my ears. It is all happening so rapidly, but time has slowed right down, and my mind processes it all, every little detail. Sam screaming, the sounds, the vibrations from the car being hit, the white spider web patterns on the windscreen as it shatters, the sensation of being showered by little squares of glass. The fragments are thick rectangles that don't hurt on my skin.

Then, I notice how the impact causes the car to skid and spin to the left, which turns the trajectory of the car towards the ravine.

Sam has her foot slammed on the brakes, but the car now has a life of its own. It slides off the edge of the road. The scream sticks in my throat. There is nothing to do, but I accept the fact that we're fucked. The car with us in it is going to fall headlong down the mountain, and we are going to crash and probably burn to death.

Suddenly the car stops.

Just comes to a sudden stop. Both Sam and I turn to look at each other, our faces white, our mouths open with terror, shock, and disbelief. By some grace of God, the car is just hanging off the road. Just hanging in mid-air.

"Jesus Christ," Sam whispers.

I swallow. "Don't move," I gasp.

"I have no intention of doing any such thing but," she replies in a hushed voice, "but we have to do something and fast."

Without moving my body, I swivel my head slowly and look around us. We are literally hanging in thin air. "Oh God!" I close my eyes for a second. The fear makes it impossible to think. I take deep breaths. "We've got to get to the backseat somehow, and crawl out of here."

"Are you kidding, one move from either of us could change the balance, and we'll go crashing down the mountain."

"Okay, how about we both open our car doors at the same time and jump out? The car is stationary so it's unlikely we'll get too badly hurt."

She shakes her head. "You've been watching too many crappy Hollywood movies, Autumn?"

"Okay, Einstein, you come up with a bright idea then," I mutter.

"Let me think." She cranes her neck forward. "What the hell is holding us up, anyway."

"Sam, can you please concentrate on getting us out of this mess first?"

"We could call the fire department?"

"You saw how narrow the road was. A fire truck will never fit."

"We should call the house. Ask for help from Rocco's staff."

"And wait thirty minutes for them to arrive? No way I'm sitting in this car for that long. I don't know whether you noticed, but the wind is picking up. The car is swaying, Sam."

She frowns. "Yeah, I noticed too. Looks like we have no choice, but to go for your crappy Hollywood idea. But first, let's try our doors to make sure they open. We'll try them at the same time so we keep the balance."

Another gust of high wind makes the car sway dangerously, and I close my eyes with fear.

"Autumn," Sam calls out. "If we don't make it out alive... I just want you to know, I really love you."

I grit my teeth. "We *are* going to make it out alive, but just in case, I really love you too."

She plasters a grim grin on her face. "Ready?"

We both very, very carefully, as if we are dismantling bombs, push down on the lever that opens our doors. Then, in unison, we push them open, just a crack. They open, and the car remains stable. We look at each other. It is too dark to see properly what is underneath us, but if we are lucky we will not have far to fall and we might fall on soft soil or the bushes will break our fall.

"Ready," I whisper.

"On the count of three?"

I nod. "One, two—"

"Hang on, hang on," she shouts.

"What?" I gasp, my hands are trembling on the door latch.

Her face is very white and her eyes are enormous. "I just wanted to say, good luck, Autumn."

I nod anxiously. "Yeah, good luck to you too. Don't worry, it's going to be fine. After we jump just try to hang onto the first tree branch or bush you roll into."

She nods back. "Okay. This is it then. I'll do the countdown."

"Hurry, Sam. This car can fall anytime. God only knows what is holding it up at the moment."

"One, two," she takes a deep breath, "three."

I push open the door and cold wind rushes into me as I jump into the blackness. I land on soft earth, roll down the mountain for a bit, then crash into some bushes. The car plunges into the darkness. Its headlights are still on, and I see it somersault down the steep slope, onto the road below, and then further and further down until the thick vegetation obscures it completely.

Everything goes quiet.

Immediately, I turn to the left to look for Sam and in my peripheral vision, I see movement, like a shadow, but blurred. Still in shock and suddenly terrified, I think it is a man moving very fast, but the phantom is gone as quick as I blink. There is nothing there. Heart racing, I peer intently into the gloom, but see nothing else move, so I put the apparition down to my overwrought emotions.

"Sam?" I shout.

"Here. I'm here." I turn towards her voice. She had less of a fall than me, and is on higher ground than me. In the darkness, her face is a pale oval. I see blood running down the side of her white face.

"Are you alright?" I shout.

"I think so. I had a soft landing."

Other than sustaining that cut she seems to be as unscathed as me. I try to stand, but my knees collapse under my weight.

"Autumn, are you hurt?" Sam calls, her voice filled with fear.

I'm shaking so bad my teeth start clattering. "I'm alright. Just a bit shook up." I push my palms onto the damp earth and push myself up again. This time my knees hold and I gingerly half-walk, half-crawl towards her. When I reach her, we hug each other tightly as if we are the survivors of a great catastrophe. We are both thoroughly shaken. I can feel her trembling and her eyes are wet.

"Fuck," Sam curses. "We could have died, Autumn. We could have fucking died."

"We didn't. We freaking survived," I croak.

She looks upwards and frowns. "Look. There's nothing by the side of the road where the car was. What was holding it up?"

I follow the direction of her gaze. She is indeed right. The car was hanging at an impossible angle over the edge. We thought it must have been caught on a tree stump or overhanging rock, but I can see now that there was nothing there.

"Maybe it was a rock and it got swept down with the weight of the car," Sam concludes.

"Yeah, maybe," I agree quietly, but I watch the car plunge into the darkness. I never saw a large rock falling ahead of it. The area in front of the car was lit by its headlights.

"Let's get back on the road," Sam says, standing up, and switching on the torch on her cellphone.

Together we scramble up towards the road. "What do we do now?"

"Well, if we go up to the house, we might get stuck there until they clear away the boulder so I suggest we walk back down and get a cab to pick us up at the base of the mountain. The walk shouldn't take us more than an hour."

Sam nods. "Okay, we definitely don't want to miss our flights in the morning."

Silently, we begin to walk down. We are both shaken, but I'm haunted more by that blur of black that had risen as if from underneath our car... and then disappeared.

For some crazy reason the shadow seemed familiar.

CHAPTER 35

ROCCO

https://www.youtube.com/watch?v=lU9p1WRfA9w
-She's Like The Wind-

I push my burnt hands into the pockets of my jacket as I reach the house. William opens the door and I tell him there has been an accident involving Autumn and they are now walking down the mountain, but there is now an obstruction on the road. He is to get the men to clear it immediately, then send Raoul to pick up the girls and send them home. He could probably pick them up before they get to the bottom of the mountain.

My back was still hurting before, but it is now throbbing with renewed vigor after I strained it by holding the car up. I dragged my pain-ridden body up the stairs to my bathroom, and hold my palms under the cold water. The skin has been burnt off and the flesh looks raw and bloody.

From behind me a face floats onto the mirror. I meet her sly eyes and try not to show the intense hatred I feel for her. The less she knows me, or how I feel, the better. I understood a long time ago, my sister has no limits. She will let nothing stand in her way.

"You could have killed her," I say expressionlessly.

"There was never a chance of that happening."

"What if one of those shards of rock had pierced the windscreen and crushed her?"

She shifts uncomfortably. "It didn't, did it?"

I close the taps and turn around to face her. She is leaning casually against the door frame and cradling a glass half full of whiskey. "What would you have done if she died?"

"Don't be so silly. There was no possibility of that. I chose the area with the softest landing. I just wanted to test if you would be able to feel when she was in danger." She shrugs. "If you had not turned up I would have 'saved' her myself."

I want to explode, to hurt her, but I cannot. Ancient rules forbid such actions. "You put her life at risk to test me?"

She strokes the sides of her glass with her long, slender fingers. "Well, that was one of the reasons."

"And the other?"

She smiles. "I was actually trying to help your cause."

"My cause?" I ask softly.

"You're losing your touch little brother. That was your opportunity to show yourself and be the savior. Every girl wants to be rescued by a knight in shining armour, a hero. And you are that, aren't you, little brother. A hero."

I walk up to her and stare into her unrepentant, cruel eyes. "I don't need help from you. I have my own way of seducing a woman. I will give her the choice. Until then, butt out of my business. Do you understand me?"

She smiles a victorious smirk. "Yes, I understand, but don't take too long. We're all suffering here."

I shake my head with disgust. "Do you ever consider anybody else's needs but your own?"

"Have the moral high ground if it keeps you warm at night, I just want my hair back."

I side-step her and start to walk away, but as I pass her I smell it. Underneath her expensive perfume... only faintly, but nevertheless present is the smell of putrefaction. I wonder if I am extruding the same stench of corruption and decay.

"She's flying to New York tomorrow. That friend of hers won an academic competition so they've been invited to attend a black-tie dinner gala," she murmurs.

I stop and turn. "I suppose you had something to do with it?"

"Of course. You have to admit it was genius. How else was I going to get her in New York?"

"Leave," I roar, hardly able to control my fury. A headache that is threatening to split my head apart has just started too.

Calmly, she discards the glass of whiskey on a table near her, and walks towards the door. As she departs, she throws out her parting shot. "See you in New York."

CHAPTER 36

AUTUMN

https://www.youtube.com/watch?v=I_izvAbhExY
-Staying Alive-

The first thing I see when I open my eyes is Sam's red curls on the pillow next to me. Her eyes are closed and her mouth is slightly open. It's been a long time since we slept in the same bed, and I feel a rush of love for her. I reach out a hand and touch her flaming hair and her eyelids flutter open.

"Good morning," I say with a smile.

She chews her bottom lip. "Autumn, I'm so very sorry I made us go up the mountain yesterday. It was very irresponsible of me, especially after you warned me that the road is dangerous. I don't know what I was thinking."

"Don't be such a dork. Main thing is we made it out unhurt."

"Anyway, I've decided to pay for you to get another car."

"No, I don't want you to do that. I don't care about the car. I'd lose everything for you."

She smiles slowly. "I'd lose everything for you too."

I smile back. "Good. Are we going to stop being so mushy and get ready to go to the airport?"

Her eyes twinkle. "So mushy it's almost moist."

I put my hands over my ears. "Ugh, stop it. You know I hate that word."

"Moist," she repeats.

I pull the pillow out from under my head and start bashing her with it. She screams and falls out of bed. I look down at her. "I hope that hurt."

"Moist," she says, and starts laughing.

I have never been to New York before. I hoped to, one day, but it hadn't been in any of my plans for the near future, but here I am.

To our delight and surprise, we are led to a waiting limo on the tarmac. We jump in excitedly, the uniformed chauffeur pulls away, and just like that we are onto an adventure of a lifetime. We are driven through the busy streets of the Big Apple. I stare out of the window with fascination.

Yellow taxis fill the roads, and an endless stream of people are either hurrying along on the sidewalk or waiting in large numbers to cross the streets. Traffic noises and strange scents fill the air. There is so much to see. So many shops, restaurants, patisseries, hot dog stands, parks, bars... gosh...

so many skyscrapers. So many different types of people. And all of them are so busy, busy, busy. Compared to this ceaseless chaos, color, and noise Hunter's Cross seems like an oasis of absolute peace and bliss.

"What do you think?" Sam asks.

I turn to meet her shining eyes. "It's loud, isn't it?"

"It's exciting."

I smile at her. "Yeah, I guess it is."

The Four Seasons is beautiful with its art décor lobby and its stunning onyx ceiling. We are shown to our suite which is pretty luxurious. There is a bottle of champagne inside an ice bucket and a basket of fruit waiting for us.

"Oh, my God. It's *Dom Perignon*!" Sam squeals.

"Wow, they really pamper the winners, don't they?" I note, as Sam tears off the foil on the bottle of Champagne.

"Well, this is the first year this competition was introduced in the campus, but long may it last," she says as the cork pops out.

Champagne flows down the bottle as Sam fills two flutes. We clink glasses.

"Well done to you, Sam. I'm really, really, really proud of you. I think if I was any prouder I would burst."

"Thank you, babe."

We go to stand on the balcony with a panoramic view of Central Park. We finish our glasses and look at each other. "Sightseeing or a visit to the spa? Not only entrance but any treatment in the spa is part of the prize. Also I believe we are allowed a visit to the hairdressers."

"Both of us?" I ask incredulous.

"Both of us. I called and checked," she confirms.

"Wow, okay. It's your prize. You decide."

"My prize comes tonight when I get to meet Professor Leon Joseph Chernyshevsky. You get to decide this one."

"Can we squeeze both into the itinerary?"

She grins. "See why I let you make the decisions."

So we do both. A bit of sightseeing and then back to the spa for a full body massage, manicure, and pedicure, then to the salon to get our hair done. Afterwards we go back to our room and change into our new dresses. Sam looks absolutely divine in a long white dress. With her flaming red hair, it makes her look as if she is a Greek Goddess. It makes my hand itch to paint her.

She comes forward and touches the amulet. "You look beautiful, but how strange that I cannot imagine you without it now. It is as if it has always been a part of you."

"That's a strange thing to say," I murmur.

"I know. Autumn, do you sometimes feel as if you are at the very edge of something? One more step and everything will change forever."

I shiver. "Don't. You're scaring me."

She laughs. At that moment, she looks undefeatable. Nothing can stop her. "I'm not scared. I welcome it, whatever it is."

I grasp her hand. "Let's go. Let's go meet this hero of yours."

CHAPTER 37

AUTUMN

I stand up and clap furiously as Sam goes to receive her prize. She looks so happy. In my heart, I wish this will be the start of something special for her, that amongst these sophisticated, well-connected people will be someone who will offer her the job of a lifetime when she finishes her education.

When the prizes have been given out, we move towards the dance floor. We are both flushed with champagne and happiness. Once or twice my mind wanders to Rocco, but I push the thought away. I will see him on Monday. And that will be the day he will tell me his secret and I will decide if I walk away or stay with him, though it's getting real hard to imagine doing the latter.

"Oh, my God, Autumn! There he is."

I turn to see a nondescript man with greying hair and thick glasses. Even from where we are I can see dandruff on the shoulders of his ill-fitting suit.

"Come on, let's go say hello," she says, as she drags me towards him.

"Hello, Professor Chernyshevsky," Sam gushes.

I didn't realize what a complete total nerd Sam was until this moment. I try not to show my amusement.

He peers at her through his thick glasses. "Ah, Miss Samantha Collins. Congratulations on winning the competition."

"Thank you, Professor. This is my best friend Autumn."

He turns to look at me as if he cannot understand why I was there.

"Hello, Prof," I mutter. The simple fact is I have as much interest in him as he has in me. I flash a smile. "I'm going to get a drink. In the meantime, both of you can talk shop."

Sam frowns. "You don't have to leave."

I frown back meaningfully. "I *want* to leave. Catch you later."

She nods. "Okay. Catch you later. But come back if you get bored."

I just about stop myself from shaking my head incredulously at her. How could anything be more boring than what she and the Professor are about to discuss?

I wander off towards the bar. As I climb onto the stool, a man takes the stool next to mine.

"Hey," he says.

He has dark hair, gray eyes, and pale skin. He is actually extremely handsome, like one of those models you see on GQ magazine, but something about him makes the hackles on my neck stand. Ignoring him, I ask the barman for a glass of champagne.

"I'm not coming on to you. I'm the organizer of this event. I'm Daniel Dupress," he says.

I turn towards him. His eyes are sly. In my peripheral vision, I can see my order has arrived. I pick up the glass and take a sip. I do not trust him. I wonder what he wants with me. "You did a great job."

"That's a beautiful locket," he says softly.

I feel my body tense. "Thanks."

He smiles, a charming, totally attractive smile. No doubt it has melted the hearts of many a girl. "I hope you don't think I'm being rude, but where did you get it from?"

I don't know why, but I don't want to tell him about Zelena. A lie forms in my throat and flows out of my mouth. "I bought it at a flea market."

His eyes flash. He knows I'm lying. "A flea market? It looks very valuable."

The lies continue pouring out of my mouth. "I didn't pay much for it so I don't think it's very valuable. I just liked the design."

"I happen to believe it might be very, very valuable. May I touch it?"

Every cell in my body recoils with revulsion, but another part of my brain wants to know more about the amulet. I grasp the chain above the amulet and hold it a few inches away from my skin. The way his eyes fix on the amulet is shocking. There is greed, there is awe, and there is something else... fear. His top lip quivers in an animal-like way as he reaches out an elegant, perfectly manicured hand. I watch with fascination as his eyes glitter with intense desire the closer his hand gets to Zelena's talisman. As his hand is about two inches away, his eyes suddenly widen and bulge, and his face contorts as if in horror. In a flash, he snatches his hand away as if the charm has burnt him.

"The fruit can't be taken, Daniel. It has to be given," a voice murmurs smoothly.

Instantly, my body relaxes as if it knows that nothing and no one can hurt me while Rocco is around. A wild excitement fizzles in my veins. Rocco is here in New York. I thought I wouldn't see him again until Monday. I watch Daniel's face lose its horror and settle back into its original slick, slightly smug expression.

"Then you should pick it, and fast, the smell of the fruit is all around the room." Daniel swivels his eyes around the room as he speaks.

I follow the direction of his gaze and see that indeed there are people watching us avidly. Their eyes drop or move away quickly when they catch my eyes.

"Are you giving me advice?" Rocco asks, his voice deceptively soft, but steely.

"Not at all. Merely, pointing out the inescapable fact that time is passing… and we are all waiting." His mouth widens. It is not a smile, but a dangerous stretching of lips.

I look up and see Rocco stretch his lips too. There is no amusement in his face.

It is as if he, Rocco, and I are speaking a secret language. A language that I cannot properly understand, but both Rocco and he are fluent in.

Daniel looks at me then spreads his hands out to his sides before he gives a courtly, extravagant bow. "Good evening, Miss Delaney. I wish you an interesting evening." As he passes close to me, a whiff of something horribly rotten fills my nostrils and I immediately pinch my nose with my fingers.

"Ugh! He just farted on us," I complain incredulously.

Rocco takes the seat Daniel vacated. He looks breathtakingly handsome in a black tux. Under the lights his hair shines and his eyes are like gemstones. Ignoring my comment about Daniel's dirty parting gift, he says, "You look beautiful tonight."

"Thank you, so do you," I murmur, taking my fingers off my nose.

A waiter comes by with a tray of champagne flutes, but Rocco shakes his head.

"Are you not drinking?" I ask curiously.

"I never consume anything for which I do not know its source."

I tilt my head and look at him curiously. "You know that is a very strange habit, right?"

"Yes. I'm fastidious like that," he says simply.

"Care to tell me what that exchange with Daniel was about?"

"It is a long story. I will explain it later tonight," he replies seriously, as his eyes drop to the amulet.

I am suddenly filled with curiosity to see how he will react to touching it. "It's very old. Want to touch it?"

He reaches out a hand and I find myself holding my breath. His hand gets closer and closer, then I feel his fingers brush my skin, as he lifts the locket up. My breath comes out in a rush.

"What are you doing here?" I whisper hoarsely. I can feel my heart beating faster.

He lets go of the locket. "I was invited."

I run my finger along the condensation outside of my glass, then look at him from beneath my lashes. "Did you know I would be here?"

"Yes," he admits quietly.

"Who told you?"

"My sister."

Understanding dawns. "Ah. And she invited you here too."

He nods.

I glance back towards the edge of the stage, to where Sam is staring with an enraptured look at the Professor while he explains something to her. Then I turn my attention back to Rocco. Suddenly, it all made sense. Something always felt wrong. A prize for a student and her friend that included being flown first class, limo service from the airport, a luxurious suite at the Four Seasons, *Dom Perignon* champagne, and carte blanche use of the Spa and room service.

I exhale softly. "Is your sister the reason Sam and I are here?"

"Yes."

If she spent that much money and trouble to get us here she must want something, something big. "What does she want with us?"

"She doesn't want anything from your friend. Just you."

I feel a cold finger of fear run down my spine. "What does she want from me?"

"I will tell you tonight. First, I need to introduce you to some people." He stands and shoots his cuffs.

"This thing you have to tell me tonight, it's bad, isn't it?"

"Like I said before, it depends on the person. Some people will love the concept and dive right in, and others will hate it with all their being."

I wrinkle my nose. "Like Marmite?"

"Not quite, but you get the picture."

"By the way I hate Marmite," I say with a laugh.

"I've never tasted it, but it smells disgusting."

I catch his hand, my voice more desperate than I expected it to be, "I can trust you, right?"

He looks deep into my eyes. "With your life."

Unless he is a complete, utter, and total psychopath I feel certain I can trust him.

CHAPTER 38

AUTUMN

"Are we leaving the hotel?" I ask, slipping off the bar stool to face him.

His eyes travel down my body hungrily. It makes my skin tingle with excitement. "We're only going to another floor."

"I can't leave Sam here," I protest, turning to look at her. She is still in exactly the same position as before, leaning in to listen to her Professor pontificate.

"We won't be long."

"Okay, let me just tell her I'm popping to another part of the building."

"That won't be necessary. If she looks up from her conversation and appears to be searching for you, that woman over there who works for me," he nods towards a young woman who is looking at us, "will escort her to the party we will be at."

My eyebrows rise. "We're going to a party?"

"I'm afraid so," he says with a slight wince.

I laugh. "I thought parties were supposed to be fun."

His lips twist. "I'll let you decide for yourself if the party is fun."

We walk side by side towards the entrance. I can feel heads turning to watch our progress. I see us in the mirrored walls. I hardly recognize myself. We look strangely regal. Him tall, blond and immaculate, and me dark-haired, vital, and somehow glossy. As we get closer I stare at myself. I know something is different about me, but I cannot say what. Then, just as we go through the door, I realize what it is. It is my skin. My skin appears more radiant, almost as if I am glowing from inside. It must be the massage and facial I had at the Spa.

We walk down the wide corridor towards the elevators, but instead of waiting at the banks he leads me away from them. We go through a door and arrive at another elevator. He presses the button and it immediately opens. Once we are inside, he inserts a card key. The elevator doors close and the car starts moving. He turns towards me. "If you ever feel uncomfortable, let me know and we'll leave immediately."

I smile "Okay. Make sure you do the same."

A strange expression crosses his lips, it seems almost like regret, then a ghost of a smile lifts the corners of his lips. "Deal."

I look up at the lights that show the floors we are travelling through and realize we are not going up, but down. Before I can ask him about it, the doors swish open. Rocco retrieves his card from the slot and guides me down a corridor. The ceiling is higher here than the floor we were on before. The walls are powder blue with very fine white plasterwork decorations.

We come upon a set of double doors with two men in costumes, like the footmen of days gone by, standing on either side of it. I can hear the faint sounds of voices and laughter coming from the other side of the doors. Silently, one of the men makes a graceful motion towards a long table pushed up against the wall next to the doors.

"Come and choose your mask," Rocco says, leading me towards the table.

"Curiouser and curiouser," I comment as I look down at the array of available masks.

There are full masks, half-masks, and those that only cover the eyes. Rocco chooses a plain white half-mask, fashioned to look like a bird with a beak. I pick a red one decorated with black crystals to match my dress. I carefully fit it over my head and turn towards him.

"What do you think?"

"Perfect choice," he says approvingly.

I realize I don't like him in a mask. It is almost a sense of loss. Suddenly, he seems like a stranger, his eyes very blue and fierce. The doormen open the doors and we walk through. Three things hit me immediately. One, every masked head in that huge, brightly lit room, either subtly or openly, stops their conversation to turn and look at us. The second thing is the overpowering smell of perfume. It hangs in the air as if someone has broken a perfume bottle in a closed place. And the third is there is something sinister, unnatural, and fearful about a room full of adults in masks.

A body detaches itself from the crowd and comes towards us. She is wearing a very elaborately jeweled full-face mask and a long, shimmering peacock-blue dress. Around her wrist is a distinctive white-gold snake bracelet. Its mouth is open and its eyes are fashioned from blue stones, maybe sapphires. She reminds me of that phrase, 'everything is brilliance and fury'. I also recognize her immediately, Rocco's sister.

"Hello," she drawls. "How lovely that you could make it to my party."

Next to me Rocco stands very still, as still as a statue.

"Hello," I return the greeting warily.

"We must get you a drink," she says, just as a waiter comes with a large tray of champagne flutes.

Rocco takes two and hands a glass to me. Rocco must know the source of the drinks, because he takes a sip. I do too. The champagne is delicious, more delicious than what I had at the party, and more delicious than the complimentary bottle of Dom Sam and I had in the room.

Isadora turns her bright, sharp, predator gaze on me. "That's a beautiful pendant."

"I bought it at a flea market. Would you like to touch it?"

A strange expression, almost fear, crosses her eyes. "My parents are dying to meet you. They're not staying long so perhaps I should take you to meet them first, and then you can mingle and dance or whatever."

I look up at Rocco.

"Yes, let's get the introductions over with," he says tightly.

We follow her shimmering body through the crowd. I notice them part to make room for us. I can feel that I am different than them. I am the outsider. Isadora stops in front of a tall couple. I cannot see either of their faces, because they are both wearing full-face masks, but the woman has a very shapely body, the kind of body a woman in her twenties would have. Even the skin on her hands are very smooth. Her enormous and magnificent blue eyes glitter with some great emotion. I cannot tell what.

The man is the exact opposite. His hands are wrinkled and marked with liver spots, but the most startling thing about him are his eyes. They are smokier, darker, and dear God, more, *much* more dangerous. There is something blank and crazy about them. Some unfathomable madness that grips my soul and makes the hackles at the back of my neck rise.

Rocco slips his hand around my waist. I realize it is a gesture of both reassurance and possession. The tension in the air can be cut with a knife.

"Autumn, meet my parents. Junia and Cicero Rossetti. Mom and Dad, meet Autumn Delaney."

"I approve. She is beautiful, Rocco," the woman says.

Rocco says nothing.

"It's a pleasure to welcome you into our family, my dear," his father says politely, but his voice is cold and emotionless.

First of all, things are moving too fast for me. Why on earth would he be welcoming me into the family when Rocco and I are only in the early stages of our relationship? Then I notice something even more strange: neither of them has extended a hand out to me. In fact, the woman, I find it impossible to think of her as Rocco's mother, carefully maintains a cautious distance from me.

"What a shame that we have to leave now, but it's good that we got to meet," she says. I notice her gaze on my talisman, but she does not comment on it.

Her hand rises, cuts the air, then lands as gently as a butterfly on her husband's sleeve. I'm mesmerized by her strange movement. I stare at her hand in fascination. Her skin is very pale against the black material of the sleeve, and her nails are long and painted in a beautiful, opaque coral polish. When I lift my gaze, I see he has turned to look at her. A look passes between them, secret, and full of meaning.

"Yes, we are already late for our next engagement," he says in that emotionless voice of his.

"No doubt we'll meet again. Perhaps you can come over for dinner," the woman says to me.

Again that sense of revulsion runs like poison in my veins. "Maybe."

She turns to her son. "Goodbye, Rocco."

Rocco says nothing.

"I'll walk you out," Isadora says quickly.

The mother steps backwards, then her husband does the same, then the three of them quickly walk away.

CHAPTER 39

AUTUMN

https://www.youtube.com/watch?v=CoZJdil0_HI&list=
PLRU2kFDUg_RLmd-GsT1v4zzYpW1TlRw5g

For a few seconds I can only stare astonished at the blank space that was once occupied by them, then I turn my head and look at Rocco. His face is taut, and the skin around his mouth is very white, making his lips look redder than usual.

"Were those people really your parents?"

He nods.

"That was the strangest encounter I've ever had. I got the distinct impression they did not like me."

"Don't take it personally, that is how they behave towards anybody that is outside their… circle."

I notice the slight pause before circle. "Why did they want to meet me while they were masked?"

He sighs. "Because they didn't want you to see their faces yet."

I shake my head, a frown on my forehead. "Why not?"

"They have their reasons."

"I know. You'll explain later, right?"

He nods. "Yes, I will. Would you like to dance?"

It is only then I hear again the classical music playing in the background. "To this music?"

He smiles slightly. "Yes, it's a waltz."

"I can't waltz," I confess.

"Just follow my lead."

"No thanks. I'm not going to go out there and make a complete fool of myself," I mutter.

"Do you really care what any of these people think of you?"

I look around and once again notice that many of them are surreptitiously watching us, actually not us, but me. I find Rocco's eyes. "Why is everyone staring at me?"

"Because they are very, very curious about you," he replies quietly.

I nod. "I need to use the restroom, but when I come back you're going to teach me to waltz."

He smiles, a genuine smile, the first one of the night. "That's more like the feisty spitfire I know."

I grin back at him. At that moment, the champagne is making my head buzz pleasantly, and everything in the world feels right.

"The Ladies is that way." He nods towards a side entrance.

"Be back in a jiffy," I call over my shoulder as I walk away.

I follow the signs and find that the bathrooms are accessed by going down a spiral staircase. After that there are two other doors before I see the sign for the Ladies. Even here, it smells overpoweringly of perfume. I use the toilet quickly, wash my hands, and go out. Once I'm outside I open the first door which then gives me a choice of doors. I no longer remember which way I came so I open the first door.

And gasp.

I have accidentally opened the door to a candlelit room. It is lavishly decorated as if it is a French brothel from the eighteen-century, with heavy red velvet curtains, vibrant art in gilded frames on the walls, a massive bed covered with a plush damask bedspread. It is so crazy. Would there be such a room underneath the hotel?

Even stranger are the two maskless people in it.

A young woman is lying naked on the big bed. Her skin looks fresh and rosy, like the skin of a freshly picked sun-warmed peach, her eyes are wide and circled with thick dark lashes, and her right hand is tangled in her long auburn hair. The only thing on her body is a thin strip of brown leather around her ankle. The anklet is fastened with a rectangular silver plate and there is something etched on the metal. Numbers and letters.

A fully clothed man is bent over her.

When they hear me open the door, both turn to look at me, but unhurriedly, lazily, as if they are in a slow motion movie. The girl's body is so heavy with desire even now her eyelids are half-closed. She shows no sign of shame and doesn't make any attempt to cover her nakedness. She looks at me without curiosity, passively, distantly.

My confused gaze moves from her to the man. He is extraordinarily handsome, has bright green eyes, and is looking at me with great interest. I want to apologize, to say I opened the wrong door, and back out, but I simply cannot tear my gaze away from the man's eyes. A deep languor invades my flesh. The air feels as if it is flecked with golden dust. It is like being in a dream.

Slowly, he straightens and begins to walk towards me. Even though his lips do not move at all, they seem to smile. I feel drawn to him in a way I cannot understand. Hypnotized and transfixed by the sight of him, I can only stare blankly at him. My brain says it can't be real. It feels like a dream or a powerful illusion, and if I pinch myself I will wake up. I am certain it is not real. He stops a few feet from me.

"This can all be yours too, sweet Autumn," he says in a soothing voice. "All of it. Just say yes."

I blink. A strange frisson runs along my skin. The pounding of my heart seems to echo all around the room and corridor. A voice hisses urgently in my head, say yes. The urge to say yes starts filling my head, like the hissing of thousands and thousands of snakes. Yes, yes, yes, yes…

But yes to what? What is happening in this room?

The girl moans softly, and he takes another step towards me, and suddenly I catch a whiff of that same nauseating odor I had detected as Daniel was leaving, but stronger with this man. Much stronger. It is akin to rotting flesh or excrement. So disgusting it turns my stomach and makes me want to vomit. The sensation breaks the hypnotic trance.

Unbidden, an image arises in my mind's eye; a cloudless, hot sky. There are vultures circling in it. Their wings are massive. On the parched earth below, I see the girl with the radiant skin. Her eyes are open, but they do not see the vultures closing in. They stare out sightlessly into an empty bit of the heavens. My body feels horribly cold and my soul hurts at the unbearable sight.

Stunned, I stagger backwards. I glance at the girl. I want to warn her about the vultures in the sky and her dead eyes, but she has already lost interest in me and turned away.

"Just say yes, and you can have it all, *all*," the man cajoles insistently in his melodious voice, but the veil has been lifted. The disgusting smell of his corruption intensifies, sickening me.

"Stay away from me," I shout, and lurch towards the other door.

I fling it open, see the circular staircase, and sprint up it so fast, I stumble in my high heels and almost fall. Grabbing the banister, I pull myself up. I look behind me nervously, but he is not chasing me. My heart is racing. I don't know what happened to me down there, but I feel as if I went down those steps without a care in the world, as an innocent, and came back up somehow irrevocably tainted and corrupted.

When I reach the large room where the party is being held I stop at the entrance, my eyes wildly searching for Rocco. I immediately spot him. Even with the horrid mask he shines like a god or some supernatural being of great beauty. A man is talking earnestly to him, but as if he has felt me arrive in the room, he turns his head in my direction. For across the room our eyes meet. The rest of the world falls away.

I am breathing hard. I open my mouth and close it. I feel so lost.

The man is still saying something to Rocco, but he turns away from the man, and starts walking towards me. His eyes never leave mine.

"What's wrong? Has something happened?" he asks urgently.

I look up at him and see his eyes flash and glitter through the mask holes. Something about them reminds me of his sister's. It sends a shiver through my body. Who to trust? Who to trust? I shake my head. "Nothing is wrong. Can we leave now, please?"

He puts a hand protectively on the small of my back. "Of course."

In my head, Zelena is saying. "Him. You can trust him."

CHAPTER 40

AUTUMN

Outside the room Rocco takes off his mask and discards it on the long table. With a shudder I rip my mine off as if it is contaminated and throw it on the table. We say nothing in the elevator. When we arrive at the room where Sam is I find her exactly where she was before we left. Nothing has changed, and yet everything has.

I look up at Rocco. "Can you wait a moment here for me, please? I won't be long."

He nods.

"Thank you," I say, and quickly walk up to Sam.

I call her name and she turns to look at me, her hand rises to cover her mouth in dismay. "Oh my God, Autumn, I'm so sorry. I've been completely ignoring you. Give me a minute, I'll just say goodbye to Professor Chernyshevsky and come with you."

I make a stop sign with my hand. "No, no, don't do that. He's the reason you were so excited about winning this prize in the first place." My voice sounds hollow. I know now that it is all fake. All of it.

"Don't be such a silly Billy, of course, I'll come with you. This weekend is about us, not just me."

I touch her hand reassuringly. "It's okay, babe. Stay and talk to him as much as you want. Rocco is here."

Her eyes widen. "What?"

I point to the man standing very still at the edge of the room. "That's him, there."

Her eyes widen further. "Holy cow, that's him? He's freaking gorgeous."

I glance back at him and see him watching us. She waves at him and he nods in acknowledgment.

She turns to me and frowns. "What's wrong with you? You seem strange."

I shake my head. "Nothing's wrong. Look, I'm going to go with him for a bit. I need to talk to him without all this noise and people, but I'll be back in about an hour. Is that okay with you?"

Her eyes sparkle with mischief. "Talk? That's what we're calling it now? An hour? Don't you dare. You stay the night with him and have a brilliant time. If I was going back with him I certainly wouldn't be coming back in an hour!"

She doesn't understand, and I can't explain any of it now, but I'll tell her everything once he explains the mystery that it would appear everyone in this room knows except me, Sam, and the staff. "If I am later than an hour how will you get back?"

"I'll hang around here for another couple of hours then the limo will pick me up and take me to the hotel."

"Are you sure about this?"

"One hundred percent. Go and have a great time. Trust me there is nothing I'd rather do than be here listening to Professor Chernyshevsky."

Now I have witnessed the terrible corruption in that room, I appreciate her clear honesty and innocence even more. I lean forward and kiss her cheek. "I love you, Sam."

"Are you practicing on me?" she teases.

I shake my head. "I'm not in love with him."

"You better not be. You just met him. You'll scare the poor guy off." She frowns. "Hang on. You don't have any condoms, do you?"

For some weird reason, I blush.

"I knew it. Here." She opens her purse, takes two silver packets out, reaches into my purse, and puts them in. Then she pulls away and winks. "There. You're all set to go."

"Somehow, I don't think I'll need them, but thanks."

She crosses her arms under her breasts. "Bet my life you'll need them."

"Stop betting your life on stupid things," I scold. "Anyway, I better go. Remember, I'll have my cell phone so call me if you need me."

"Stop worrying about me. I can take care of myself. See you early tomorrow. Breakfast is at eight. Remember we have a full day before our flight."

"I'll be there well before that," I promise.

"I'll be expecting details in the morning," she calls gaily, as I walk towards Rocco.

I lift my hand in a wave without turning around.

There is a midnight-blue Rolls Royce waiting for us outside. He opens the door closest to the sidewalk and settles me into the seat, before walking around to the other side. The inside of the car is very plush and redolent with the smell of new leather and Christmas candles. I sink into the soft leather with a sigh. The man and the girl in the room seem like a dream, or a mirage I created in my imagination now.

I touch my temples. I must have drunk too much alcohol. There is an incessant throbbing in my head.

"Headache?" Rocco asks.

"Just a slight one," I admit. "Sam and I have been on the champagne all day long. If you have a couple of headache tablets that would be great."

"Lie back and relax. I have just the thing for you in my apartment."

I lay back and close my eyes. The car journey is very smooth, but I feel my headache getting worse and worse. Thankfully, not too long later, I hear his voice say softly, "We're here."

I open my eyes and look around. We are parked in front of a tall building. There is a doorman in a long black coat at the door who rushes forward to open my door and greets me politely. We walk to a lift with chrome doors. The doors open and we enter.

Rocco inserts a black card into a slot above the console and the car begins to move. Silently, we ride up to the penthouse on the 67th floor. The doors open to a sort of foyer, or a layer of security between the elevator and apartment. Rocco puts a different card key into the heavy door and we enter his apartment.

The ceilings are at least twenty feet high and there is an amazing glass staircase leading up to the first floor.

"Have a seat while I get you something for your headache," he says over his shoulder as he disappears from view.

I move into the vast space. It is exactly how I imagined a very rich bachelor would live. It's all polished glass, black leather, and chrome. The only thing that stands out as different is the artwork, for the walls are full of stunning old masterpieces. Some I have seen in books, and some I have never ever seen, which can only mean they have never been recorded. They have just belonged to his family ever since they were painted.

As I am standing under one that I think looks very much like a Vermeer, but the world has never heard of, he returns holding a glass with a brownish liquid in it.

"What is that?"

"Just some herbs and leaves. It will keep you from getting a hangover."

"Are you sure it's not some date rape drug?" I tease, taking the glass.

His lips twist. "Do you really think I need a date-rape drug?"

I sniff it. It smells very herby. "Does it taste horrible?"

He shrugs. "Depends if you prefer having a headache or two seconds of bitter medicine."

"Oh, I forgot to tell you that Sam and I tried to come up the mountain to your house on Friday, but halfway up, a huge boulder broke off the mountain and came crashing down on the road. It crashed only a few meters in front of us. My car skidded and nearly went off the road. It was terrifying for a few moments I really thought it was the end of us, but as you can see, we made it out alive, though my car is history. But it's okay, it was an old car. The main thing is we were both safe. The amazing thing is by the time we walked down the mountain, your men had cleared up the road, and Raoul was driving down the mountain on his way to the bar. He stopped and gave us a lift home."

"Yes, Raoul told me about your accident. Since it is my fault for deliberately keeping the roads dangerous and unstable, I have replaced your car."

My eyes widen with astonishment. "You did what?"

"It is parked behind the gallery."

I shake my head. "You bought me a car!"

He looks amused. "Yes. The keys have been delivered to the gallery. Now drink up."

I pinch my nose and gulp the brew down. "That was actually not too bad," I say, before my knees turn to jelly. As I drop into soft blackness, a pair of strong hands catch me.

CHAPTER 41

AUTUMN

https://www.youtube.com/watch?v=wo07t6XjNO4
-Too Lost In You-

I awaken on a wide bed. There is a glass ceiling above and through it I can see the stars in the night sky. I blink and turn my head. The vast room is lit only by moonlight. It is very beautiful, but for a second I do not understand where I am or how I came to be there. Then it comes back, Rocco's apartment, the drink…

I take a deep breath. How strange. My headache is gone and I feel as fresh as if I have dove into a cool waterfall in summer. I rise to my elbows.

"Ah, you are awake."

I realize my dress is very crumpled as I sit up and face him. He is sitting on an armchair. He has on only his dress shirt from the night before, the collar unbuttoned and the sleeves rolled up. In the pale light of the moon he looks other-worldly. Too magnificent to be real. A wild fantasy that few women ever expect to meet in their lifetime.

"Where am I?"

"One of the bedrooms in my apartment."

"How long have I been sleeping?"

"No more than an hour."

"Wow, I feel like I slept for hours. That brown brew of yours is powerful stuff. I feel *amazing*. Thanks."

"You're welcome. You can take a bottle back with you. Just dissolve two tablespoons in a glass of water and voila…"

"Thanks, I will. Sam will almost definitely need it tomorrow."

"Just make sure there is one hour for her to sleep it off."

In the ghostly light from the moon, he sighs.

"So this is it," I whisper. "Time for you to spill the beans."

He nods slowly. "Yes, it's time, but first may I tell you a little story?"

I pull the silky sheets around my shoulders. "I'm all ears, Rocco."

He drops his head and his wonderful hair glows in the moonlight. How I long to run my fingers through the silky strands.

"A very long time ago, in a far-away country, a very lonely man found a baby pigeon in the woods. It had fallen out of its nest. It was a poor thing, half-dead, a leg was mangled, and its wings were caked in mud. He took it home in his coat and nursed it as if it was his child. He woke up many times in the night to feed it warm milk from his palm. When it looked like it would die, he kept it inside his shirt, and prayed for it to survive. And it did. It became an adult. It always limped and it never really learned to fly. Something was wrong with one of its wings. Nevertheless, he loved it with all his heart."

Rocco looks up at me, a strange expression in his eyes. "One day, he went again into the woods and he found a box with a baby hawk inside. Hawks were precious in the country he lived in. Only kings and royalty owned hawks and there are only a few of them left in that land. They could fetch many pieces of gold in the market. He guessed the box must have fallen off the horse of a hawk merchant. There was nothing to be done, but to take the hawk home. The hawk was nothing like the pigeon. It was wild, fierce, aloof, and almost reptilian in nature. It didn't want to snuggle in his shirt. It was born to be a predator, so he began to train it to hunt.

"He would hold a dead rat in his hand, and the hawk would fly towards him and land on his gloved hand. Then one day, the leather contraption that was attached to the hawk broke, and the hawk soared away towards the tall trees at the edge of the woods. He knew he had to get the hawk back down quickly, or it would fly away and eventually get tangled in a tree branch. Hanging upside down it will starve to death. He called to it and showed it a dead rat, but it refused to come to him. A storm was brewing. Big drops of rain had already started to fall. He was desperate. He needed to do *something* to bring the hawk back."

His voice has dropped to a whisper and I lean forward to hear. Something about the story makes the hairs on my hand stand. I know it's not just any story.

"An idea hit him. It was a brutal idea, but he was desperate. He didn't know what else to do. He ran into his house, took his pigeon from its cage, and went back out into the storm. He held it up high over his head and called to his hawk, but it wouldn't come. Tears began to pour down his face. He lowered the pigeon down. It was wet and bedraggled, and looked at him with an uncomprehending look. He stroked his finger along his throat. He knew it couldn't fly, but he could throw it into the air, and the frantic flapping of its wings would surely be irresistible to the predator instinct of the hawk. He would fly towards it and tear the pigeon to bloody pieces. At that moment he would be able to recapture the hawk. The pigeon would of course be killed. It was a terrible sacrifice, because he loved the pigeon, you see. It was his only companion. But anybody at all would have made the same decision. The hawk was precious, rare, and worth so many pieces of gold. He could always buy or find another pigeon."

Rocco rakes his fingers through his hair. "The pigeon gazed at him with its dear, innocent, round eyes. It couldn't understand why he had brought it out into the rain. It couldn't understand why he clutched it so hard. Tears came into his eyes. He had loved it with all his heart all its life. It was impossible to explain to anyone else how he felt. Yet, no one could blame him. Without him, it would have died long ago. He remembered the day he had found it, how tiny and helpless it had been. Then he remembered its adorable habit of gently rubbing its beak against his nose. It loved him. It was a soft and gentle creature. It ate directly from his palm. Not the hawk. The hawk was a proud thing. It would never concede even to be his friend. Let alone love him. He closed his eyes for a second. In that second he made up his mind."

I throw the silky sheet off me, clamber off the bed, and run to kneel next to him. I put my hand over his mouth, and beg, "Don't tell me anymore."

He stares at me, his eyes as inconsolable as I had imagined the man who had the terrible decision to make.

He takes my hand off his mouth. "I have to tell you, Autumn," he whispers brokenly. "You have to know what you are getting into."

"I know. I know. There are too many unanswered questions around you, your family, and those people at the party, but not tonight. Tonight is for me. You see, I already know that what you have to tell me will mean I have to walk away from you, but just tonight, I want to have you. I want you, Rocco Rossetti. Tonight, make me yours."

"Are you sure?"

"I have never been more sure of anything else in my life." I smile. "I've got two condoms."

He closes his eyes. "Oh, Autumn. You are so pure." He opens his eyes. "I dread the day you begin to hate me."

I lay my hand on his smooth cheek. "No matter what I will never hate you. Maybe I won't be able to be with you, but I will *never* hate you."

He looks so deeply into my eyes, it is as if he is looking into my very soul, and cherishes me beyond all else. But I can't understand it. How can that be the case when he knows so little about me?

"Don't say that yet," he whispers. "If I start to believe that it will make me very sad if you start to hate me."

"I won't hate you," I insist fiercely. "No matter what you tell me, I won't hate you."

His lips are inches away. So close. "Let me tell you everything now, Autumn. It's the right thing to do… before you give your body to me."

My heart pitter-patters in my chest, but my voice is sure and firm. It is neither colored nor muddled by alcohol. This is what I want. "You will tell me when we get back to Hunter's Cross, and I will find a way to walk away from you. I can do it because I've always known you do not belong to me. You are too beautiful, too exotic, too special, too mysterious, but just tonight I want to pretend you're mine. Now, kiss me Count Rocco Rossetti."

CHAPTER 42

AUTUMN

https://www.youtube.com/watch?v=4vKsSGyQf-M
-Wicked Game-

His powerful hands suddenly shoot out to grip my arms and roughly pull me to him. A shocked gasp flies out of my mouth. He swallows it as he crushes his lips hungrily against mine. His kiss is wild, ferocious, and triumphant. If I didn't know better, I would have thought it to be a declaration of possession. A man claiming his woman. Whatever it is, it is nothing like the previous occasion our lips met. Vaguely, somewhere in my head, flashes of the realization that he must have been holding himself back the last time.

This, this is the *real* him.

His scent, earth and morning dew, fills my senses, intoxicating me. As the kiss deepens, his taste begins to filter into me. He is delicious. It pushes away all my confused thoughts about him and makes me feel as if I am lost in a sweet dream. The edges become hazy, as if I am in a fog. But this is real, I tell myself. And yet it seems fantastical, unreal. Even my body feels like warm butter. Fluid and boneless.

With my eyes clenched shut I swing my arms around him. I'm determined to have my fill before I lose him forever. We are wrapped in a cocoon of dangerous attraction and molten lust. He slips his tongue into my mouth. It is like being zapped by a bolt of electricity. My whole body starts humming as dormant desires wake up and an insistent throbbing begins between my legs.

Blindly, I suck on his tongue.

It takes me to another plane of bliss and intimacy. The barrage of emotions and sensations are overwhelming and I was actually frighteningly dizzy. I feel as if I'm close to passing out.

Suddenly, a low growl comes from deep inside him, and he grabs my hands, pulls them away from around his neck, and holds me still. Very, very still, and for a moment, not quite fear, but an instinct for self-preservation rises inside me, warning me.

"What is it?" I whisper, staring up at him. In the moonlight his pale skin seems to glow.

His haunting eyes lock with mine, and I'm unable to look away. I'm mesmerized by them. There is something dangerous in there. The naked girl with the leather anklet flashes into my mind. She should have run. I know that, but it was too late for her, as it is for me. I'm bewitched by his glittering eyes. Instead of fleeing from him, desperately I try to press myself against him.

My body writhes uselessly inside his steely hold.

His fingertip touches my bottom lip and I feel myself go numb. Gently he pulls it away from my teeth. His finger feels chilled and I shiver and instinctively lick my lips. I taste his finger. A trace of champagne from earlier, and something else. Something intriguing. I feel a type of intoxication move over my mind and body. It confuses and disorientates me. It is like I'm a prisoner in my own body, watching from within. I see my body arch languorously, sensuously, invitingly… there is only one thought in my head. I want him to have it all. All of me.

But he leans forward and whispers, "Do not give in, Autumn. Wake up."

And the spell is suddenly broken. I stare at him, with widened eyes. "What happened to me?"

"You just wanted me too much," he murmurs, as he starts to undress me. His movements are sure, confident, and quick. He dispatches my bra effortlessly, and pulls my panties off my legs. It is clear he has done this many, many times. A prick of jealousy makes a small sound escape from my throat.

He stills. "I won't hurt you."

I stare at him mutely. Inside, I am shaking like a leaf.

He lifts my naked body up into his arms like it weighs no more than a fly, and carries me towards the big bed. He deposits me on it and stands looking down at me. The moonlight is no longer on his face, and I cannot see his expression or his eyes. But I can tell that his shoulders are tense, his whole body is tense. I can feel the tightly coiled power radiating from him.

My nipples throb painfully. They are crying out for release.

Then he bends from the waist and I feel his palm rest on my stomach and his skin doesn't feel cold the way his finger did when he touched me in my dream state, instead it sears into me. I clench my teeth with anticipation. He doesn't stroke, or squeeze, just lets his hand remain there, owning the flesh under it. Slowly, he moves it up until it comes to a rest, cupping my breast. Again, he lays his claim.

"Open your legs, Autumn," he commands.

I take in a trembling breath, and part my legs.

"Wider."

I obey, opening my legs as wide as they will go. I cannot see his eyes, but his head turns towards my exposed pussy. A small growl erupts from his throat. Then his hand travels down to my wet and swollen sex, and he covers it entirely, owning it.

My hips jerk helplessly against his hand.

He sucks my nipple hard as he pushes two fingers deep inside me. I am so wet they make a squelching sound. His thumb pushes hard against my clit and moves rhythmically around the hood, pushing it into the bone below. It is all too intense, too wanton. My head starts to swim.

"I'm going to come," I cry.

Instantly, he moves his hand and his mouth away. Cold air brushes against my open pussy. Fully clothed, he gets on the bed and kneels between my legs. He pulls my pussy lips apart with his fingers and dips his tongue into me. A deep sigh of satisfaction runs through his body.

"Sweet," he murmurs, almost to himself.

Then he uses his tongue to explore between the folds. Using the tip of his tongue, he nudges my clit, up and down, side to side. The pleasure is indescribable. My hands claw into his golden hair as I writhe and moan under him. My body is screaming for a climax. If only he would touch my clit, just once, I could come. Feverishly, I beg him to let me come.

But he doesn't allow me.

He just eats me out. Penetrates my sex with his tongue, fucking it, his teeth biting, his lips sucking and pulling at my throbbing flesh. Every nerve in my body is alive and on fire. Then he places his mouth over my engorged clit, and sucks it deep into his mouth. I feel his teeth at the base, trap the sensitive nub, and my orgasm blasts through me. All the blood rushes to my pelvis, my eyes roll back and I can't stop the piercing scream that rushes out of my mouth. My voice sounds far away and I can hear him greedily drinking my juices.

I remain weightless and lightheaded, as I look down at Rocco. My juices are smeared all over his lips and chin and he is rubbing small, soft circles around my clit. Again, pleasure begins to spread through my veins like a drug and I twist my hips shamelessly against his face.

His expression is so beautiful as he inserts three fingers into my soaking, swollen pussy.

CHAPTER 43

ROCCO

https://www.youtube.com/watch?v=r3Pr1_v7hsw
-I Want To Know What Love Is-

My cock is so fucking hard it hurts. My fingers are still buried inside her sticky, pink pussy and her muscles are clenched tightly around my fingers. The pretty little thing is throbbing and pulsing for my cock. We are playing an age-old game, but she is small and there is no way not to hurt her.

I swirl my thumb around her clit and instantly she cries out, "Isn't it your turn yet?"

"It will be soon. First, I need to get you good and ready, baby," I whisper as I taste her smoky sweet cream again. I suck her hard and finger fuck her until she climaxes again. Her body arches right off the bed and her juices gush out of her this time.

I stand and quickly undress and slip on a condom.

Her eyes move down to my erection and they widen. "Wow! That's really very impressive." She drags her gaze away from my cock back up to my eyes. She bites her bottom lip. "Is this going to hurt?"

"Some," I admit, "but I'll be gentle."

I lay down next to her and roll her on to my body. Then I grab her by the waist and position her so she is straddling my thighs. I feel her pussy spam against my thighs.

"Ride me," I command. "This way you can control how much of me you take."

Autumn

I look down at him. In the bluish light of the moon his hair glints like gold and his body is pale and absolutely flawless, not a mark on it. If not for his red lips, he looks almost like a marble statue.

But good God, he is big. Huge.

I can't imagine him fitting inside me. The biggest thing I've ever had inside me is my small white vibrator. And yet, my sex is clenched with excitement and anticipation. I'm eager to take him inside me.

Getting onto my knees, I hover over him for a few seconds. Then I start to lower myself until the head of his shaft pushes aside my soaked folds. My mouth opens in a silent gasp as it penetrates me. For a second, I freeze as my body stretches painfully to accommodate his girth.

Then I resume impaling myself on him.

As the inches of hard flesh slip into me the feeling is unlike anything I've ever experienced before. It feels almost as if my wet core is sucking him in, and the sensation of being stretched to the limit isn't at all how it started out. It is addictive! It makes me want more and more of his thick, full cock inside me.

"Fuck, you're so tight," he mutters, as his hands come out to grasp my waist. His eyes narrow as he holds me halfway down his cock. I look down and see my juices running down his shaft, making it glisten. His cock feels so good, so natural, so perfect inside me, I can't believe how long we've waited to do this.

"You okay?" he asks, his voice thick with lust. I realize then he is holding himself back with almost superhuman effort.

"Yes," I whisper.

"Ride me," he commands.

Gazing into his mysterious, shining eyes I feel almost hypnotized. In a haze of desire, I place my hands on the taut muscles of his stomach. The skin under my palms burn, as I slam myself on him. He loses control then. With an animal growl, he grabs my ass and spreads the cheeks so I am even more open as he plunges upwards into me. It is a thrust of pure possession. He is claiming me as his. I stare at him astonished.

"This dripping pussy belongs to me," he says.

My mouth opens soundlessly at the indescribable sensation of pain and pleasure. Of being so full of cock. I urge him to fuck me harder and harder, flattening my thighs and pushing my sex onto him, until I can hardly bear it and yet I do not stop him.

I'll fuck you anyway I want because you're mine, his body says.

I am wide open and taking every inch of his massive cock. It hurts, but I twist and grind my swollen clit on his pubic bone.

Rocco

The feel of her soft, silky skin against me as she slowly rocks her hips back and forth, rubbing her velvety mound against me, is like nothing I've ever dreamed of. Her pussy feels like a hot, damp, fist around me. She pushes her groin into me desperately.

She needs this as much as I do.

She leans forward and presses her breast against my mouth. My tongue draws to the rosy peak and flicks lightly across the hard nipple. As I savor the sweet sensation, she leans close and whispers, "I can't believe I've taken all of you. You are so damn big."

I catch her nipple in my mouth and begin to suck it hard.

She moans and begins to bounce on top of me, her young flesh shimmering in the moonlight as she rides my swollen cock. Then, from somewhere deep inside I feel an ancient fear, rising to the surface, warning me to beware.

Did you ask permission?

Yes, yes, I did. She *wanted* me to.
Did you trick her?
Never. Never. It is not her who is my prisoner, it is me who is hers.

I look at her face; it is contorted with primal craving. Her eyes are closed and her body arched. I call her name, and she opens her eyes and stares down at me, and for a second I am shocked. Her eyes are almost silvery. She is powerful. I see it now. She is powerful and she doesn't even know it.

It is not just a legend. She is real. The prophecy is real.

My thoughts blur and swim as the animal lust of her tight pussy squeezing my cock rushes into my head. I grab her shapely ass and slam her up and down my cock. I forget to be gentle. I forget this is her first time. I forget the world outside. I forget everything. I even forget I am the devil.

I see only the goddess I had glimpsed in her eyes a moment ago. I only know where I belong. Inside Autumn. I fuck her as hard as I can, hurting her, hurting her, hurting her. A roar fills my ears, like an inferno of destruction, as she rides me uncaring of her own safety.

I hear her scream. She's climaxing too. I have taken her with me. It is pure bliss. I'll never let her go. She's mine now. Forever.

The explosion comes and I howl her name again and again. Mine. Mine. Mine.

CHAPTER 44

AUTUMN

As dawn starts to light up the sky, Rocco moves away from my body and lies on his back and closes his eyes. He must be tired. We never slept the whole night. Most of it feels like a fantasy now.

Him, going down on me as I lay back on these very sheets, teeth clenched and cresting toward another orgasm. Him, kissing me tenderly as he pushed into me with long, slow, delicious strokes. Me going down on his big, pale cock, until he grabbed me and turned me into a panting, sweating, desperate mess.

It is, without doubt, the most amazing night of my life. And now I know what all the fuss is about. Sex is wonderful. There is not one part of the night that hasn't been mind-blowingly-incredible. I climaxed so many times I can no longer remember how many.

I turn to look at Rocco and my heart clenches. There is something soft and angelic about Rocco with closed eyes. He looks younger and somehow vulnerable as if he has suffered greatly, which of course, must just be a trick of the light. Rocco is the most privileged person I know.

I reach out to lightly trace my fingers over the curve of his sensuous mouth. Such an insatiable mouth. A smile slips onto my face as I remember how much he loved eating my pussy.

His eyes flutter open and he smiles as he meets my gaze.

The smile is sweet and kind, and it tugs at my emotions. "I should go. Sam will be waiting for me," I whisper.

"Before you go…" He gets onto his side and parts my legs.

I should protest, my pussy is still swollen and sore, but I remember the amazing pleasure he can give with his mouth and tongue. I'm not late. There's still time. I close my eyes and moan as he begins to work his magic.

He slides his tongue in and out of my pussy, mimicking what his strong cock did all night long. My hips start to move, begging for more. I want to be stretched again. To feel so full and tight. Then he starts to eat my pussy in a way designed to tease and torment. My voice becomes hoarse with groaning, calling his name and begging him to let me come. The heat inside me mounts and mounts. I become incoherent with desire, my hips grinding restlessly against his mouth.

"Please, Rocco. Please." I mewl at him as my body writhes and twists.

"Not yet, Autumn. Not yet."

Then I feel a sensation of electrifying power run through me, and my body arches off the bed. The climax is so strong my eyes roll upwards and my mouth opens in a soundless scream. I feel my spirit soar as if out of my body. It is the most incredible feeling. When I come back my body feels like lead. I don't want to leave him, but I know I must go.

"Rocco." I touch the cool skin of his face softly. "I have to go."

"I know." He rises from the bed and pulls me up. Then he sits as silent as a statue and watches me get dressed in the dim, bluish light. When I am ready, he presses a bottle into my palm.

"For Sam," he says quietly.

I look down at the bottle. It is the tablets I took last night. "Thanks."

He nods in acknowledgement, and escorts me to the elevator.

"There is a car waiting outside for you. Go safely."

The doors open and I walk in. He stands watching me. There is a strange expression on his face. One of great longing. For some weird reason, it feels like the last time. Like it will never be like this again. Before the doors can close I dash out of the elevator and throw my arms around him. I lift my face to his and he crushes my mouth with his. The kiss is hard, demanding and hungry. It is as if we have not spent all night together, but we are lovers meeting after many years apart yearning for each other.

"I don't want to leave," I whisper, as he trails kisses down my neck.

"It's okay, Autumn. Go and be happy. We will meet again on the mountain."

He steps back and I turn away and walk into the elevator again. "Bye," I whisper as the doors shut.

He doesn't say anything, just looks at me as if it is the last time we will ever be together again. I stare at my own reflection in the shiny doors. I look different. My lips are swollen and there is some knowledge in my eyes that was never there before.

The doors swish open and I walk out into the foyer. The night security guard nods politely at me. I walk through the front door and Rocco's Rolls is waiting for me. The driver is standing next to an open door. I'm about to slide in when something makes my skin tingle. I look up and I see Rocco standing on the balcony. It is too dark to see him clearly, but I can make out his shape leaning down as if he is desperate to catch a last glimpse of me.

I lift my hand and wave at him. He waves back. Then I climb into the car and the chauffeur closes the door. I stare out of the window at the still darkened streets. New York never sleeps it seems. There are people around going about their business.

I cannot help feeling as if I left something behind in Rocco's flat. It feels like it might have been my heart.

CHAPTER 45

AUTUMN

W hen I get back to our suite, Sam is lying diagonally across her bed. I drop two tablets into a glass and pour some water over them. The tablets immediately begin to dissolve into a light brown liquid. Then I climb onto her bed.

"Oh shit! My head is splitting," Sam groans without opening her eyes.

"I've got something that will help."

She opens one eye and looks suspiciously at the glass in my hand. "What the hell is that?"

"It's fantastic for hangovers. I promise."

"You know I won't even take Tylenol. No chemicals or drugs. I've drank lots of water. I'll be fine in a couple of hours."

"It's pure herbs, Sam. Take it, please," I insist.

"No."

"This is ridiculous. You're just suffering for no reason. Do you think the champagne you were drinking last night was pure grapes? There were chemicals, probably toxic, in there too."

"Stop being logical so early in the morning," she grumbles, getting onto her elbows.

"Come on, babe. They're just herbs. I promise you will feel wonderful afterwards. I did when I took them."

"You drank it?"

"Yup, last night and trust me, you will feel amazing when you wake up."

"I can't sleep too long. We have a full day."

"I'll wake you up in an hour," I promise.

She takes the glass from my hand and downs it. "That didn't taste too bad actually."

I watch as she gently falls back on the bed and sleeps. Taking the empty glass out of her slumbering fingers I put it on the bedside cabinet. Then I lay next to her and think of Rocco. He should have been a fantastic secret that I held to my chest. Something so wonderful, so fairytale like, that I have to pinch myself to see if I am in a dream, but all I can think of is that there is something very terrible he needs to tell me. Something so terrible that I will have to walk away from him forever.

I try to think of all the terrible things he could tell me. Then I think of his sister and a shudder goes through me. She has done nothing bad to me, but I know instinctively that she is dangerous. Across my closed eyelids, I see the young girl with the leather anklet. There was something very pathetic about her.

I remember once going to a friend's house and being told that the turkey walking around in her backyard was the turkey that they would be eating for thanksgiving. I went outside and stared at it. It spared me a glance before it went back to diligently scratching the ground for worms. It had absolutely no idea its death was imminent.

For some bizarre reason the girl reminds me of the turkey. I wonder what she is doing now.

My thoughts turn to Rocco's parents. There was more than a hint of something very odd, downright strange, about them. Both of them. If Rocco's sister had not introduced them as his parents, in his presence, I would never have believed it. Their friendliness was false, and they appeared so removed from their son. There was definitely no love there. In fact, I detected impatience and resentment. It was as if he was doing something they found despicable or beneath them.

It makes me wonder if Rocco seems so despairing and lonely because of his family. I think of all the things he did to me during the night. Even now just thinking about it makes my body begin to throb. Quickly, I move my thoughts away and try to figure out what Rocco's secret might be. Why would his sister want to poison me? Did they not want me in their family? Was it because I clearly wasn't high born, one of them? I remember the mother's eyes. The way they had raked over me, assessing and hostile. I remember Zelena telling me to beware of his family. That they were dangerous.

As I lie there listening to Sam's even, peaceful breathing a plausible scenario forms in my head. Rocco is bound by some family tradition. He cannot choose his own bride. He cannot offer me anything but a quick fling and that is why he was so insistent I knew about it before we slept together. He was trying to be fair to me. He didn't want to cheat me.

Figuring out his secret doesn't make me feel any better. It actually makes me feel really sad. I always knew I couldn't have him for real, but it was nice pretending that he could be.

Next to me, Sam stirs. I turn my head and watch her eyes open.

"Autumn," she whispers.

I smile softly at her. Thank god, I have her.

She rubs her eyes. "Wow, you were right. I feel really, really amazing."

My smile turns into a grin. "Told you. I took it last night, never slept a wink, and I don't feel tired or sleepy even now."

"What kind of herbs are those?" she asks curiously.

"No idea. Rocco gave them to me and I was too busy with other things to ask."

She curls her body towards me, and puts her hands under her cheek. "I bet you were too busy to worry about herbs. Did you use the two condoms?"

"Yup."

"Well, well, the virgin becomes a woman. Come on then, tell me everything."

So I tell her. I tell her about the amazing sex. Then I tell her about my plausible scenario theory about his family. Reluctantly, she agrees with my guess. She links her fingers with mine and tells me not to worry or give up hope. She believes Rocco will stand by me. She believes given enough time Rocco will fall in love with me and he will not forsake me.

After that we get ready, have breakfast, and go out into the freezing smoky Big Apple. There is so much to see and do before we fly back to our separate destinations. We eat hotdogs, we laugh, we take a million photos, we talk to strangers.

I cry at the airport. I don't know why I cry.

She hugs me tightly. "Stop being such a wuss. I'm just a phone call away."

"I know. I'm just going to miss you."

"Love you, Autumn. Love you so much."

I'm so choked with emotion I can't even say the words back to her.

The last call for her flight comes through the loudspeaker system.

"That's me," she says brightly. "Send me a text when you land."

I stand there watching her walk away, her red curls bouncing recklessly. I don't know why I feel so sad to let her go, maybe it is because of my insecure situation with Rocco.

My voice comes back and I shout out, "I love you, Sam."

She stops, turns around, and blows a kiss at me. Then the crowd swallows her.

CHAPTER 46

AUTUMN

The next day I go back to work and other than the lovely surprise of the new car Rocco bought for me, life settles back seamlessly into its old pattern. Brianna from the bakery comes in for a chat with some doughnuts and coffee. She ends up buying a small garden sculpture of a fairy. After she leaves, I clear up the mess. As I wipe down the table Sam calls.

"Whatcha doing?" she asks.

"Cleaning the table after eating some sugary doughnuts."

"Ugh… sugar. It's ten in the morning. How could you do that to your body?"

"Well, I tried your cereal and it was disgusting, so I got Brianna to come over with some real food. Oh, and I'm packing it all up and mailing it to you."

"Don't you dare," she warns.

"How's it going with you?" I ask with a smile.

"I'm on my way to class, and I'm a bit late, but I just wanted to call and hear your voice. By the way, guess what I—"

Her voice is cut mid-sentence at the same time that there is a loud bang. She must have dropped the phone, because the sound of it hitting hard ground was so loud in my ear I have to jerk the phone away from my ear. For a second, I stare at the phone in confusion. Then I snatch it back to my ear and scream, "Sam! Sam, are you all right?"

Sam doesn't answer me, but I hear other people screaming, moving, shouting out desperate questions and frantic commands.

"Oh, my God."

"Call 911. Someone call 911."

"Is she alive?"

"For fuck's sake move out of the way."

"Did anybody get the car's registration?"

"It's a hit and run."

"Sam," I scream.

Someone picks up her phone and says, "Hello."

"Hello, what's happened to the girl with the red hair?" I ask frantically.

"Hi, I… uh… were you talking to her before the accident?"

"Yes, yes," I nearly scream. "Is she all right?"

"I'm so sorry, but she's not moving at all. Someone's called 911 and asked for an ambulance, we'll have to see what they say."

"Can you stay with me on the phone till they get there?" I beg.

"Yeah, sure."

I stand in the middle of the shop for about fifteen minutes, then I hear the sounds of sirens. Authoritative voices ask people to move. I wait, hardly daring to breathe.

"What's going on?" I finally whisper.

"I don't think she made it," the girl whispers tearfully. "They're... Oh, my God, she's dead."

"No. Noooooo."

I kill the connection and look around me in a daze. It cannot be. It cannot be. I walk towards a painting and straighten it. It's a lifelong habit. I *hate* paintings that are not straight. It gets on my nerves. I walk away from the painting and stand in the middle of the gallery. My gaze slides around the other paintings, my mind feels strangely blank. Larry comes downstairs.

"I'm going to Old Joe's. Want a burger?"

"Yeah, sure."

"With extra cheese and mustard."

I nod. "Yeah."

I stand in the middle of the gallery and watch him walk across the road. A woman pushing a stroller goes by. Her baby drops its pacifier and she bends to pick it up. I watch them without expression. How long I stand there I do not know, but eventually, Larry comes back.

"Here's your burger. I'll have mine upstairs."

I take the brown paper bag from him. "Thanks." I put the Out For Lunch sign on the door, then take my burger to the backroom. I put it on the table and switch on the radio. A song I do not recognize comes on. I open the small fridge and pull out a can of Coke. Then I sit at the table, unwrap the burger and stare at it.

I can see that Joe has been really generous with the cheese. It has oozed on to the paper bag. I take a bite of the burger. It tastes good. I take a sip of Coke. I don't believe Sam is dead. The girl is either playing a cruel prank on me, or she did not see clearly. She's not a doctor. How can she know? Sam will be taken to the hospital and the doctors there will take care of her. They will mend her again. She is young. She will survive.

I take another bite. A song I like comes on and I sing along and bob my head to the rhythm. I look at my phone. No messages yet. It's early yet. Obviously, I have to give the doctors time to work on her. They may even need to perform surgery on her. I wonder if I should call the hospitals around that area and find out exactly what is going on with her.

No, just give it a bit more time.

I take a swig of Coke. I'm not hungry, but I take another bite. It is a shame to waste good food. I wipe my mouth with the napkin and chew. In fact, I was wrong, the burger doesn't taste as good as it usually does. There is almost three quarters of the burger left. I wrap it and put it into my bag. I will give the rest to the raccoons.

I go out front and take off the Out For Lunch sign. Then I sit at the table. There are no thoughts in my head. My mind is oddly empty, which is strange. I find my fingers tapping impatiently on the surface of the table. I jump when my phone rings. I run to it to pick it up. I am sure it is Sam, she is calling me from some hospital, but it is not. I freeze next to it. I stare at the lighted screen in horror. The lighted words read:

Sam's Mom

I don't move until the phone stops ringing. The message icon starts blinking. I pick it up and hold it to my ear.

"Autumn, it's Sam's mom here. I've got some bad news. Sam… Sam," her voice breaks. There is a pause where I hear her take a deep breath. Then she continues in a strange robotic monotone. "Sam's gone. It was a hit and run. She didn't suffer. She died on the spot. I'll call you again about the funeral. Goodbye, dear."

CHAPTER 47

AUTUMN

Slowly, I put the phone back on the table. I clasp my hands together to stop them from trembling. I don't believe her. I can't believe her. She can't be right. It's impossible. I saw her last weekend for God's sake. I think I stood there for hours, but I cannot say, because time had lost all meaning for me. I must have been in shock. I was startled into movement by the sound of the bell above the door.

Lifting my head, I walk into the gallery. It is the lady from the boutique where we bought our dresses. She is carrying a large white box.

"Hello," I greet, my voice sounds strange. "Can I help you?"

"I'm here to deliver this dress to you. I'm sorry I'm a day late. Someone accidentally left an oily finger print on the skirt so I had to have the stain professionally cleaned. It is now flawless again." She smiles.

I frown. I feel so confused. I can't even think straight. "I didn't order a dress."

"Well, somebody did. It's all paid for. Enjoy," she says, with a wink. She leaves the box on the table. "Give me a call if you need to make any alterations."

I stare down at the box.

"Bye," she calls as she exits the gallery.

I open the box and part the tissue inside. It is the green dress in the window. I take the envelope and pull out the card.

I simply couldn't resist.
I knew it would be perfect for you.
Make sure you don't let Mr. Ghost tear it in his haste though. LOL
Send me pics as soon you as you get this.
xxxxxxx
Sam

A thin, high-pitched, completely foreign sounding wail flows out of my mouth. It is such an eerie sound I hear Larry running across his office. He runs down the stairs and appears in the gallery an anxious look on his face.

"What is it?" he asks urgently.

I can't answer him. Tears are running down my face.

"Autumn, what the hell is going on?"

"Sam's dead. Hit and run." The unbearable words come out in an odd scratchy voice.

As his jaw drops in shock. I feel the card drop back on top of the tissue, and my legs start moving as if they have a mind of their own. I run out of the gallery and down the road. I run without knowing where I'm going. Sam's dead, but she bought a dress for me. People turn to stare at me, but I don't care. Nothing matters anymore. Sam is gone.

I run until I get to the bar. I stop and go inside. It smells of beer and fried fish inside. There are only a few customers seated at the tables. I take a seat at the bar.

"I work at the gallery, but I haven't brought any money with me. Could I have some drinks now and pay for it tomorrow, please?"

The bartender takes one look at my snotty face and nods. "No problem. What would you like?"

"Vodka neat. Make it a double."

His expression doesn't change. As if he's used to grief-stricken women coming in alone in the late afternoon to order vodka doubles. "Gotcha."

My throat hurt. My eyes hurt too and there is a horrible, horrible pain in my chest. Shit. Shit. Shit. Why did she have to go and die on me? How could she? My eyes are so full of tears the bar becomes blurry.

"Here you go," the barman says.

I pick up the glass and throw the Vodka down my throat and it spreads its warmth into my belly. She was supposed to outlast me with her superfoods, healthy breakfast smoothies, her careful study of food labels before she deemed them good enough to put into her body. She might as well have eaten ice cream and cake for breakfast, drank full fat Coke, and stuffed herself with fast food for lunch and dinner. My gut burns with rage. She was cheated. I was cheated.

I slam the glass on the counter. "Another one… please."

"Coming up."

I throw a few back. My head spins slightly. I stand. "I'll be back tomorrow to pay the tab." Then I leave the bar. Outside the setting sun hits my eyes and makes me squint. I sway for a few seconds as I get my bearings. I must have drunk far more than I thought, or maybe it was just because I drank on an empty stomach.

"You all right, hon?" a man asks. His face is leather, and his brown eyes are kind.

I nod, then I start to walk in the direction of my caravan. It's a long walk and my shoes start to chafe and hurt. I take them off and walk in my bare feet. It gets dark and I stumble along blindly. My body feels hollow. I cannot accept she is gone. I refuse to. I keep thinking of how she looked at the weekend. The way she had laughed when I clowned around at the hotel spa. She had been so happy, so excited about the future.

The caravan site comes into view. As I walk past Joe's caravan, I see him sitting on the step drinking a beer.

"Howdy neighbor," he calls out.

I completely ignore him and walk on. When I get home, I get my bottle of Vodka out of the cupboard, and go sit outside. I swig a mouthful straight from the bottle. Then I lean my head back against the cold metal of the caravan and close my eyes.

"Oh Sam," I whisper brokenly.

"Hey, you all right?" Joe's voice asks.

My eyes snap open and I frown at him. "Get lost, Joe."

In the darkness his eyes glitter dangerously. "Why are you being like that? I'm just trying to be friendly-like."

"Go back home, Joe. I'm really not in the mood to chit chat." I stand with the intention of going back inside, but he moves fast, and suddenly he is standing in front of me. I'm trapped between him and the chair.

"I'm a good listener, Autumn," he says softly.

"Then you should have fucked off by now, because I've already asked you to leave three times," I snarl.

"Woah," he says, widening his eyes in mock fear, "watch it Joe, this cat has claws."

"For the last time, *move*," I mutter between gritted teeth.

He grins, his teeth flashing like a Cheshire cat. "Why? I like where I am. Let's go inside your caravan. I promise I'll make you feel real good."

I take a deep breath, then I knee the moron as hard as I can right in the balls. His mouth opens in shock, and a guttural, choking, almost inhuman sound comes out it. Then his knees give away and he drops to the ground. He curls himself in to a fetal position at my feet while clutching his groin. I step over him, go into the caravan and lock my door.

"Oh Sam," I whisper in the dark.

CHAPTER 48

ROCCO

His hands are still cupping his groin, his mouth is muttering curses, and his curled body is rocking gently to dull the pain when I step next to him. His eyes widen with astonishment when he sees the shiny leather of my shoes come out of nowhere and appear so close to his face. His gaze flies upwards to my face.

"Who the fuck are you?" he blurts out incredulously, fearfully. My noiseless approach has, naturally, freaked him out.

I say nothing, just stare down curiously at the pitiful creature that he is. Never in my life have I ever seen fit to mingle with or expend any energy on a creature such as him. A useless eater. I knew, of course, men such as him existed, and existed in vast numbers, but I'd never before come so close to one.

Suddenly, he understands. He knows what I am here for. His eyes bulge with terror. He opens his mouth as if to scream, but to his shock no sound comes out of it. I continue to look at him. Tears fill his eyes and run down the sides of his face. Thinking I am the angel of death his eyes beg me silently for compassion. He makes silent promises to be better, to do better. Mutely, he apologizes feverishly for his past misdeeds. He pleads for forgiveness. Then he begins to call to God, the very God he had spurned in his miserable life.

I bend down and grasp his neck. It snaps like a twig, and the annoying, begging light goes out of his lying eyes. I lift him easily and haul him over my shoulder. Dry twigs crunch under my feet as I carry him and his bottle of beer towards the fence surrounding the trailer park. At an appropriate part of the fence I hook one of his legs between the wooden slats, and let his body fall on the ground.

Tomorrow someone will find him.

They will assume he fell and broke his neck. I toss the beer bottle next to him and I look around. The hour is early, but it's Monday night, so there seems to be no one around. Without taking another look at the vermin, I sprint back to the edge of the forest directly opposite Autumn's caravan. I slide behind a tree and from the shadows I return to my task of guarding her.

Nothing and no one must harm her.

CHAPTER 49

AUTUMN

I hear Joe move away as I'm sitting outside my cupboard and taking all my clothes and shoes out. Once everything is out, I climb into it, and close the doors. It is reassuringly dark inside. When I was very young, I used to sit in the cupboard all the time. I enjoyed being in the dark, enclosed space. It made me feel safe. My child's mind had convinced myself no monsters could get inside.

But it is a very strange thing to be doing when one is an adult. I hug my knees to my chest and gently sway backwards and forwards. Then a strange sound begins to come from my mouth. I have no control of the sound. I have never learned it, or practiced it, but it sounds a bit like one of those songs sung by the Celtics to call their sheep to them. I once heard it on a video on Facebook.

I realize my body is calling. Not to sheep, but to Sam. I am calling her back to me. I call and call, my voice becomes hoarse, but she does not come. I climb out of the cupboard, my body cramped and my heart lost.

Restlessly, I open the food cupboard. I have no appetite but I should eat something. The first thing I see is the organic cereal she bought for me. I reach out and touch the box. She touched this... while she was still alive. It seems impossible that she is gone never to return. I will *never* see her again. My hand recoils from the box as if bitten by a snake. A strangled cry of horror blows out of my mouth, then my knees give way, and I collapse to the ground in a heap.

The pain of losing her is indescribable, terrible, unspeakable, unbelievable. I have never felt such pain. Nobody who has not lost someone they truly loved would understand. I didn't. I knew it must feel horrible, but I could never understand the absolute horror. Sam was my best friend, my sister, my only source of love. The only family I had. We spoke every day. No matter what we found a moment to talk.

Now she is gone. I will never speak to her again.

I think of her laughing, I think of her staring enraptured at that Professor, I think of her saying, "I love you," when we were hanging on the edge of the mountain. So many images flash into my head. Then suddenly, an image floats into my head. Zelena saying I will suffer a terrible loss. I stand and rush out of my caravan. I can see her light is on. I dash to her caravan and bang on her door urgently.

She opens it, stands back, and silently allows me to enter.

"The terrible loss has happened," I hiss.

She closes the door and nods sadly. "Yes, I can see."

"Did you know? Did you know my best friend was going to die?"

"No, I only knew it would be a great loss."

"She didn't even get to finish her sentence," I gasp brokenly.

She opens her arms out to me. Something snaps inside me and I rush into them. My broken heart understands that here is sanctuary, a soft place where I can grieve. Hot tears pour down my cheeks, and I sob until my body heaves, and I feel as if I will break.

"That's it child, you'll make yourself ill. Let's us have a cup of tea," she says gently.

Weak with sorrow and sobbing, I let her lead me to the table. She pulls out a chair and I slump on it with my face buried in my hands. The hurt is terrible. I close my eyes and rock my body. I am aware of her boiling water, opening containers, spooning tea, pouring the boiled water into cups, and moving towards me. She puts a cup in front of me and the other on the opposite end. Then I hear her sit down opposite me.

I raise my head and look at her. "I'll never know what she wanted to say to me."

"What she wanted to say to you is unimportant, the only important thing is, her soul wanted you to be the last voice she heard before she went."

"What do you mean?"

"We make contracts before we come to earth. We agree to certain things, certain indignities and certain sufferings, because we know it will advance our evolution. One of the things she agreed to was a short life, but she wanted that brief life to end with one last time hearing your voice."

I stare at her through tears. Hope trembles in my voice as I ask, "Can you do a séance? Can I speak to her?"

She shakes her head regretfully. "I'm sorry, I don't do séances, but I can tell you this. She lived an honest, blameless life, so she has nothing to regret, and the place she goes to will reflect the clean life she lived."

I press my lips together tightly to stop my chin from quivering. "Why did she agree to such a short life?"

"Perhaps her job is done."

"How can her job be done?" I demand almost angrily. "She was so young and she had so many dreams. She never got to fall in love, have children, be a grandmother, and she never got to have the career she wanted."

"Those are earthly things. You think they are important, but they are not. She has done what she came to do and now she is gone."

"You don't understand, she *wanted* to live. She lived such a healthy lifestyle, she was worried she would outlive me and be alone for too long."

"The mind is not the soul. Those were not the things her soul wanted to experience in this incarnation. She has done what she was supposed to do," she insists quietly.

"What has she done?"

"It is not for you or me to judge. She's the lightning before the thunder. There is a storm coming, Autumn. I warned you, remember?"

My mouth opens. "You didn't tell me it would involve her."

"I didn't know, but she has done what she came to do. One day you will understand."

"I will *never, ever* understand why she was taken away from me," I cry bitterly.

"The day you will understand is coming sooner than you think."

I'm in such a distressed state I do not think to question her mysterious words. "Oh, Zelena, I miss her so much. I don't know if I can bear it."

"I know. I know you're hurting now. Drink your tea, child, before it gets cold. It will do you good."

I lift the cup and drink the brew. It tastes of nothing. I wipe my eyes with the back of my hands. "What do I do now?"

"Now you sleep, but tomorrow you will go back up the mountain and continue your painting."

I frown. "How did you know I was painting him?"

"You are an artist and he is a marvelous subject. Of course, you are painting him."

I sigh deeply. "I have no desire to paint."

"Work will heal your heart."

There are other questions gnawing at my brain, but I feel too exhausted to deal with them. My eyelids start to feel heavy. I glance at her bed. It looks orderly and neat. My caravan is full of memories of Sam. Even the bed will smell of her.

"Why don't you go to sleep on my bed?" she offers kindly.

"What about you?" I mumble half-heartedly. I'm so sleepy and drained I can hardly keep my eyes open.

"I never sleep at night. I make my potions and only snatch a few hours of sleep in the afternoon. Go on. I will wake you early in the morning so you won't be late to work."

I walk to the bed and as soon as my head touches the pillow I am gone to a place where there is no pain.

Zelena

I pull the duvet over her sleeping form and for a long time, stand looking down at her innocent face. This is a tragedy she will never get over. The way I never got over the death of my daughter. Always, she will mourn for this senseless loss.

I think of her trusting eyes filling with horror at what I must do. I wish with all my heart there was a different way, but there isn't. I harden my heart.

Betrayal, I must see in her eyes.

CHAPTER 50

ROCCO

I see Zelena's door open, but it is not Autumn that comes out. It is Zelena. She walks to the edge of the field and makes a beckoning motion in the general direction of the forest. Immediately, I start walking quickly towards her.

From the moment Raoul reported that she was not at the gallery, I knew something was wrong. Pure instinct alone had lead me to the bar. I had waited in the dark for her and followed her home, keeping enough distance that she never felt my presence. I knew she was devastated, but I didn't know why. And I knew not to approach her. If she had wanted me, she would have called me, she would have come to me. I bled for her as she walked barefoot on the road. Her gait swaying and unsteady.

It did not surprise me when she went into Zelena's, but it did surprise me when she didn't come out.

"What's going on?" I ask urgently as I reach Zelena.

"I put her to sleep. They killed her friend today. Hit and run," she says quietly.

247

"Sam?" I breathe incredulously. I never expected that.

She nods stiffly. There is some strong emotion inside her, but she makes a great effort to hide it from me. I am too furious to wonder what it is.

"How can you be sure it is them and not a coincidence?"

"Because I am Zelena and I know things others do not."

"Why would they do that?" I ask through clenched teeth.

"I can think of no reason to do that. Ask your sister."

"Take care of her," I say and begin to run. I run back to the parking lot of the bar and get into my car, then I drive so fast to the city, the scenery outside my windows blur. My hands grip the steering wheel so hard, they hurt when I eventually arrive at my destination, and release the steering wheel.

Her housekeeper opens the door. She takes one look at my face and cowers away. I don't need her to tell me where Isadora is. I stride through the ostentatiously luxurious house and kick down her living room door.

She makes a great show of looking unconcerned.

She was flicking through a magazine and she looks up and smiles. She is wearing a white silk trouser suit and gold high-heeled sandals. There is something undeniably and heart-breakingly beautiful about her, and she may even possess the loveliest eyes of any living creature, but this is a complete mirage. The truth is rotten.

I stride up to her, grab her wig, pull it off her head, and fling it across the room.

There. This is the truth. She is not beautiful at all. In reality, she is ugly beyond description. Every atom in my body recoils from the sight of her. The skin on her head has become even more revolting. It is red, with brown boils that weep with liquid and pus. Not like a skin disease, but like something evil. The disgusting smell of rotting and death rising from her exposed sores fills my nostrils. It is so over-powering it actually makes me want to retch.

"Why?" I snarl.

She shrugs nonchalantly, stands and walks towards her wig. Bending down she picks it up and fits it back on her head. Then she faces me. Her eyes glitter wickedly, daring me to hurt her. Yes, she'd like that. She'd like to push me into making a mistake and give her a reason to trap me into her malevolent plans.

"Sometimes I think mother must have dropped you on your head when you were a baby, little brother. Isn't it obvious? Losing her best friend will only push her closer to you. You should be thanking me. I just made it easy for you."

"She had nothing to do with any of this."

"I care less for her life than I do for a bug I squash under my shoe. You will see for yourself in the coming days what I have done for you."

I am so furious I want to destroy her, but I know I can't. Anyway, it won't solve anything. My parents will take her place. If I destroy them, others will take their place. I have to find a way to defeat them all. I take a deep breath, and holding myself tightly in rein, I take one last look at her. The corruption in her cunning eyes, her cruel mouth, her smooth skin… then I start to walk away.

"You think you can survive everything?" she flings at my back. "She might be important to you, but is she all that matters? Don't we matter? We are your blood."

I turn back slowly. Her hands are clenched at her sides, and her eyes are hard and cold. I feel nothing for her. I feel nothing for any of them. My words are slow and measured. "You know I have never believed in the greater good. See where it got the Incas. All those hearts sacrificed, that river of spilled blood flowing down the temple steps, and their civilization was still obliterated, gone without a trace." I turn away and carry on walking towards the door.

"We are in the same boat as them, Rocco. We, you won't survive this unless you give her up."

I don't turn back. I don't break my stride. I don't care if I don't survive. I will never sacrifice Autumn to her.

Some kind of shudder rises from inside me, or perhaps it is a long-suppressed piece of knowledge. I know now Autumn is no longer safe. I am dealing with a mad woman. A woman who will stop at nothing, and do anything to survive.

I have to tell Autumn everything as soon as possible, and if her answer is what I think it will be, then I have to be prepared to fight all of them.

They cannot win. I won't fucking let them. I'll perish before they hurt a single hair on her head.

CHAPTER 51

AUTUMN

By the time I am gently shaken awake, the sun is already streaming in through the windows. I look into Zelena's wrinkled face and blink with confusion. Then I remember coming here last night, and why I came, and pain is instant, and like a dagger in my heart. With a cry of sorrow, I sit up, and swing my legs to the floor.

"Thanks for letting me sleep here. I was so tired last night."

"It was the tea. A sedative concoction I made. You needed it."

I nod blankly. "Yes. I suppose I kinda lost it last night."

"Go to work now, child, then go up the mountain to paint. Work will occupy your mind and keep the pain away."

I stand and look at her. "Thanks again, Zelena. I feel a bit better this morning. It was the shock. It made me go crazy." I scratch my head. "I was in such a state I think I even kneed Joe last night."

She smiles. "I'm sure he deserved it."

"Yeah, well, I'm off."

"Take care of yourself, little one."

I go back to my caravan. The first thing I see is the box of organic cereal. I swallow hard and rush to the shower. I get ready as fast as I can and walk to work. When I get to work Larry is already there. He is actually moving the vacuum cleaner around. I stare at him with astonishment. It is immediately clear he has never vacuumed anything in his life, and he looks ill at ease and to be honest quite ridiculous.

"What are you doing here?" I shout above the noise.

He starts and tries to switch off the vacuum, but fails to find the button. I walk up to him and turn it off. The room falls strangely silent.

"Uh, I didn't know if you would be coming in today in light of..." he trails off uncomfortably.

I shake my head. "It's okay. I'm here now. Work will do me good."

He steps back awkwardly. "I'll be... er... upstairs if you need me." He takes a few steps away from me, then turns back. "I'm really sorry for your loss, Autumn."

I bite my lower lip so hard it hurts, and I nod. No words are possible. I realize then that pity is the worst thing for me. Zelena is right. I've got to work, keep my hands and mind occupied at all times. I walk to the vacuum cleaner and switch it on. I see the box with the green dress in the backroom and it hurts, but I deliberately walk towards it and carefully put it away into the backroom cupboard where my painting of the castle is.

Then I carry on cleaning. I clean and clean, stopping only to call Rocco's number at about ten thirty. He doesn't answer so I leave a message that I will be driving up to see him after work to paint him. Then I find other things to do right through lunch. The afternoon is easier. Two customers and an artist comes in and it keeps me busy.

As I am closing up, Raoul walks in. He nods silently, and I nod back. I follow him out silently, and he drives me up the mountain. At the place where Sam and I hung over the edge, I feel a terrible sense of loss. I squeeze my eyes shut and think of something different.

William opens the door for me. "Good evening, Miss Delaney."

"Good evening, William."

"The Count is waiting for you."

He takes me to the room where Isadora had offered me wine. Rocco looks at me, and it is unbearable to see pity shining in his beautiful eyes. I guess Larry must have told him when Raoul found me gone from the gallery yesterday.

"I'm so sorry, Autumn," he says softly.

"Yes, I'm sorry too." My voice breaks, and I have to swallow the hard ball of pain in my throat. I want to run to him and let him hold me, but I'm afraid. I know I can't use him as my crutch. I know he doesn't belong to me. "Can we... can we... get on with the painting?"

"Autumn, I know you're grieving, but we really need to talk. It's important. You need to know."

I run to him and throw my palm across his mouth. "Please, Rocco. Don't. Not yet. I'm already so broken, I just couldn't take another blow. Not yet. Just let me finish my painting, and then I promise, I'll hear what you have to say."

"Oh, Autumn, I would have given everything I own to protect you from this pain."

"Don't pity me, Rocco. Please. Just let me paint you. I need to occupy my hands and mind. Otherwise, I fear I will go mad with fury and sorrow."

"Would you like some food first?" he asks gently.

I shake my head. "No."

"When was the last time you ate?"

I realize I haven't eaten all day. The last thing I ate was yesterday, part of a burger. And yet I do not feel hungry.

"You must eat something," Rocco insists.

"I'm not hungry," I protest.

Gently, his fingers touch the thin skin under my eyes. "Either you eat or you do not paint."

I nod. The whole world seems alien to me. All day I have been waiting for her to call me. Tears fill my eyes and run down his fingers. A look of terrible sadness crosses his eyes.

"You are mine, Autumn. No matter what happens, you are mine." Then he scoops me into his arms and carries me to the sofa where Isadora had sat. He lays me on it. The tears roll down my face. I want to stop crying, but I can't. "I loved her," I whisper.

"I know."

"I feel so hurt, so devastated. Nothing makes sense anymore. I just want her to come back."

"She's not coming back, Autumn."

I beat his chest. "It's unfair. It's unfair," I sob.

He pulls me towards him and holds me tight. I don't know how long I stay like that, but eventually, he pulls away. "It's time for you to eat. It's just soup and bread."

I don't remember him calling anyone, but almost as if he had, someone comes in with a tray bearing soup and a hunk of bread. The soup is yellow with a circular pattern of cream in it. I take a spoonful. It tastes of nothing.

"Keep eating," he instructs.

I take another. And another. He tears a bit of bread, dips it in the soup, and holds it to my mouth. I let him feed me, as if I am a baby. To my surprise the bowl becomes empty, and the bread is reduced to crumbs.

"Feel like painting now?"

I nod.

We move to the library. He takes up position and I start to paint, and to my great surprise Zelena was right. For the first time since Sam was snatched away from me, I forget to mourn and yearn for her. In fact, I forget everything. There is nothing but my painting, the thick viscous paint, the right brush, the rag, the turpentine, and the subject... that I must now confess I am in love with.

CHAPTER 52

ROCCO

Outside it has begun to rain. I walk up to her. "That's enough for tonight, Autumn. It's time you were in bed."

She nods silently and wipes her hands on a rag.

I take her upstairs to her bedroom. "I'll run a bath for you," I say, and go into the bathroom. When I come out she is sitting on the bed looking lost. I walk up to her. "Stand," I instruct.

She stands quietly.

Like a child, she lets me undress her. Then I carry her into the bathroom and lower her into the scented bath water. She leans back against the bath. For a while I let her be, then I begin to wash her. Meticulously, tenderly, with infinite care, as if I am a mother with her newborn baby.

Her tears mix with the water. "I can't bear the pain," she sobs.

"I know," I whisper, and lift her out of the water. I stand her on the ground, and dry her body down with a towel. Then I carry her to bed and lay her on it.

She holds her arms out to me. "Fill me, Rocco. I'm empty. So empty."

"You're not empty, my darling," I say, as my gaze moves down her creamy stomach to the soft nest of curls. "Open your legs and show me your pussy."

Her thighs part to reveal her opening, full of wet swollen flesh.

"That's a good girl," I say, and part her thighs as far as they will go. Then I put my mouth on her sweet heat and make her forget her pain.

For hours I make love to her and afterwards I give her a small glass of fruit brandy laced with a mild sedative.

I let her drink it, and watch her fall into an exhausted sleep. I stay on guard next to her until five minutes before her alarm is set to go off. Then I slip away quietly.

Afterwards, I stand at the window of one of the empty rooms facing the driveway and watch her get into the car with Raoul. I wait until the car goes out of view and is lost to me before I go about my business.

CHAPTER 53

AUTUMN

Two days pass.

Every day I go down the mountain to work at the gallery, then Raoul picks me up and takes me back up to *Ze Dem Adelar*. I paint, then we eat together, speak of anything other than Sam, then we go to my bed and have the kind of sex that makes me forget the world and Sam. I fall asleep in his arms, and wake up alone. I get ready and another day repeats.

Once Rocco tried to remind me that we need to talk, but I turn on him like a wild animal and kiss his mouth. He forgets what he wanted to say, or just understands I am not ready. Maybe I won't ever be ready, because I feel certain now that hearing what he says will mean I will have to give him up and I can't lose him. I cannot hear the ending of the story of the hawk and pigeon. I know now, I am the pigeon and his family are the hawk.

I can't let go of him yet. Not yet. Not when I am so horribly fragile. Sometimes when I am in the middle of making love with Rocco, I think I will break. And I will cry out and he will immediately stop and hold me tight.

But by the third day, I know I have to steel myself and go back to my caravan. There is food becoming moldy in my fridge, and I am bothered by something else. It is crazy, but I have never dreamed of Sam. I think of her all day so I should dream of her at night. At least once, but I never do. I feel as if she can't come to me when I am at Rocco's place.

After Larry leaves for the night, I go to the back and pull out my painting of the castle. I should finish it, but I have feelings for it. It seems dull and amateurish to me now. I put it back into the narrow space it was resting in and decide to clean the gallery first. That way I won't have to do it in the morning. After I have cleaned downstairs, I carry the vacuum cleaner upstairs to Larry's office.

His office is small and it only takes me a few minutes before I'm done. I switch off the vacuum and in its dying growl, I hear a sound downstairs. It is unmistakable. Glass breaking. I still and listen carefully. Someone is working the lock. The rusty bell tinkles.

The shuffling of feet… hushed men's voices… there are men in the gallery! More than one.

I can lock myself in here, but what if they have heard the vacuum and know I am up here.

I creep silently to the door, crack it open, and crawl along the short corridor. Then I hang my head over the top of the stairs and… see three men. All dressed in black. Two of them have knives. My heart starts hammering in my chest.

Suddenly, one of them swivels his head, looks up and sees me. For a second we stare at each other. He has the hard face of a thug. Then he breaks the stare. "Upstairs," he tells his friends.

A scream escapes my throat, and I'm on my feet in a flash. I run for the sanctuary of the office. It has a lock. I reach it, slam the door shut and turn the lock with trembling hands. Placing my body against it I debate what to do. Call the police or open the window and try to climb down the pipes.

But I can already hear the thud of their footsteps running up the stairs. I need to barricade myself first. This door is too flimsy. I make a mad dash to Larry's desk and push it forward until it rams against the door. The men start trying the door handle, then banging on it. One of the men slams his body against the door.

I take a frightened step back. Clearly, the desk won't be enough to hold them back. I look around desperately: the metal filing cabinet. I hurry to it and push it with all my might towards the door. When I am close enough I shove it onto the desk. It falls with a crash. I jam it against the door.

My body is shaking as I find Larry's phone under some papers on the floor and call 911.

"911, what's your emergency?"

"Oh no, girlie you don't want to do that," one of the men outside says.

"Spokane gallery has been broken into. There are three men inside. They have knives and they are trying to break down the office door. I am alone. Please send some help quickly," I plead.

"What's your Zip code ma'am?"

"Uh… I'm not. Wait." I place a hand to my chest to calm myself down enough to think and speak. "75169. Please hurry. I'm in terrible trouble."

The thin wood at the upper half of the door splinters. They push through a rectangular hole. I see a man's face in it. He has dark hair, hazel eyes, and a wide mouth.

"Is she alone?" I hear someone ask.

"Yeah," he says. His voice is frighteningly emotionless.

I rush to Larry's golf bag and take out the golf club with the thickest head. Then I rush to the door and swing it wildly at them. "Don't come in here. There's no money or safe in here," I shout.

I heard someone swear.

"Keep breaking the door," another voice instructs calmly.

I'm sweating adrenaline, but there is absolutely nothing I can do. My fantasy of climbing out of the window is just that, a fantasy. There are no pipes to climb down. I'll just break my neck, but I will attempt it if I see the men look like they will make it through the door before the police get here.

It is nearly ten o'clock at night and there is no one on the street, but I rush to the window, open it, and begin to scream at the top of my lungs. They swear, but they don't stop their efforts to break through my barricade. In fact, they redouble their efforts. Their unshakeable determination is scary. If they were ordinary robbers they would have left by now. At that moment I know, they have come for me. But the police station is not far and I begin to count the seconds until I hear even their sirens in the distance.

Suddenly, the pounding stops.

Then to my astonishment I hear a heavy crash. Then dull thuds. It sounds like someone rolling down the stairs. I stand frozen by the window, still clutching the golf club, and staring at the door in shock. What the hell was happening outside?

"What-the?" I hear one of them say, before what sounded like a blow follows. A grunt of pain. Thudding, hasty footsteps, more dull thuds, and then two further crashes ensue. It all seems to be happening too quickly, that I almost can't keep up. Have the police arrived? But I haven't heard a single siren.

Suddenly everything goes quiet. I don't move. I dare not even breathe.

I listen, as still as death, but there is only utter silence. I don't even blink.

What has happened? Who has come in to help me? Could Larry have returned for some reason? But he is too unfit to take on three armed and clearly dangerous men.

It takes me a few more seconds to once again summon the courage to speak. "Hello," I call.

Nothing. I swallow. What if it is a trick to get me to come out of the office? Freezing cold air coming from the open window makes me shiver. I am so terrified I can't move. I just stand there, heart crashing into my rib bones, until I hear police sirens in the distance. The adrenaline that had kept me alert is still fizzing in my blood, I rush to the door and push the cabinet off the desk, then the desk.

In minutes the police are through the front door. Immediately, I unlock the door and run downstairs only to come to a shocked stop. The three men are out cold and in a neat heap in the middle of the gallery floor. I look at the cops in shock.

"What happened?" one of them asks me.

I start blurting out what happened.

"I see security cameras. Can we see the footage?"

I don't have access to them so I call Larry. He's there in less than ten minutes. He rushed up to me. "Are you sure you're okay?"

I nod. He takes us all upstairs to the small room next to his office. We gather around him as he takes the tapes back to the moment I carry the vacuum cleaner upstairs, then he forwards to the moment the men come in. We watch in silence as they go upstairs. The camera shows an empty room for a while, then we see a man, dressed all in black with a hooded sweatshirt come in. He must know about the cameras because he keeps his face turned away from it or downcast.

I inhale sharply. I know that man. One moment he is standing at the door, the next he has streaked up the stairs, but so fast he is a blur.

Larry gasps.

"What the fuck?" one of the cops mutters, and they all lean closer in amazement.

Suddenly one of the intruders comes crashing down the stairs, followed by another, then another. The hooded man comes down the stairs, lifts the men and tosses them all together onto the floor, as effortlessly as if they were rag dolls. His movements are too swift; it is as if the film is on fast forward. Once the men are in an unmoving heap on the floor, he moves to the entrance and stands there silently, his back turned away from the cameras. He is so still it is almost as if he is a statue or a shadow. A few minutes later he slips out of the door. Then the police rush in. It is obvious he had waited to hear the sirens before he left.

"Do either of you recognize him?" an officer asks.

I look at Larry.

"No," he says, shaking his head. He looks completely sincere so he must not have recognized Rocco.

The officer looks at me. I shake my head slowly. "No."

The officer looks at me suspiciously. "Are you sure? Because it seemed as if he was protecting you."

I shake my head again. "No, I've never seen him in my life."

"Right. We'll arrest the intruders and take a statement from you in the morning." He turns to Larry. "We'll need those tapes too."

"Of course," Larry says.

After the police leave, Larry asks if I need a lift back.

I force a smile. "It's okay. I could do with the fresh air."

He screws on a temporary extra lock he had upstairs, and I get into the car Rocco gave me and start to drive. I drive without thinking, purely on instinct. As I park the car, William appears at the doorway.

He nods at me.

"Where is he?"

"In the study," he says in his formal voice.

I walk to the study. Every step feels like I am coming closer and closer to the edge of a cliff. I open the study door and Rocco is standing with his back to me. He is looking out of the window. He turns. He is wearing a black shirt and black jeans.

"I'm ready to hear the truth now. Who are you? And what do you want from me?"

CHAPTER 54

ROCCO

https://www.youtube.com/watch?v=k4A5XuMz_Tw
-Killing Me Softly With His Song-

"Come in and sit down, Autumn," I invite softly. My body feels rigid and tense, but it will be a relief to finally get it out.

She walks forward and sits stiffly at the end of the chair opposite my desk. Her back ramrod straight with dread.

I remain standing. "Who... or what am I? I am the descendant of an ancient race of immortal beings who can live for many thousands of years. Our kind have lived on earth alongside humans since the beginning of time. It's a long story, but human history is not as your rulers have taught you. Anyway, our relationship with mankind was peaceful, and we were viewed as benevolent guardians, and with fear. We were called the Shining Ones, and there were many glowing accounts of us in your most ancient texts and could be found in all great libraries, but they are all buried under the sea now.

"Originally, we were the keepers of knowledge and guardians of humanity. Especially, whenever there are extinction event cataclysms on earth that happen in cycles, every twelve to fourteen thousand years. When one of these catastrophes, which we call EMPOCs, happen, the damage is unimaginable. There is death and destruction everywhere. Everything is obliterated. Huge parts of continents sink into the sea, drowning all its inhabitants and leaving not even a trace of their civilization, while other parts of land full of sea creatures will rise from the ocean. And sometimes the earth burned for days, obliterating everything in its path.

"The bible tells one story of a people who were devastated by a great flood, but there have been many other such cataclysms that have befallen earth. During this time, all technology is lost, and the trauma and shock is so all encompassing the survivors collectively suffer a mind wipe of sorts. They walk around in a daze and it has always been our kind who guided them in the rebuilding of their destroyed cities. We brought seeds that we had saved in underground vaults and taught them agriculture.

"If you've ever wondered why archeologists sometimes dig up artifacts that carbon date back to hundreds and thousands of years, but those items show signs of being cut by laser machinery or made by some other historically impossible technology and advances, it is because the real history of the earth has been deliberately hidden from you. Humankind has attained greater heights during other cycles of civilization."

She stares at me, her face white and incredulous. Her body frozen in shock.

"During the golden age of Egypt, my descendants took a wrong turn. The same way the fall of humankind was caused by Eve being tempted into eating the forbidden fruit, one of us was seduced by the dark magic of the powerful priesthood of that age. She let one drop of human blood fall on her tongue, and all of us lost the ability to fly. We fell into the sin of craving blood above all else. And there we have remained ever since."

Autumn's eyes widen with shock as she gasps furiously, "No. This cannot be true." She shakes her head in disbelief and puts her hands over her ears. "No, this is a sick, sick joke. Vampires do not exist."

"It's not a joke," I say calmly. "In your heart, you know it is true. You saw me lift your car. You just didn't want to believe your own eyes so you blocked the memory. You wanted to pretend to yourself for a little longer. There is no more pretending, Autumn."

She closes her eyes, then reopens them. All the light in them is gone. She looks at me dully. "You're a *vampire.*"

Shame fills my body, but I don't look away from her. I am what I am and she is what she is. Nothing will change that. "When we fell, we became the exact opposite of what we had once been. Our skin that was illuminated and glowing with white light was taken away from us, and sunlight became deadly to us. Even the weakest ray of sun can seriously burn our skin. Physically, we were still beautiful, but we had become creatures of the night. Predators, who had to hide our true natures from humanity.

"Blood lust is something no human can ever understand. Yes, there are humans who become Satanists and they drink blood at ceremonies, and they probably quite enjoy the wickedness of it all, but it is not like that for us. The only way you can even begin to understand how it feels, is if you try to imagine you are starving.

"You haven't eaten for days, then someone puts a wonderful, favorite hot meal in front of you. You can see it, and smell it. It is right in front of you, but your hands and feet are tied and your mouth is taped shut. As I stand here now I can hear the blood rushing in your veins and I can smell it. Smoky sweet and seductively innocent. You had onions at lunch. And the adrenaline from your encounter with those intruders is still flowing in your blood. Adrenaline is like a drug. A drug far, far more addictive than the purest heroin.

"Do you want to drink my blood?" she asks, her voice shaking with horror.

"Yes, I want to," I admit brutally. "And I cannot stop the blood lust, just like you cannot stop your heart from beating, or your kidneys from doing what they are supposed to do. You see, our greatest punishment is not that we lost our light, or we have to slink and slither by night and can never feel the wonderful warmth of the sun again. It is having to endure the curse of this relentless clawing thirst for blood, day and night... for eternity."

She shakes her head in rejection at my words. "No. No. Oh, my God, no. I cannot believe this. This is just so incredible, so unbelievable. And to think I laughed when I read *Interview With A Vampire* at the absurdity of vampires going around killing humans every night. As if they wouldn't be found out. And here you are telling me you and your family are going about doing just that."

"You were right to laugh, because that is not how it is done. We couldn't, as you put it, go around killing humans every night, or we would have quickly aroused suspicion, become known to the communities that we blended into, and eventually destroyed. The solution was obvious. We had to have our own supply. Like the *Massai* tribes who drink the blood of the cattle without killing them."

She presses the heel of her hand to her head in disbelief. "Oh God, you *own* humans?"

"I don't, not anymore, but my family and the others of my kind do."

She frowns. "How? I mean where are these poor people kept?"

"In underground facilities."

She covers her gaping mouth, and shoots to her feet. "Jesus, I have to get out of here!"

"You cannot run from this any longer, Autumn. I know you are shocked and horrified, but please sit down and let me finish. I have to tell you everything because you have to know everything, no matter how distasteful. It is the truth."

Slowly, she lets herself fall back on the chair.

"When I say underground facilities, I don't mean sordid little prisons dug into the ground. Earth is not a solid ball, it is more like Swiss cheese with many deep tunnels, and massive secret underground caverns, some are humongous with ceiling heights as tall as a New York skyscraper. Some of these spaces are owned by humans and called DUMBs (deep underground military bases), but they are mostly owned by Vampire families who bought up the land above these caverns a long time ago, then built homes with secret elevators that travel into the caverns underneath.

"Some of these settlements are so big they are spread out over areas bigger than Hunter's Cross. They are powered with electricity, have rail networks, and are fitted with sophisticated aqueduct and filter systems that purify and distribute water and air. There are schools, shops, offices, coffee shops, a bar, a club for the young, a Church, a Police station, and a clinic.

"People live in comfortable units fitted with all mod-cons and have access to beautiful parks with tame birds and animals. Each person is given a hydroponic allotment garden where he/she can grow their own food if it so pleases them. They have no bills to pay, and food is plentiful so they have no need to work or produce anything of value, unless they want extra credits which will allow them to shop at the luxurious stores.

They are free to spend their time on leisure activities; painting, sewing, making furniture, distilling whiskey, playing video games. There is no crime. The inhabitants fall in love, marry, bear children, and bury their dead. They have no idea about life on the surface of the earth and yearn for nothing. Once a month they go to the clinic and donate a pint of blood. They don't know why they do it, but it has always been done that way."

She tilts her head and looks at me the way someone would if they rescued a stray kitten the night before and have walked into their kitchen and found a fully grown, hungry panther prowling around. "And your family has one of these... settlements?"

"Yes. It is called The Parallel."

CHAPTER 55

ROCCO

She looks at me intensely, her eyes shining. "Do the inhabitants of these settlements wear a thin leather anklet with a metal plate clasp that has numbers and letters inscribed on it?"

I stare at her, surprised. "Yes. How did you know?"

"I saw a naked girl wearing it in one of the rooms underneath the party you took me to. Were all those masked people vampires?"

"Yes."

"What do the letters and numbers on the metal clasp mean?"

"Not as much as you think. The anklet's real role is only one. It signifies compliance. Any human that takes it off is marked as a trouble maker and quickly removed from the settlement before he can infect anyone else."

"I see." She bites her bottom lip and looks down. Her face is troubled. "Is that girl dead now?"

"Yes. If they are brought up from the settlements, they are to be used at blood drinking orgies or hunts."

"Hunts?"

"Usually, reserved for trouble makers. They are brought up to homes, where they are allowed to think they can escape, then they are hunted down in the grounds and killed."

"Why?" she cries.

"Because some of us are addicted to adrenaline soaked blood."

I see a shiver go through her and she hugs herself pitifully. "But you yourself don't keep humans as livestock?"

"No, but I did avail myself to The Parallel until the seventeenth century."

"Why did you give it up? What do you do for blood now?" she lashes out. I understand her anger. It comes from hurt. This is not what she wants to hear from me. Unfortunately, there is worse to come.

"In the seventeenth century, I was living in Paris, in the court of Louis XV. There, I met a young girl, a maid. A simple country girl who had left her village to work at the King's grand palace. She was only seventeen and she had the lowly job to light the fire every evening and take out the chamber pots every morning, but compared to pampered, powdered shallow creatures that populated the circle of aristocrats at the Palace she was special beyond compare.

"She had rosy cheeks, clear blue eyes, and a laugh that reminded me of little bells in winter. She was honest and so innocent she went to bed with a little toy rabbit. And I wanted her. Really wanted her, which shocked me, because it was the first time I'd felt an emotion other than the intense lust for blood.

"Suddenly, I saw humans in a different light. My upbringing had made me view them solely as a means of feeding my powerful need. Even though I befriended them, dined with them, played cards with them, and had amorous liaisons with them, they were never more than sustenance to me. I was a lion with a full stomach playing with baby kudus until I was hungry again.

"Polly was the first baby kudu I wanted to keep for myself. To take care of and shower with all the wonderful things she had never known. I moved her into my castle in Bavaria. You will be surprised to know that it looked exactly like the castle on the rock you painted. The more I knew her, the more I began to love her. She was pure, everything I was not. One day she became pregnant.

"We share the same original core DNA as humans so children are possible, however our ancient rules are unambiguous and immutable. We are allowed to mate with humans, but progeny is strictly prohibited. The reason for it was self-preservation. Our ancestors knew we needed to keep our numbers carefully controlled. The chain is only as strong as its weakest link. Bringing irresponsible additions to our ranks would eventually mean the end of us all. I didn't care. I was willing to break our most sacred laws and become an outcast. I was determined to marry Polly and have our child."

I turn away from Autumn because I don't want her to see how furious I still am. I stare unseeingly out of the window. Time rolls back. I see her still body. Inside her my unborn child. I tore her belly open. I thought I could at least save the child. He was fully formed and beautiful, but his heart had stopped beating. I pulled his tiny wrinkled eyelid up, and his dead blue eye stared back at me. Grotesque. Grotesque. Grotesque.

I clench my fists and continue speaking. "But it was not to be. My parents had her killed. They thought I would forget her and go back to being the way I was, back to my blood thirsty ways, but it was too late. The real reason the Council had forbidden breeding with humans was the fear of how mixed bloods will change the ideology of our kind. How could you drink the blood of a human, how could you kill a human, when your own son is half-human? I couldn't go back to seeing humans as a great sleeping mass of throbbing hearts inside warm bodies.

"The blood lust was still there, day and night, but I had changed. And irrevocably. In the same way a vegetarian decides not to eat meat. Not because the desire for meat is gone, but because the desire to protect animals is the stronger desire."

"Does that mean you no longer drink blood?" Her voice trembles with hope.

I shake my head and see the disappointment in her eyes, but she has to know the truth. All of it. No more hiding. "I have become capable of going for months without blood, but I still need it or I feel my strength ebbing away. I get the blood from blood banks and drink it cold. That way, it does not excite the blood lust inside me."

"After all this time you still crave blood?"

She would never understand, and I never wanted her to understand the bottomless nature of the desire. I nod. "Yes."

She flinches as if I have hit her, but I note that she appears unafraid of me, and that is something to be positive about. "If the food you consume gives you no nourishment why are you so careful with what you eat?"

"There was a time I could eat the same food as humans, but since the second industrial revolution the food humans consume has slowly become more and more polluted with pesticides, preservatives, additives, heavy metals, and toxins until they are literally poison. When I turned away from my true nature, I diminished myself. Though it may seem to you as if I am much stronger than any man you know, I am not what I should be. The others of my kind are stronger, faster, and more resilient than I am. Without blood as my main sustenance my body has become less mighty, and those pollutants will make me fatally sick."

"Garlic," she says suddenly. "I've seen you eat garlic bread. It's not true that it wards off vampires?"

"Garlic has no effect on us, but the myth might have its roots in the fact that too much garlic makes the blood taste bitter. Consequently, it is not introduced as a food into the settlements."

"And the Christian cross. Is that a deterrent?"

I shake my head. "No. The only deterrent is sunlight and fire. Nothing else."

She raises both hands and presses her temples. I watch her quietly. Then she stands and begins to pace the floor. She stops abruptly, and her hands make a chopping movement. "Okay. You and your family are vampires. I get that. That's very clear. But what do you all want with me?"

CHAPTER 56

AUTUMN

https://www.youtube.com/watch?v=k2hGmoWFzaA
-Everybody hurts-

He moves away from me and sits on the leather chair behind the desk. Swinging slightly away from me he leans back and stares out of the window. There is an expression on his face I cannot describe. Perhaps it is sadness, perhaps it is longing for something he cannot have.

"It was written in our ancient book that a very, very long time ago an oracle had foretold the demise of our species. The vision warned that our corruption would become so boundless we would be unable to reproduce and we would slowly rot away. Ever since we have feared and waited for the prophecy to manifest. We didn't know how or when it would begin, or what form it would take, but fifty years ago the revelation began to manifest.

"At first the effects were slow to show, and they could be easily hidden, a sore here, a boil there, some signs of ageing, but as the years passed the decay became more and more obvious. In some cases, it was no longer even possible to hide or go out in public without attracting undue attention. The reason you were invited to a masked party was because some of us have become so unbearably hideous and repulsive it would have shocked and frightened you. Not only are our bodies breaking down, but recently we have also started to reek unbearably of decomposing flesh."

"Yes, I smelled that," I whisper, remembering the nauseating stench coming from the man I met in the room below the party. "Why are you still beautiful and why do you not smell?"

"When you witnessed me, in bed wrecked with pain, that was not a disease I caught in Asia. That started fifty years ago when all the others began to show symptoms of decline and ruin. I don't know, I might still start to stink as the end comes closer. For the moment the worst signs of decay seem to be in those who partake in human hunts."

I stare at him transfixed. The things he is telling me is beyond belief. It feels as if I am caught in a fantastic nightmare. The thought of him as a vampire is too fantastic, too horrible, and yet every piece of the jigsaw puzzle that so confused me has neatly fallen into place. Now I can see all the parts I could not figure out. Knowing all of this doesn't make me love him any less. In fact, I love him so much it hurts. Even so, I realize that I may not be as important to him as I thought. Perhaps, I am not important at all. He clearly just needs something from me. I am afraid to ask, but the words gather in my mouth and come out in a whisper.

"How do I figure in all this?"

He turns his beautiful eyes towards me, and I can see now there is no longing for something he cannot have in them. There is only a quiet resignation and a great sadness. He looks exhausted. There are blue shadows under his eyes. How could I have missed how tired he looked? The thought of him dying fills my heart with terrible pain.

"The ancient texts give us a way to stop the decay," he says softly, his eyes never leaving mine. "It was long foretold that before the next EMPOC comes, a child will be born, a human child, and she will hold our destiny in the palm of her hand. It is the law of this world. As you have sowed you will reap. Just as we have held the lives of so many humans in our heartless hands she will decide the extinction or salvation of our species."

For a second my eyes go blank. It cannot be. Surely, he doesn't mean me, but his eyes, his eyes tell me I'm not wrong. The word shoots out of me and hovers between us, "Me?"

He nods slowly. "Yes, you. Little, unassuming Autumn., you. You and you alone have the power to decide whether to preserve my kind or stand over their demise."

"How can that be?" I blurt out incredulously. "It must be a mistake. It can't be me. I have no powers at all. I'm nothing."

"It is not a mistake. It is you. The power is in your blood."

"What?"

"Yes, you carry something in your blood, a little genetic aberration that could regenerate my entire species."

"How do you know that?"

"There is something else about me you do not know. I bear the title of Count in the human world, but in our world, I am a Prince. One day I will be King. It was foretold that it would be me who would lead our kind towards salvation and redemption, or termination. For hundreds of years I looked for you. I would close my eyes and search for your blood. One day, I locked in on you. You were two years old then. Ever since that day, I've watched you, taken care of you, and protected you from the shadows."

My mouth feels dry and my voice sounds hoarse and rough. "What exactly do I have to do?"

"You must be willing to offer your blood to me in a ritual, but it is not as easy as it sounds. I must warn you that if you do, there is no turning back, you will become one of us, immortal but forever cursed with blood lust."

I walk to the chair opposite him, the horrendous weight of his words is too much to bear. I slump into it. "I will become a vampire?"

"Yes," he says simply.

"And if I say no?"

"Nothing will happen. No one can force you, Autumn. It is our immutable law. We can trick, lie, and cheat humans into interacting with us, but we must obtain their permission before we take anything from them. If your blood is acquired by force it will be of no use to any of us."

I nod slowly, even though there is nothing to nod at. "What will happen to you without my blood?"

He shrugs. "It doesn't matter. I have now told you everything. I have done the right thing, my duty to you and to my species. You must think about what you want to do and tell me your decision. Until I have your answer, I suggest you do not leave *Ze Dem Adelar*. Some of my kind do not seem to understand the concept of 'willingly offer'. William has prepared your room for you. I bid you goodnight, Autumn."

Then he stands and walks away without looking at me as if he thinks I find him too deplorable to look at. There are so many questions in my head, but I let him go. I let him go because I don't want him to see me cry. When I hear the door close, the tears fall. Now I know he never cared about me. It was all about my blood. It's the creed by which they live. They can trick, lie, and cheat humans into interacting with them as long as they ask for permission. Never in a million years did I ever think I would be in a position like this. I don't even have Sam to call and talk to. I feel so horribly, horribly alone.

For a long, long time I just sit there, my mind playing back all the incredible, fantastic, unbelievable things he had said to me. Then I stand and go up to the observatory. The house is utterly silent and my shoes echo. I walk past a large painting of a stern man from a past century who it seems to my fevered imagination to malevolently stare down at me.

I know exactly where he is. Not because I am guessing but because I can feel him. I can feel him.

I run quickly and lightly up the circular staircase until I arrive at the observatory. The circular roof is open and Rocco is sitting on the pedestal. There is a bottle of wine and a glass half-filled with red wine next to him.

He turns to look at me and I feel something inside me break.

CHAPTER 57

AUTUMN

https://www.youtube.com/watch?v=3YxaaGgTQYM
-Bring Me To Life-

"Would you like some wine, Autumn?" he asks politely, distantly. It is as if we are strangers. As if New York never happened. Or he never held me through the night when my heart was shattered by Sam's passing.

"No thank you," I say equally politely. "I want you to tell me the ending of the story of the hawk and the pigeon."

"The man chose the pigeon. He had loved it for too long to sacrifice it." His voice is deliberately flat. It's impossible to believe that he is thousands of years old. He looks so young, so beautiful… so human.

I walk up the pedestal as he takes a sip of wine and sit next to him. "Tell me what will really happen to you if I say no."

"You shouldn't concern yourself with that. I will probably outlive you."

"You don't understand. I want to help you, you will never know how much I want to... to be honest I don't even care about the blood lust thing, if you can do it, then so can I, but it goes against everything I believe in to make your sister, Daniel, your parents, and all those people at the party strong and powerful again so they can go out and hunt more humans."

He holds the glass of wine out to me. "Try it. It's really good."

I take a sip of the rich red liquid. Suddenly, I think of blood. The thought of him drinking blood makes a shiver of revulsion go through me. I give the glass back to him. "Yeah, it's good."

He puts a hand out and touches my cheek gently. "You've been crying."

I bite my lip. "It was a bit of a shock to find out you were a... vampire."

"Hmmm... yes. Shall I tell you a secret?"

"What?" I whisper.

"I never wanted you to do it." He hands me the glass of wine.

I take a sip. "Why not?"

He takes the glass back, refills it, then shrugs. "Because I was alive when they were sacrificing virgins to Pagan Gods believing it was for the greater good of their society, and I didn't agree with that either. Besides, I've long wanted to stop my parents and sister, but they always had the right of our laws behind them so I had no means. Until now."

"I love you, you know," I blurt out.

He nods slowly and looks away. I don't know why, but I feel as if he is dying right before my eyes. "I know that, Autumn, but you know we can't be together, right?"

I try to not let him see how hurt I feel. "Why not?"

He smiles ruefully. "Because my kind are not only blood-thirsty, they are also vengeful and spiteful. They will not allow us to ride off into the sunset together while they decay slowly and horribly. In fact, once they know they have nothing to lose anymore, they may even try to force you to take part in the ritual. Done that way, you will certainly die a painful death."

An icy finger runs down my spine. "What does the ritual entail?"

"Basically, I consume your blood," he says impassively.

"That's it?"

His lips twist. "As far as you're concerned, yeah. The most important thing for rituals is timing. The ceremony can only be done when the alignment of stars is favorable. The next window of opportunity is in four days, and the one after that will be in twelve years. That is the reason my family was so anxious for me to tell you as soon as possible. None of it matters now, you will be gone before that."

"Where will I go?"

"You are going to disappear without a trace. I have your new identity ready to go. Social Security number, passport, drivers license, bank account and credit cards."

Even though I am in a strange state of disbelief and shock, I feel anger rise in me. At the thought of all these decisions being made for me as if my life was no longer my own. Other people were deciding everything for me. I snatch the bottle of wine by the neck, take a swig, and turn towards him.

"So you knew I was going to say no?"

"I would have been disappointed if you had said yes."

"The decision is harder than you think. Every fiber in my body is screaming at me to save you. I have to fight with myself to say no."

He looks down. "I have made sure you will be wealthy for the rest of your life. The hard part will be to never contact anyone from the past. Also really important: you must never again send your blood to any company promising to do a health check on you, or allow anyone to do a DNA test on you. The instant your details are uploaded onto anyone's database they will be able to track you."

I push my hair out of my face. "Where am I going?"

"Los Angeles."

"Los… Ange… les," I repeat slowly. "I've never been there."

"You'll be living in Los Angeles, the art city of America and with the greatest concentration of artists, but you'll also own a pretty cottage five minutes from the beach in Martha's Vineyard, Massachusetts."

I push my hands through my hair. "God, I feel so lost. I can't take any of this in. I think I'm still in shock."

"You have two days to get used to the idea and you must never leave this house until then."

I swing my head towards him. "What about my work at the gallery?"

"You can never go back there, Autumn."

"It's not a coincidence that I came to work at Larry's gallery, is it?"

"No. I arranged it."

"So Larry lied to me."

"No, he didn't. We are able to subtly hypnotize humans and compel them to do certain things without them knowing why they are doing it. It's a form of glamor. I put the desire to come to Hunter's Cross into your head and put hiring you into Larry's head."

I remember the way Larry had literally run out of the restaurant that first night. He felt so bad he couldn't even look me in the eye the next morning.

I stare into Rocco's beautiful eyes. "Did you never feel anything at all for me?"

His jaws clench so hard a little muscle ticks in his cheek, and he speaks, his voice strained. "Yes, of course. It is only natural."

His answer hurt me in a way I cannot describe. I swallow hard. "Do you still love Polly?"

He turns to look at me and smiles sadly. "Polly? It's been more than two hundred and fifty years since she was mine, Autumn. For many years I lived alone and without servants in our castle. Even as it began to crumble around me I spent the nights roaming the empty corridors like a madman. Even when bats and wolves came to live within the walls I didn't want to leave, but in the end the worst of the pain was gone, and I left Bavaria never to return. Still, she will remain in my heart until the day I am no more because of how she changed me."

And then I do something stupid. Something really, really stupid.

CHAPTER 58

AUTUMN

https://www.youtube.com/watch?v=9X_ViIPA-Gc
-I'd do Anything For Love-

I put my wrist against his mouth, and softly say, "Go on, drink. Drink my blood."

He leaps away from me so fast, he is a blur of movement. He stops about ten feet away, his face white and fierce, and his eyes blazing with… hunger. A hunger so feral it shocks me. He had described it, but I never imagined, never understood it could be like this. Blood lust is frightening.

He stood before me, a predator!

In a flash I feel ashamed of myself. He had turned away from his own nature because he wanted to be good, to be compassionate to my species. He chose to walk a difficult, lonely path untrodden by any of his kind. And what did I do? I gave in to a childish, petty impulse to provoke him and in doing that threw the great sacrifice he had made back in his face.

"Why did you do that?" he snarls.

I stand and take a step towards him.

Breathing hard, he takes a backward step. He is so furious I can barely recognize him. "Don't come any closer," he warns, his nostrils flaring.

"Rocco," I whisper, full of remorse.

He puts a hand out, palm facing me. "Just stay there for a moment. Don't move. Don't say anything. Calm yourself. Your heart is beating too fast."

It is true, in the strange silence of the room I can hear my heart racing. I freeze and try to compose myself, but I can see him losing the struggle to control himself. For hundreds of years he had held back the terrible need, and now it has come crashing into him. Reminding him it was never gone. It is as if I had put a syringe full of heroin in front of a junkie.

He takes a step towards me, but his eyes are glazed and unrecognizable. I feel a flash of fear. Instantly, I see a corresponding reaction in him. It makes his eyes glitter dangerously. He takes another step, but this time I face him bravely. I know he is not lost to me. He is mine. I will never be afraid of him. Not when I know I can reach into his head. We are connected. I didn't have to look for him tonight. I knew exactly where he was. And I had painted the castle that was the symbol of his greatest pain.

I stare into his eyes and in my head, I whisper, *Rocco.*

He stops in astonishment.

I never take my eyes off him, even when they fill with hot tears.

I'm sorry. I'm really sorry. I know it was a terrible thing to do. Please forgive me. I wasn't thinking. I'm just so confused and scared. I've just lost Sam and now I'm being told that being with you means helping your family carry on the monstrous practice of hunting down humans for eternity. It's no excuse, I know, but I just wanted you to stop being so cold and horrible to me. If I have only got two days left with you, I want us to be as we were before. All I'm asking is for a few good memories. That's all.

Tears roll down my face.

His clenched hands unclench. The molten fire in his eyes cool as his hunger fades. His breathing becomes calm and even. He runs his hands through his hair. "Don't ever do that again."

"I won't," I promise. Slowly, I walk up to and bury my face in his chest.

His hands claw into my hair. He breathes my scent in deeply, and rasps, "Truly, you play with fire, Autumn. You have no idea. No idea."

"I didn't understand," I whisper. "I'm so sorry."

"It's okay. I'd rather die than hurt you."

I lift my head and his mouth crushes mine, and he kisses me, deeply, passionately, hungrily. And I know he doesn't need to tell me he loves me. He loves me. A man has to love a woman to kiss like this. As if his heart is broken and the world has stopped turning. I fall into the familiar vortex of desire. I don't really realize when he lifts me off my feet and carries me in his arms to his bedroom.

He puts me on the bed and looks down at me. "You are so beautiful, Autumn, and I will miss you when you go."

Between my legs I am soaking wet. I reach out a hand and touch his leg. "Just today, can we not use the condom?"

He frowns. "No, what if you become pregnant?"

"Then I will take care of it. It will be part of you."

"What if he is born with blood lust? You won't know how to control it. Let my species die out, Autumn. It is right that we do. We have brought enough suffering and pain on this earth."

Tears fill my eyes again. "Okay, we will use the condom."

He begins to undress me. His movements are swift but gentle. My work blouse lands on the floor, my skirt is gently pulled out from under me. My bra and panties follow. Very gently he moves his palm over my hardened nipples. I gasp. The moonlight throws strange shadows on his face. I will always remember him as the man I found on the other side of midnight. An angel of the night.

I reach for the zip of his pants, but he catches my hand.

"No, not yet," he says thickly, he begins to undress himself.

CHAPTER 59

ROCCO

I rake her nipple with my teeth and she cries out. Then I spread her legs wide so she is completely exposed to me. Her little pussy quivers. I run my middle finger down her belly and over her clit then plunge my thick digit into her drenched pussy.

Her little hips writhe with anticipation.

I circle her swollen clit with my thumb and her body begins to buck. "Not so fast, baby," I growl.

I need ownership of her. My intensity for her is like nothing I've ever known. It's unquenchable.

I drop my weight on her trembling body, pinning her to the bed, trapping her underneath me. I want her under me forever. Lust ripples through me as I fist my cock. Then I bend my head and lap up her juices before I capture her mouth. As my slippery tongue thrusts into her mouth, I plunge deep into her tight pussy. She gasps at the intrusion, but as I continue to pump into her, mewling noises fall out of her mouth.

I withdraw and slam back in so brutally, she almost bangs her head against the headboard.

Bending forward, I capture her mouth and slip my tongue into it. She likes that. Likes sucking my tongue while I fuck her. While she sucks my tongue greedily I ram into her. It's a hard, frenzied fuck. My hardness filling her over and over again while those mewling noises she makes that I love so much are echoing around us.

We come together. So hard, I see stars.

Autumn

He doesn't say a word, but his eyes are full of lust and triumph. The possessive expression is beautiful. I never want it to change.

"I want to give you a blow-job," I whisper huskily, as my deviant hands reach for his cock. It is so hard it jumps out into my hand.

I kneel at his feet and as I move my head closer, he stuffs the hard shaft into my mouth.

Then he rocks his hips a few inches at a time, feeling out my mouth and gauging the distance to my throat, so he doesn't thrust into my gag reflex. There is still about three inches or so of his shaft outside my mouth.

Hearing his groans sends quivers of pleasure down my back as I kneel at his feet worshipping his cock. How strange, but it satisfies me in a way I would never have expected. The groans being torn out of his mouth are food for my heart and soul. With his fingers threaded through my hair, he gently pulls my head onto his cock further and further. Feeling him grow in my mouth makes me happy and excited beyond reason. Even once when I gag on his cock it makes me yearn for more.

I feel powerful and sexy. Deep in my heart, I know I belong to him, but I can see he is holding back. He doesn't want to hurt me. He doesn't want to come in my mouth. And I want him to. I want to push him over the edge, make him lose control and come in my mouth, and then I will know he belongs to me just as much as I belong to him.

I become lost in the act. I breathe in his scent, and taste his essence, as my whole focus goes on Rocco's cock and the lusty animal sounds rising from his mouth. I forget everything except becoming that carnal, sensual woman that makes him explode deep inside my throat.

As I slide down his cock, my whole body trembles with desire. He must have felt it, because he slides out of my mouth. He puts a condom on, then picks me up, I wrap my arms and legs around him. My pussy is wet and throbbing.

He plunges his big hard shaft into me. "You're so tight," he rasps.

He always feels so big when he first enters my pussy. I take deep gasping breaths as I remember the exquisite torture of taking all of him.

He keeps me impaled on his cock as he walks us back to the wall, knowing that my clit and pussy would be stimulated with every step. He bends his head and swallows my whimpers and mewls of delight with a deep engulfing kiss.

Immediately I feel the need to climax consume me. I don't know how it is possible, but his cock seems to move even deeper inside me. My clit and pussy are being caressed simultaneously by his rock-hard cock. Each step sets off another round of excruciatingly pleasurable explosions inside me.

"I'm going to come," I gasp.

"Not yet," he instructs.

I don't want to deny him, but the pleasure is unbearable, bordering on cruelty. I clench my teeth to try and hold back the flood of my orgasm, but it starts.

"I can't hold back," I gasp.

He pushes me hard against the wall of the bedroom and fucks me hard and deep as I continue to come for him. Each crest is more searing than the last. With the wall of the bedroom supporting me, one of his hands is free to slide into my hair and grab a fistful. He jerks my head backwards, exposing my neck. For a second I think he is going to use his teeth, but he growls against my skin, then sucks at it. He is marking me. Claiming my neck.

I feel my throat throb beneath his lips in this primal act of domination and submission. My exposed neck tells him that I trust him implicitly. My orgasm rocks my whole body as he continues to fuck me hard and deep.

"Y ou're mine, you belong to me and you always will," he growls.

Yes, I am yours," I hiss.

"Mine," he groans. "Mine."

CHAPTER 60

AUTUMN

https://www.youtube.com/watch?v=p0MdP8KeAII
-It Must Have Been Love-

I run a finger down the two faint reddish scars between Rocco's shoulder blades, his skin is cool and smooth under my finger. His whole body is flawless, except for these two marks.

"What are these lines?" I ask softly.

He turns to face me. "They are a leftover from the days when we had wings of light."

I sigh. I still can't get over the fact that I have two days left with him and I will never see him again after that. "Rocco?"

"Yeah?"

"You're not going to outlive me, are you?"

A ghost of a smile lifts his lips. "Probably not."

"How long do you think you have?" I whisper. It makes me feel terrible, because I know it is my decision that is going to destroy him. His goodness, his beauty, his kindness. It doesn't seem right.

"I don't know, but our symptoms have become more pronounced, and the decomposition greatly accelerated. In my case, I can feel each attack becoming more painful and lasting longer."

My eyes fill with tears and I dash them away. It's almost impossible to believe that a being of such vitality and magnificence has so little time left. "I'm sorry, I've become such a crybaby. Ever since Sam was taken away from me I've become so emotional."

"You cry because you have a soft heart. It is nothing to apologize for. But don't pity me, Autumn. There are things worse than death."

"But it is so unfair. You've tried so hard to be good," I wail.

"It's not unfair. I've lived for thousands of years, and I can tell you my sweetest and best victory was to conquer myself."

"You know important people, right? Why can't we ask them for help? This is big enough for the President of the United States to know."

"Presidents can do nothing for us, Autumn. All political leaders are puppets who exist simply to absorb the anger and frustration of the populace for a given number of years. There are far more powerful hidden hands behind them directing the world. And those hands know about us, but they have no interest in our activities as they know we are not permitted to get involved in human evolution, and they are free to take humanity down any path they choose."

I exhale loudly. "Holy hell, that's one conspiracy theory I always thought was one of the craziest. What's their big plan for humanity, then?"

His eyes turn bleak. "There is nothing you can do to change their plans. Telling you about them will only sadden you."

"So that's another dead end." I pause and swallow hard. "Can you not sometimes come and see me in Martha's Vineyard, or wherever it is I will be living?"

He turns on his side and faces me. "No, Autumn," he murmurs gently. "Once you leave here we can never again meet. Even if by chance you see me somewhere you must pretend you do not know me."

"I find it impossible that I will never see you again. You are a part of me." I cry. "I feel so cheated. I would have done anything, gone anywhere, given up everything for you, but how can I give away the lives of other humans without living in guilt for eternity?"

"We have two whole days left, let's make the most of it, no more talk about how sad and lonely life will be once we part. The decision is made and it is a good one. Now, what do you want to do tomorrow?" His conviction is firm, strong, and he seems utterly convinced of the rightness of my decision.

"I want to go to The Parallel," I say slowly.

"Why?"

"I want to know what life is like for them. Will you take me?"

"I haven't been to it since I met Polly, but I will take you there tomorrow night if that's what you want."

"Yes, that's what I want."

"What do you want to do in the morning?"

"Breakfast in bed, then we're making love for hours, and after that I'm going to finish my painting of you. It's my gift to you."

"That sounds like a very good plan, but it's not tomorrow yet and there is so much I want to do to you," he murmurs, swooping down to take my nipple in his mouth.

CHAPTER 61

AUTUMN

https://www.youtube.com/watch?v=b_zHQ6kFuQ0
-The Power Of Love-

Out of habit I wake up at my usual time, but in foreign surroundings. However, there is no moment when I feel disorientated. I know exactly where I am. In Rocco's bed. And I am not alone. I turn my head slowly and look at him. His face is turned towards me, but his beautiful eyes are closed in sleep. I stare at him in the gloom. His breathing is so slight it is almost undetectable. With his golden hair, flaw-less skin, and perfect features, he looks like an angel.

But he is a vampire. A living, breathing vampire. But one that doesn't hurt humans.

I feel a great sadness descend on me. There is today and there is tomorrow, then I will never see him again. I bite my lip at the terrible pain the thought causes me. I tell myself, I will have my whole life to be sad about losing him, but today and tomorrow I will live more intensely than I have ever before. I will treasure every second, and hoard it away in my head. Never to forget.

As quietly as I can I start to move away. As soon as I do, his eyes open. There is no sleepiness in them. They are as clear and as blue as they always are.

"Good morning," I greet, reaching out to touch his red lips.

"Where are you going?" he murmurs.

"I have to make some calls, then I'm getting us breakfast in bed," I say with a soft smile.

"Breakfast in bed? I've never had that."

"Well, that's what you're getting today."

He smiles and there is regret in his eyes, but all he says is, "Hurry up then. I've got a surprise for you after breakfast."

I pop a kiss on his mouth and jump out of the deliciously warm bed.

He gets on his elbow, and drawls, "Come back fast, Sexy."

God, I love him so much, it actually makes my stomach clench. I grin at him. "You can bet on that."

I pull on his shirt, button up, and run downstairs where I find William coming in from the foyer.

"Good morning, Miss Delaney," he greets crisply.

"Good morning, William. I wonder if it would be possible for me to take a breakfast tray upstairs?"

"I can send a tray up to you," he suggests.

"Well, can it be sent up to Rocco's bedroom?"

"Of course. What would you like?"

"Whatever Rocco usually has for breakfast and for me, a toasted bacon sandwich and a glass of orange juice please."

He nods. "I will bring it up as soon as it is ready."

"Thank you."

He walks away and I run into the study where I had left my purse last night. I dig out my cell phone and call Brianna. She always starts early at the bakery and I know her days off are Monday.

"What's up, babe?" she says.

"Hiya. Listen, remember how you said you were sick of the smell of vanilla and cinnamon and you wished you could work somewhere glamorous, like a gallery instead? You still think that?"

"Yeah."

"Something's come up and I have to leave Hunter's Cross for good so I was wondering if you want my job."

"Oh my God, yes. I do," she says immediately.

"Great. Let me talk to Larry and get back to you."

"Autumn, is everything okay with you?"

"Yeah, everything is just fine. I'll phone back once I've spoken to Larry."

I then call Larry.

"Autumn?" he asks in an oddly husky, sleepy voice.

"Yeah, it's me. Look, I'm really sorry, but after what happened last night I'm too afraid to come back to work. I'm actually going to leave Hunter's Cross."

"What?" His voice loses its drowsy, dreamy quality. "You're not coming back?"

"No. I'm really, really sorry about the short notice, but the good news is I'm not leaving you in the lurch. Brianna, the girl who works at the bakery, is more than happy to step into my shoes."

"That blonde girl from the bakery?"

"Yup. That's her."

"Hmmm... yeah. Okay. Ask her to give me a call and I'll set an interview up today. Now what about all your stuff? You have all your things in the backroom, right?"

"I only want the painting of the castle and the big white box with the green dress in it. I'll send someone to pick them up this evening. The rest Brianna can have or she can just bin it."

"Where is the painting and the white box?"

The painting is leaning against the wall on the right of the backroom, and the box with the dress is in the cupboard by the sink. Thanks so much, Larry, I'm really sorry to do this to you."

"Don't worry about it. I know it's been hell for you, first with Sam's accident, and then the shock of those men looking for you last night. Have you figured out what they wanted?"

"No," I say, and wince. I hate lying to Larry. He's been really good to me.

"I'll miss you, Autumn. You've been one of the best staff I've ever had."

"I'll miss you too," I say, and my voice sounds as small as a child's.

"Keep in touch, huh? Let me know where you go and if you are okay."

"Goodbye, Larry."

"Take care, Autumn."

I end the call and stare out of the window. One by one all my bridges were being burned. Then I left the study and went upstairs. Rocco and I have a large breakfast, and I lie back and enjoy my surprise. Afterwards, we go downstairs and I paint him until lunch. After lunch I go back to working on my painting. By tomorrow I will be finished. We have an early dinner then we set off for the Parallel.

CHAPTER 62

AUTUMN

The Parallel is located in a desert in Utah, right in the middle of nowhere. We fly to a private airport a few miles away then drive to it. At a certain point down a deserted road, Rocco turns into a narrow road marked Private No Trespassing. A few minutes on the bumpy dirt path and I see a structure rising from the horizon like a dark shape. But as we get closer, the car's headlights show it to be an abandoned, dilapidated farmhouse. I had imagined the entrance into another world with electric fences and armed guards.

"This is it?" I whisper.

"This is it," he echoes. "The best way to hide a secret is in plain sight." He opens the car door and gets out and I follow him. The air smells dry. We go into the house and it is in total darkness, but it would appear Rocco can see in the dark because he takes my hand and walks confidently into the inky blackness. Somewhere inside the house, on the ground floor, he opens a trap door that leads to the cellar of the house. We climb down the steps into an area that is even more frighteningly dark. Here not even the shapes of objects will detach themselves from the darkness. It is also very cold. I switch on the torch on my phone and find Rocco pulling what seems to be a false wall aside. It reveals a metal door. He puts a key into the door and it opens into another room fashioned from wooden panels. There are two wooden boxes on the floor.

He walks to the west wall, pushes the panels in a certain pattern, and part of the wall slides away to reveal what looks like elevator doors. I look at the boxes.

"What's in them?"

"Treasure. If someone gets as far as this room, the gold and silver will distract them and stop them from searching further," he replies, as his fingers move quickly over the keypad by the side of the doors.

The doors open and we step into a metal pod. The doors close soundlessly. I don't know what I thought, but it seems only seconds pass, before the doors swish open to a marble room full of light. I look at Rocco in astonishment. "I thought you said we are miles deep."

"We are. The system is built with technology still undiscovered by the humans currently inhabiting earth. Remember, we have lived through many planetary destructions and during some of those civilizations ancient humans rose to greater heights than they enjoy now."

He takes my hand and I follow him. We go out of the marble room into a beautiful house. There are servants walking about and they greet us politely, showing no surprise at our presence. I feel instantly that there is something... off about them. I cannot put my finger on it, but something is wrong.

We leave the house and go out into a sort of Japanese garden. Made out of small, perfectly raked white stones and a few well-placed brown rocks. There is a bridge and a pretty fountain that makes a soothing noise. I notice that the air is not cold, but just warm enough for me to be comfortable. It also feels clean and fresh, as if mountain air is being piped into this space.

We get to a street with rows of shops on either side of it. Everything is so clean and pretty. There are no cars, but lots of bicycles and a kind of tram on rails goes past us. We meet people who immediately smile and wish us a good evening, but again I have the same sense of disquiet that there is something not right about them. And it's not the ubiquitous leather anklets the women wear, or the leather bracelets the men sport. It is more profound than that.

They seem to be without depth, like NCPs in a video game.

There are no annoying traffic noises, no dirt anywhere, or people behaving badly, but there is such a cardboard quality to the order and tidiness that I can't help feeling as if I am taking a tour of a fake town built in a movie studio. A woman carrying her small child approaches us from the opposite direction. I see her glance at Rocco, and a flash of fear passes in her eyes. Then she quickly schools her face, and with a smile wishes us good evening. As she hurries past us, I notice she clutches her child closer to her body.

"Want to have a drink? They made good margaritas when I used to come here," Rocco says, pointing towards a bar. Music is coming from it. I recognize it to be a track from the seventies.

Feeling bemused, I nod, and we walk over to it.

Inside, it is clean and pretty. There are people seated at the tables. There is no one talking loudly, laughing or looking like they may have had too much. When we walk up to the bar, the barman smiles at Rocco. Even though it is a small community where everyone must know everyone, and Rocco and I are clearly strangers, the barman displays more NCP behavior. He shows neither surprise nor curiosity and instead utters the line he must have uttered thousands of times before.

"What can I get you, Sir?"

"Two margaritas."

The barman nods. "Two margaritas coming up." He turns away to begin making them. I look around me and to my surprise I see a riot of red curls. My heart stops. Sam! Then she stands and I see that it is not Sam. Of course, it isn't. Her friend stands too and they start to make their way towards a sign that says, restrooms. And I suddenly realize she is not wearing a leather anklet or bracelet.

I look at Rocco. "I need to use the restrooms."

It is as if he can read my mind because he frowns. "There are hidden cameras everywhere so be careful what you say to anyone."

I nod, and follow the girls. When I open the door to the restroom, the other girl is in one of the cubicles and only the redhead is at the mirror. Her eyes slide over to me.

"Good evening," she says, smoothing down her unruly red curls. Now that I am so close I can see she looks nothing like Sam, even so, I feel close to her. A desire to protect her fills my chest. She must be about the same age as me.

"Good evening," I reply, and pretend to check my appearance in the mirror.

"Are you from one of the other settlements?" she asks curiously. In her eyes I see the lively spark that is missing from all the other inhabitants of The Parallel.

It's just a small white lie, and it slips out easily. "Yes."

She pulls out a tube of lip gloss. "Which one?"

"Where's your bracelet?" I blurt out suddenly.

She stops and turns towards me. If I had said something that was intrusive and tactless to a total stranger on the surface, they would have turned around and told me to damn well mind my own business, but she doesn't.

"It didn't suit this dress so I left it at home," she explains politely.

The door of the cubicle opens and her friend comes out. She takes one look at me and steps back in fear. Her eyes dart to her friend, then back at me. "Look," she says. "We want no trouble. I've just had a baby and April has sick parents she has to take care of."

"It's all right, Daphne, she's from one of the other settlements," the redhead says, frowning at her.

"No, she isn't. I saw her come in with one of them."

The redhead's eyes widen and her face becomes pale.

I place my forefinger on my lips to indicate they should remain silent, and walk up to April. I lean close to her ear and whisper, "Always wear your leather bracelet. Tell everyone that. It is how they choose who is next to be taken away."

She nods dumbly, her green eyes shocked.

I smile at her, then I go out of the restroom. In the bar, I see Rocco standing by the bar where I left him. His eyes meet mine. "Let's go," I mouth at him.

He stands and comes over to me, and we leave the Parallel immediately.

CHAPTER 63

AUTUMN

https://www.youtube.com/watch?v=9YrsH5hT4yM
-You Don't Have To Say You Love Me-

The night flies in a daze of desire and pleasure, and before I know it dawn is already in the sky. This will be my last full day with Rocco. Tomorrow evening, after the sun goes down, I will be leaving. I look into Rocco's marvelous eyes and I want to cry with sadness. I don't know how I will be able to walk away. During the night, I'd dreamed I said yes to him. He grew fangs and bit into my neck and then all his family gathered around and bit me too. It was horrible, and I woke with a start.

"What's the matter?" he whispered in the dark. It never failed to surprise me how quickly he awakened at the slightest movement or sound.

"Just a dream," I whispered back, and kissed him.

He wrapped his arms around me and I lost myself in the taste of him. Soon this will be no more, a voice said in my head. Greedily, I sucked on his lower lip.

Now I stare into his eyes in the faint light of the dawning day. "It's my last full day with you."

Something flashes in his eyes, but so fast I do not catch it. "What do you want to do?" he asks.

My painting is nearly finished. The last few strokes I intend to execute tomorrow morning. "Well, if Raoul can go collect some stuff from my caravan for me, I want to stay in bed all day with you, go downstairs for a lovely dinner, then fall back into bed with a bottle of champagne."

"That can easily be arranged, Princess," he says with a heart-breaking smile.

So that is what we do. I send Raoul to collect my stuff and also put a note in through Zelena's door. She is a kind soul who helped in a time I was in a terrible state and I didn't want to abandon her without saying goodbye.

Then I get back into bed. For lunch we have a large perfectly cooked Spanish omelet. Rocco opens a vintage bottle of champagne. The alcohol fizzles in my veins as I lie back on the bed, my legs splayed open, and Rocco splashes freezing bubbly wine between my legs and eats me out.

I giggle until I giggle no more.

That evening I decide to wear my green dress to dinner. I wash and dry my hair so it falls in waves down one side of my neck, and apply some lipstick and mascara, then I get into the beautiful dress carefully.

I cry a little when I see myself in the mirror. I don't know where she is, or if she can see me, but I whisper, "I'll always love you."

Outside the wind howls like a wolf. I walk towards the window and see my own reflection in the glass. I still remember my first night here, and the waif who had warned me to leave before it's too late.

"Well, I'm leaving," I whisper.

Tonight is my last night. It seems unbelievable to think once I leave this house, I will never see Rocco again. I put on the only good black shoes I have and start walking towards the stairs. Rocco is waiting at the bottom. He exhales in a rush when he sees me. He stares at me as he cannot believe his eyes. The look is so intense I feel myself blushing.

"You're so beautiful, Autumn," he whispers.

"Not as beautiful as you," I whisper back, and it is true. He is an extraordinarily beautiful being. Whenever I have been with him, I have noticed everyone openly staring at him.

We have dinner in the dining room. It is lit with hundreds of candles the way it was the first night we dined here. We eat, we drink champagne, we talk, we laugh, we flirt, but inside I am so sad I want to cry. As I am eating my delicious chocolate torte that feels like clay in my mouth, tears begin to run down my face.

He comes to me, kneels down, and puts his arm around me. "Don't cry, Princess. You made the right decision, and I'm so proud of you."

I stare at him through my tears. "I think I've changed my mind," I mutter.

"Stay strong, Autumn. Don't do anything you will regret for the rest of your endless life."

"I can't. I just can't leave you."

"Will your great love for me be forever bathed in the blood of countless innocent humans?"

I flinch at the ugly thought. I know he is right. I'm being selfish.

"I'm sorry for being so weak, but it's so hard to leave you. I can't even bear the thought," I sob.

"You are young. In time you will forget me and find," he swallows hard, "someone else and you will fall in love, marry him, and have a family of your own."

I look deep into his eyes. "How will I ever find a man to equal you?"

He doesn't hesitate. "You will love again, of that I am sure. You are too beautiful not to."

I stroke his marvelously golden hair. "I know you probably don't love me like I do you, but can you just pretend and say you do. Just for tonight. It will make me feel better."

He clenches his jaw hard, and then he forces the words out, "I love you."

And I realize why he never said it, because hearing the words doesn't make me feel better at all, it breaks me. I begin to sob inconsolably. The loss of Sam and now him, it just overwhelms me. I cannot stop. The pain comes from deep inside me and I wail like a mother who has lost her child. I beat his shoulders, my hands clawing into his flesh.

I cry until I feel like a hollow drum. There is nothing inside. No pain, no love. Just emptiness. He carries me upstairs to his bedroom and lays me in his bed. We don't even make love. He just holds me and rocks me.

"Tell me about your childhood." I whisper.

"No," he says gently. "The less you know me the better. You must start to forget me, Autumn."

"All right. Maybe you're right, but I don't want to end my last night with you like this. Let's go up to the observatory and have a drink. Get drunk together on old wine. I want to remember us happy."

He smiles. "Okay."

We go upstairs and get drunk together, well, at least I do. The alcohol doesn't seem to affect him at all. I get so sloshed I do a clumsy striptease for him. There is a strange expression on his face as he watches me. Greedy, hungry, but sometimes I see flashes of pain and sadness. We make love on the pedestal under the stars and the nearly full moon. Afterwards, he gives me those herbal tablets and I fall asleep in his arms.

I wake up in Rocco's bed when it is nearly dawn. I can see the first tinge of light is already in the sky. I turn my head and see him watching me.

"Good morning," I whisper, feeling strangely calm. Perhaps, I have resigned myself to my fate, or perhaps it is the calm before the storm.

"Good morning," he whispers back.

"Did you not sleep at all?"

"No."

"Why don't you nap for an hour? I'll go down and put the finishing touches to the painting and we can spend the rest of the morning and afternoon together."

"Okay, come up when you've finished. I can't wait to see it."

I kiss him gently, tenderly, and slip out of bed. He watches me as I put on his discarded shirt. It's cold against my skin, but it still smells of him. Downstairs, I can hear the servants moving about in the other part of the house as I make my way to the library. I don't waste time. I immediately set about finishing my painting.

Finally, I stand back and examine it critically. It is without doubt my best work. He is beautiful, from his flawless skin to his sensuous red mouth, and yet somehow, I have managed to capture the loneliness and despair I sometimes see in his eyes.

I put my brush down, and see a spider, small and transparent hanging from a silver thread from the table with my painting equipment. I walk to the bar and pick up a glass, then I walk to the table and pick up a piece of paper. First, I trap the spider under the glass, then I slide the paper under the glass and pick them up together so that the spider is inside the glass with the paper as a lid. I walk to the window and open it. The sun has risen and a new day has started. Time to wake Rocco up.

Carefully, I set the spider free on the window ledge. "Be safe, little one."

Fresh, morning air hardly warmed by the sun, blows into the room as I stand watching the spider crawl away. Go have a good life, little man. My good deed for the day, I look up into the superbly manicured gardens. To my astonishment, I see a baby deer caught in the branches of a bush at the edge of the garden. I look around and see no sign of its mother.

Instinct takes over. My legs start moving. I have only one thought to free the poor animal. I run from the library and out of the front door. I sprint as fast as I can around the side of the house, then loop around towards the tall hedges of the garden, and under their cover head towards the trapped animal. I don't want to scare the helpless little thing. It is caught fast and fighting valiantly to escape.

As I get to it, I suddenly realize, to my amazement and confusion, that one of the fawn's front legs has been tied to the branches of the bushes. I fall to my knees, next to the struggling, frightened animal, and quickly begin to work at the ropes. The knot is not too complicated, and I'm pretty sure I can undo it.

Suddenly, a shadow falls over me.

I whirl my head around and see a man looming over me. He is big with a tanned, grim face and bottomless black eyes. Too late I remember Rocco telling me, I must never leave the house. He pulls a syringe out of his jacket pocket.

I gasp in shock and try to stand, but before I can even begin to rise, he grabs my arm and plunges the needle into it. I try to open my mouth and call out for help, but my tongue feels heavy and my body starts to lean sideways.

Then blackness descends.

CHAPTER 64

ROCCO

https://www.youtube.com/watch?v=YCYaALgW80c
-Stay-

Autumn!

My eyes snap open. I vault out of bed and stand, couched, tense, and listening. Everything is quiet and still. Ordinary. But I know...

She is in danger.

I close my eyes, and taking a deep breath, try to lock into her energy signature. I can still feel her, but only faintly. Something sluggish and strange about it. There is not a second to waste. Buck naked, I open my eyes and run through my bedroom, into hers, and towards the window facing the front of the house. My eyes scan the grounds and I see the man. He has her slung over his shoulder and he is running towards a waiting car.

My face twists.

I take a few steps back, and with a roar of fury, I run forward, straight into the window. The ancient glass on the window smashes into smithereens as I crash through it. I feel the air rush against my naked skin as I jump from the first floor. I land feet first on the ground and I roll once, before I right myself. Then I begin to run. The man is almost to the car. The sun is already in the sky, and I can see that soon I will be outside the shadow cast by the house.

The car door opens from inside and the man throws her in, turns back to look at me, then jumps into the front passenger seat. The car shoots forward. I know I can still reach her. I can run faster than they can drive down the mountain.

I reach the end of the shadow cast by the house, and run directly into the morning sun's deadly rays.

Instantly, my skin begins to blister, where my skin is cut, my blood actually bubbles as it is boiling. The pain is indescribable, but I can't stop. I keep running even as my flesh fries.

I try to run, but the damage has now started to cook my muscles. Every step is agony. My knees give away and I drop to the ground. My shoulders and back feel as if they are on fire and my eyes feel as if acid has spilled on them.

On my knees, I scream her name.

There is not a thing I can do as I watch the car turn the corner and go out of sight.

There is a tree about six feet away, and I start crawling towards its blessed shade. As I crawl, I feel as if my skin is melting. I get to the shade and curl up. My head feels as if it is splitting, but my shoulders have taken the brunt of the damage. They feel like they are being poached. But worse, far worse than the physical pain is the unbearable agony of knowing they have her. She was so close to escape...

"My Lord," I hear William's voice say anxiously from above.

It is impossible for me to even open my eyes anymore. The pain is excruciating. Then I feel a big, thick blanket fall over my head and body. The friction against my burnt skin makes me shudder.

"Quickly," he says. "Let's get you up to the house."

Unable to open my eyes, I allow him to lead me back to the house. Once we get indoors, he helps me up the stairs to my bedroom. He sits me on my bed.

"I will fill the bathtub with ice water," he says.

"No," I say. "Get me a glass of whiskey." My skin is burning, but inside I am as cold as ice.

He goes out and comes back in a few minutes with a glass generously filled with amber liquid. I take it from him and knock it back. I give him back the glass. Our eyes meet. "How long have you known?"

"Ten years after I came to work for you," he says quietly.

I nod. "Thank you, William."

"Can I get you anything else?" he asks, his voice polite and unruffled.

"No."

He leaves and I walk to my cupboard and open the doors. I press the buttons on a panel at the back of it and the secret door opens. I walk into the tiny room behind the cupboard. There is nothing there but a fridge. I open the door and pull out three pints of blood from it. Standing there, I drink it all.

One by one. Cold, unappetizing blood runs down my throat and into my stomach and starts to warm my insides.

I look at my hands and already I can see my skin start to heal. The regeneration process is quite beautiful and I stare a while at the way the cells weave together. The new skin is flawless, not a mark on it to show the damage it has suffered.

When the pain in my head subsides, I walk out of the cupboard and shut the panel. There is no need to hurry anymore. That old romantic plan that she could simply slip away and never be seen again is gone, but all is not lost. True they have her, but they will not hurt her, and they need me to work the ritual. Without me it would be a shot in the dark. Something they would only attempt if I do not present myself at my father's house.

I get dressed and go downstairs to my library. I can feel heat radiating from my stomach making me stronger and stronger. I walk towards the painting. I promised her I would not look until she was ready to show it to me. That day was today. I stand in front of it. The painting is marvelous. Superbly executed. A far cry from her painting of the castle. She's made me beautiful, and god-like, even though she knew I was a parasite who preyed on the life force of humans.

For a long time, I stare at its terrible beauty. Then I go to my study. I write letters and I trigger the chain of events that should play out in the event of my death.

William comes in to ask if I would like lunch, but I have no hunger.

"No," I tell him, "but come in and sit down."

He sits opposite me and looks at me politely, as he always does. As if he had never seen me in the state I was earlier. I feel a great affection for him.

I push an envelope towards him. "I'm going out this evening and I may never come back so I want you to have this. You may continue to live here for the rest of your life as the master of the house. The household bills will be paid from a trust account and you will get a yearly income that will allow you to travel and live a leisurely life. Or you could even decide to use the check inside the envelope and live a completely different life in a different part of the world."

"I hope you come back. I hope you come back with Miss Delaney. That is my greatest wish," he says quietly.

I smile at him. "I've been blessed to have you."

"No, the honor to serve you was all mine," he says loyally.

"Thank you, William. Now I have a few more final arrangements to make before I leave."

"Good luck, my Lord," he says softly. Then he stands, and walks away quickly.

CHAPTER 65

ROCCO

London

https://www.youtube.com/watch?v=XXYlFuWEuKI
-Save Your Tears-

My father's butler greets me by name, "Good evening, Count Rossetti. Your father and mother are in the Rose room."

He has never seen me before so I imagine he must have recognized me from that family portrait my mother keeps in the living room. He opens the door to the Rose room, announces me formally, and closes it behind me.

The dusky pink and gilded walls are the same, albeit a little faded. It is impossible to imagine that more than a hundred years have passed since I was last here. My father and mother are sitting on a long sofa. His deterioration is remarkable, his eyes are sunken, and his skin wrinkled and mottled, there is a seeping sore on his cheek. My mother looks unchanged, but I realize, like my sister, she is wearing a wig. Even standing two meters away from them I can smell the putrid stench of rotting flesh.

"Come and sit down," my father invites cordially.

I sit opposite them. "What's the plan?"

"What it always was," my father replies coldly.

"Where is she?"

His hands tremble slightly as he reaches for his glass of sherry. "You will see her tonight… at the ritual."

"You're forgetting something very important. She has refused to willingly take part in your ritual."

My father lunges forward suddenly, like a striking snake, his eyes glittering with cold fury. He may look weak and aged, but the ancient power and might is still coiled up inside him. "That's because you didn't do your job properly. Sometimes I wonder if you are truly from my loins. You turn away from your own nature, and now you fail at the one duty your lineage expects of you. It was a simple task. Make one human female fall in love with you, but you even managed to fuck that up."

My mother touches my father's sleeve. "Calm down darling. Rocco is more like me. He has a kind heart."

My father leans back. "Stop deluding yourself, Junia. Our son is the one who persuaded her not to take part. One look at her and I can see she is deeply in love with this fool. She would have done anything for him. I know he persuaded her not to. He wants to destroy us all."

"Yes, it's true," I snarl. "I didn't want her to do it. I want us all to die off. We don't deserve to live. We are cursed parasites."

In a flash, my father streaks across the space between us, his fist raised to deliver a blow to the side of my head. I duck easily, and he flies face-first into the sofa. I stand and move back. My mother takes the opportunity to stab her syringe filled with very strong sedative directly into my arm.

I turn and smile at her. She is breathing hard and afraid I might retaliate, but she has nothing to worry about. It is exactly what I expected from her and it is the only way I will see Autumn again, the only chance I have of saving her.

I sink down on the sofa and let the sedative take over.

CHAPTER 66

AUTUMN

Scotland

I wake up feeling strange. My head feels as if it is full of cotton wool and my tongue is stuck to the roof of my mouth. There's light from a lamp on the bedside table. Confused, I squint and look around me groggily. I am in a beautiful, but unfamiliar bedroom. And then I remember. The horror floods my mind.

The deer, the man, the jab in my arm.

Oh Rocco! I'm so sorry. I've been so stupid.

I look down and see that somebody has dressed me in a long white dress. There is a window on one wall, and I scramble out of bed and hurry to it. It is pitch black outside, but it is clear I am very high above the ground.

The door opens and Isadora walks in wearing a long red robe with gold embroidered on it. It looks grand and ceremonial. She smiles at me. "Ah, you're finally awake."

"Where am I?"

"In my father's castle on the Scottish highlands. It's a pity you woke up so late. Otherwise I could have shown you the grounds. It's very beautiful around here."

I stare at her in amazement. Scotland? They brought me all the way to Scotland. "How long have I been sleeping?"

"Would you believe a whole day and a half." She shakes her head as if scolding a child.

But clearly, they drugged me because they wanted me to sleep for all this time. "Why have you brought me here?"

She shrugs, her voice sultry with meaning. "For the ritual."

The strong scent of her perfume floats over and fills my nostrils. I straighten my spine and my voice rings out clear and loud. "The ritual cannot be done if I do not agree to it."

"Yes, that's right. Would you not like to see Rocco?"

My jaw drops in shock. "Is he here?"

She smiles again, a condescending, knowing smile. "Of course."

"Yes, I would like to see him," I whisper.

"I will take you to him, but look, the clouds have passed and you can see the moon. Isn't it beautiful?"

I don't turn to look. "Please take me to see him, Isadora."

"Follow me." She turns and goes out of the room.

I hesitate for a second, then I run barefoot after her. She moves extraordinarily fast through the castle and I have to run to keep up. My stomach is churning with sick dread as I tail her down stone steps past gloomy gray walls. There are heads of animals mounted on the walls. They stare balefully at me. We get to the main part of the castle and I can see how vast the main living room is. It has a great big fire roaring in a massive stone fireplace that is so big it is almost like a small room. There is a long dining table and a feast is set out on it. In the middle is a roasted suckling pig with an orange in its mouth.

She turns to me and winks. "We are having human guests after the ritual. Obviously, you're invited."

An icy finger of fear runs down my spine. I am not sure what she means, but no matter how I look at it, it makes me feel cold with dread. We pass the ground floor and go down a circular set of steps. It seems as if we are going right into the bowels of the castle. Here the stonework is rough and there is a strange smell in the air. All of a sudden she comes upon a door, stops, and turns to me.

"Here we are." Then she opens the door and walks in.

The floor is cold beneath my feet. I take a deep breath and come what may, follow her. I gasp at the scene before my eyes. In the lights of thousands and thousands of candles I see that we are in a large cavern-like space. The sweet smell of incense is thick in the air, and the walls consist of orange brown rock. At the far end of the space there is an altar with a thick wooden slab of dark wood on it.

Rocco is lying on it and his eyes are closed. There are metal shackles around his leg and wrists.

I fly to him and throw my arms around his chest. "I'm so sorry I left the house," I sob.

"Listen carefully," he whispers. "You have no choice now but to go through with the ritual, but afterwards I will make sure that none of them ever takes another human life."

I raise my head and look into his eyes.

"Did you understand what I said?"

I nod.

He smiles encouragingly at me. "Don't be frightened. It'll be okay. I'll never leave your side."

"I love you," I gasp.

"I love you too, Autumn… so much."

A shadow moves in my peripheral vision and I swing my head fearfully in that direction. To my shock I see Zelena. My eyes widen with astonishment. "What are you doing here?"

"She's here to carry out the ritual," Rocco's sister drawls.

Suddenly, I realize what that statement actually means and I shake my head in disbelief. I stupidly sent her a goodbye note because I truly cared about her, but she told them I was leaving. I grasp the pendant she gave me, rip it from my neck, and fling it towards her. It hits her belly and falls at her feet. Still she does nothing. Says nothing. For some weird reason her betrayal really cuts. I had trusted her implicitly.

"You betrayed me," I scream. "For what? Thirty pieces of silver?"

"Immortality. That's what is on offer tonight," Rocco's sister answers for her, looking at me with avid eyes. It is almost as if she enjoys seeing me hurt and in pain.

I ignore her and turn to Zelena. "Are you going to become one of them? Hunt humans down and suck their blood?"

Rocco's sister laughs. "After tonight you'll be one of us too, little sunshine. To be honest I really can't wait to see how high and mighty you are when the thirst for human blood comes upon you."

"I'm not going to give in," I say through clenched jaws.

She throws her head back and laughs uproarious. "Tell her, little brother. Tell her what it's like."

"If you want her to be willing you sure are going about it the wrong way," he snarls at her.

That makes her sober up quick. She forces a smile on her face. "I was just kidding. It was a joke. You know, to lighten the air." She turns to Zelena with a frown. "Isn't it nearly time?"

"Yes, it's nearly time. Your parents are on their way down and should be here any minute now. We'll start in less than half an hour."

There is a noise and the door opens. His parents walk in, both wearing red robes similar to the one worn by Isadora. I stare at them in shock. His mother appears as young as Isadora, but his father looks as if he is a hundred years old.

"Shall we begin?" he says, in his cold voice.

CHAPTER 67

AUTUMN

https://www.youtube.com/watch?v=0iAzMRKFX3c
-The Wind Beneath My Wings-

Zelena opens a big book and begins to chant. Her chanting is strange and yet hauntingly beautiful. I listen to her voice and feel almost hypnotized by it. I have to force myself not to fall into the spell she is casting. I try, but it's hard, I start to feel light-headed.

I look at Rocco.

"It's okay," he mouths. "It will hurt less."

"I love you," I mouth and let myself go. Instantly, I feel a strange warmth in the region of my solar plexus. The warmth rises until it is in the middle of my chest. It becomes stronger and I burp loudly. I look around me confused.

"Yes, let it all out. All the old blocks," his mother coos eagerly.

And suddenly out of nowhere comes a horror of what I am about to do. It makes my body shake. Out of my mouth comes the words, "I can't."

Zelena continues to sing her song. She has betrayed me, but a little voice inside me says, listen to her. She will lead you to the right path.

My body convulses. This is wrong.

"I can't," I blurt out.

His father moves so fast I do not actually see him. All I see is the glint of the knife as it flashes, then blood, a fountain of red blood pouring out of Rocco's wrist.

"What have you done?" I yell as I run towards the altar. I try to hold closed the gaping wound but blood seeps through my fingers and flows onto the dark brown slab. I turn to Zelena. "Help him," I scream.

But she doesn't take any notice of me. She just sings in that hypnotic voice that makes my insides throb. I am so frightened I feel as if I am floating above my body.

"Only you can help him now," his father says. "Give him your wrist before it is too late and let him drink your blood before he dies."

I take my wrist and lay it on his mouth. For a second he does nothing and my gaze moves to his eyes. He kisses the inside of my wrist, then I feel his sharp teeth break my skin. It doesn't hurt at all. All I can hear is Zelena's voice and all I see is Rocco's eyes. I thought I would see greed or a great hunger as the blood thirst takes over. He had denied that urge for centuries. I was even afraid I would be disgusted, but to my shock I see tears fill his beautiful eyes and run down his temples into his golden hair. I stare at him astonished. He is crying! I have never seen him cry. But here he is. Crying. Because he has to drink my blood.

"Now," Zelena commands, her voice ringing out.

And things start happening around me. The speed with which his parents and sister move is incredible. Three red flashes at the edges of my vision, and suddenly, they are upon me. His parents on either side of my neck and his sister on my wrist. The pain of their fangs inside my flesh is unbearable and I open my mouth to scream, but only a strange strangulated gasp comes out because the horrendous smell of them makes my body dry heave uncontrollably. More than the pain, it is the smell that overcomes me.

I see the terrible fear and shock in Rocco's eyes, before he turns away from my wrist and yells at Zelena. "Stop them. They are going to kill her."

She answers him calmly. "Not yet. They have not had enough."

"They are going to kill her," Rocco roars, as he tries to yank himself out of his steel bands.

Zelena doesn't answer him.

He begs her. I hear bits of his begging and pleading. He offers her all his wealth on top of the promise of immortality that his family have offered her, but she ignores him and carries on singing.

The skin on my arms turn pale with the loss of blood and I start to feel faint and cold. So cold. Even their awful smell no longer bothers me. I know I am dying. I look into Rocco's eyes. I love you, I tell him even though I am already too weak to speak. How greedily they drink from me. Like starving beasts. I feel my heartbeat become fainter. I know I am dying, but a part of me feels glad I will never be like them.

I will die a human being.

I do not know why, but I am drawn to listen to Zelena's voice. Even though she has betrayed me and Rocco, the songs she is singing are oddly familiar and dear to me. I feel as if I have heard them before. Where I do not know.

In my mind's eye I see tall weeds swaying in the wind and hear the sound of water rushing by. "Autumn," a woman's voice calls. I've heard her voice before. It is sweet and full of love. Is it an angel coming to collect me? I know I should go with her, but not yet. Let me say goodbye to my Rocco first.

More and more blood flows out of me and into their rapacious mouths, and I feel my life force ebbing away into their bodies. I can even feel them becoming strong with my blood. They have won, but I have no one to blame but myself. I sent the note to Zelena, and I left the house when I was commanded not to.

The edges of the room start to go black. It's almost like the way a photograph burns. Now the middle starts to yellow. Soon it will be all black. And I will be dead.

In a daze of pain and resignation, I look into Rocco's horrified face. He cannot believe his eyes. He fights against the metal constraints, but they are thick, meant to hold down mighty vampires. I want to tell him it's okay. Not to be sad. I don't mind dying. I never wanted to live forever. And I definitely didn't want to be a creature of the night.

I can die in peace because I know now that he loves me. I try to open my mouth to speak, but I am already too frail. I'm so cold my body is shivering. The voice in the reeds calls to me again.

"It's me, Autumn."

I gaze at Rocco's face, and let all the love in my heart shine in my dying eyes.

"No," he roars, the veins in his neck are bulging as he rails against his metal trap.

Then, suddenly, without warning, his mother jumps away from my neck with a scream of terror. Clutching her chest, she falls on the ground and starts to writhe and roll in agony. Both her husband and daughter instantly cease drinking from me, and turn to look at her.

When they let go of me, I am so weak I cannot even stay upright. I collapse on top of Rocco. Disorientated and half-alive, I watch them as if from far away. I cannot understand what is happening. Something must have gone wrong.

"What the hell is going on?" Rocco's father demands, looking from the horrible sight of his wife writhing and choking, to Zelena.

She has stopped singing and looks at him expressionlessly. "She drank without permission."

"You told us to," Rocco's father shrieks like a madman. He no longer looks old and withered, but nearly as young and powerful as Rocco. His eyes are frightening.

"I lied," Zelena says softly.

"You, you, worthless gypsy traitor," he screeches incoherently.

With blazing eyes, he picks up the same knife he'd used to cut his own son and lunges wildly at her. He stabs her in the stomach. Then his dangerous eyes widen, and he seizes his own chest and falls to the floor where he twists and writhes in extreme agony. Isadora grabs her throat and stares at her parents in horror. Then she too begins to twist on the floor in agony. Rocco's mother starts to vomit. What comes out of her is like bits of egg pudding, only they are the reddish brown color of liver. More horrendous clots heave out of her.

"Quickly, set me free, Zelena. I have to give Autumn my blood before she passes out," Rocco shouts, and I hear the desperate panic in his voice.

Blood pours out of Zelena as she crawls slowly towards us. When she arrives, she pushes me gently onto my back.

I look at her with love. She didn't betray me. I was right to trust her. My pendant. I threw it at her. Tears fill my eyes.

"Don't cry," she croaks.

"Let me loose, Zelena," Rocco begs urgently, his hands shake furiously inside the steel bands.

"It is not your blood she needs. It is mine."

"Don't do that, please. You will kill her. She needs my blood to survive," he cries frantically.

"You do not know who she is, my Prince. She was never meant to drink blood." She pulls the knife from her chest and her blood rushes out of her wound. Uncaring of her own blood loss she uses the tip of the knife to make a small cut on my chest.

"You are my granddaughter. I am your grandmother. And this was foretold," she crones in a hypnotic voice as she mixes her blood with mine.

QUOTATION

This is my command: Love each other.

-John 15:17

CHAPTER 68

AUTUMN

https://www.youtube.com/watch?v=BoXsxYf2UMA
-Sacrifice-

A strange thing happens.

Where her blood touches mine, I feel its warmth. A wonderful heat that spreads through my body. I no longer understand what is happening, but I feel my body changing. There are sounds, rushes, gurgles inside me. In the background, I can hear Rocco talking to Zelena.

"Who are you?" Rocco gasps.

"We are the great old ones, beings who have been called upon to stand in the place that was once held by your species. We are humanity's guardians now, and we agreed to lend some of our own to earth, to help and guide them during this difficult period in their evolution."

Then she reaches out a hand and unclasps the metal band closest to her. Immediately, Rocco frees himself from the other bands and moves to cradle my head in his lap.

"What's happening to her now?" he asks, looking down anxiously at me.

"She is regenerating."

A wailing sound comes from his sister as she thrashes on the floor.

"And my family? What will happen to them?"

"They will die, slowly and horribly. Unless you hasten it by stabbing them in the heart with the silver dagger in my bag."

"What about the rest of my species? What will happen to them?"

"They will all die. You will be the last vampire on earth."

"The life is ebbing out of me, but remember, hold my grand-daughter until she wakes. Do not shake her or move her even if she stops breathing," Zelena says, her voice trailing feebly.

"Zelena," Rocco calls, but there is no reply from her. Her breath comes in short gasps, then she takes no more breaths.

Suddenly, I see the weirdest, craziest thing. I see her rise from her body, but she is not old and ancient, she's tall and beautiful. She shines with white light. She reaches down and touches my body and I too begin to rise from my body.

"Am I dead?" I gasp in shock.

"No, you are not, but there are things you must see which you cannot see while you are in your human shape."

I look at Rocco and I see him holding onto my body, his face is creased with worry lines. When I look up I find that the cavern walls are fading out and another structure is taking its place. It seems almost like a cathedral with a lofty ceiling made of glass and crystal walls. A light without a source is pouring in from every direction and other beings like Zelena are flooding into the space. They are all mesmerizingly and indescribably beautiful.

Inside their midst a figure moves forward. She doesn't look like them. She looks human. My heart fills with joy. It is Sam. She smiles at me. I reach out to touch her, but my hand goes through her.

"I love you, Autumn," she says.

"I miss you so much," I tell her.

"I know, but everything is as it should be. Don't mourn for me. I am fine. Do what you came to do. We will see each other again." Then she smiles at me, turns and disappears back into the midst of the beings.

One of the beings moves forward. "You have sixty-three years left on earth." She touches the space between my forehead, and says, "This is what is going to happen to humanity in your lifetime."

"Nooooo," I cry in shock.

She retracts her finger from my forehead.

"Is there a way to control it, to make it friendly?"

"No."

I stare at the luminous being desperately. "Can they just not turn it on?"

"Unfortunately, it is too late for that."

"What is to be done then?"

"Wake humanity up."

"How?" I whisper. I could not even begin to imagine how I would stop the terrible future I was shown.

"To move a beach, start with a handful of sand. Begin immediately, tell your friends, teach their children, but don't tell them what you have seen, or their fear will make it a self-fulfilling prophecy. Show them the true power and light that lies hidden inside a human being. Wake them up to their own beauty. The evil cannot manifest when there is love."

The shining being takes a step back. "We must take our leave now."

The being that was Zelena, steps forward and smiles gently at me. There is so much pure love radiating from her. I feel a strong reluctance to let her go.

"Do you have to go?"

"Yes, my work here is done, child."

"I'm so sorry I was rude to you before. I trusted you and it hurt me terribly when I thought you had betrayed me."

"I know. Now go back into your body and hold the light for humanity. I will return for you in sixty-three years."

Suddenly, I was back in my body. The lofty cathedral-like space, Zelena, and all the beautiful beings were gone. I was back in the cavern.

"Autumn," Rocco calls.

I open my eyes and look at his pale concerned face. "Rocco," I breathe.

"Why are you crying?" he murmurs.

I touch his face sadly. "Because I have seen the tyranny that is coming on earth."

He frowns. "What did you see?"

"The singularity," I explain. "The point where human and machine intelligence becomes indistinguishable, and humanity is plugged into a global A.I. network. There will be no privacy or freedom, and all humans will be born slaves."

"Yes," he confirms gravely, "that is what our ancient books have foretold."

"But it doesn't have it to be that way," I say fiercely. "The future is not set in stone. We can still change it."

Our conversation is interrupted by a wet sound coming from one of the bodies of his family. I sit up and see their bodies moving jerkily as more and more blood clots come out of their mouths.

"Stay here," Rocco instructs, as he stands. I notice, to my surprise, that the deep cut on his wrist has completely healed over. The same has happened to me. All my wounds have healed without a trace.

I don't look as he stabs them in the heart with Zelena's silver dagger. One by one, they breathe their last. Then he comes to stand over me.

"It's finished," he says softly. Then he holds out the little pendant I had torn from my neck and flung to the ground.

I curl my fingers around it and bring it to my cheek.

"Can you walk?"

I stand, and it appears as if I have suffered no ill-effects at all from everything that has happened. "Yes, I can walk."

"Let's go," he says, as he gently gathers Zelena's inert body into his arms. We go upstairs and find the main room is full of people. They are beautifully dressed and in a celebratory mood. When they see us, they turn pale and shrink back as if they are afraid of us.

Frozen with horror, they watch us walk out of the castle.

CHAPTER 69

AUTUMN

https://www.youtube.com/watch?v=bjrOcrisGyI
-Up Where We Belong-

I do not know how Rocco managed it but we are allowed to bring Zelena's body with us back to the States. William opens the door for us.

"Welcome back, my Lord, Miss Delaney," he says, stepping back from the front door. His voice is as polite as it always was, but his eyes shine with a secret joy.

Rocco nods at him. "It's good to see you again, William."

William swallows so hard, his Adam's apple bobs in his throat. "At your service, my Lord."

Before we let ourselves feel the relief we have of coming home we bury Zelena. In the darkness, Rocco himself digs a grave in a special spot in a sunny corner of the garden facing south, so I can see her from our bedroom every day I wake.

Rocco holds my hand as I say a prayer for her. I can't help the tear that runs down my face. I understand that she has finished her job on earth and I understand I will see her again, but she was my guardian angel. Rocco wipes away the tear with his thumb.

Then we walk back to the house hand in hand.

We go upstairs and lay on the bed. I turn to look at Rocco. The soft light from the lamp falls on his cheekbones making them glow. God, I love this man so much there are butterflies in my belly.

"It feels as if a lifetime has passed since I was last here," I breathe.

"You'll never know how terrible I felt when I saw that man drive away with you. The helpless rage I felt when I couldn't come after you. I never want to be without you again, Autumn. It was unbearable."

"Oh, Rocco. I'm sorry I made you suffer, but you'll never be without me again, my love. I belong to you."

He rises from the bed and goes to his cupboard. He opens it and comes back holding a black box. I sit up and watch as he opens it and puts it in front of me. There is a diamond ring inside. It looks very old and very valuable.

"Where did you get this from?" I murmur, staring at the stunning stone.

"From my art dealer. I didn't think I would ever be able to give it to you, but I accidentally saw it in his suitcase when he came to show me a new work of art he'd acquired for me."

"So it's not a family heirloom. You bought it for me?" I ask, looking up into his face.

"Will you marry me, Autumn Delaney?"

I exhale in a rush, and start grinning from ear to ear. "Thought you'd never ask, Count Rossetti."

"Is that a yes?"

"Yes, that is a big, fat yes," I shout happily, flinging my arms around his neck and clinging to him like a monkey and kissing him. He tastes like home. Finally, he is mine. And only mine.

Eventually, he puts me down on the bed and slips the ring on to my finger. "I love you, Autumn. I never thought I could love someone the way I love you. Without you, life has no meaning. I was ready to end it all if things went wrong in Scotland."

I wind my fingers in his silky hair. "I know exactly how you felt. I didn't know how I would carry on without you in God knows where."

"We will never be apart again."

"Does that mean… we can stop using condoms?"

He laughs, a rich dark sound. "Yes, I've been alone so long I want at least a dozen children running these lonely hallways."

"You better get started then, hadn't you?" I say cheekily, pulling my t-shirt over my head. Out of respect for Zelena's body we haven't had sex since we left the castle and I'm dying to have him inside me.

"Thought you'd never ask?" he says, reaching for his belt.

I take off my skirt and underwear and stare up at him as he undresses then, crouches down in front of me. Spreading my legs apart he impales me, his buck naked, hard shaft ramming into me so suddenly that there isn't time for me to adjust to his size. It shocks me into a long whimper of submission.

That drags a rumbling animal growl from his throat.

I love the way his skin feels inside me. Like hot silk. Every inch of me feels like it is on fire. My hips push upwards as my hands grab his firm, strong buttocks and shove him deeper into me, our bodies slam together and he is in, balls deep. At that moment I feel a flash of primal possession. He fought for me and now he is mine.

And only mine.

I scratch my nails down his spine like a wildcat and wrap him so tightly to me it feels as if we are melded together. I know exactly what I want. I want every last inch of him inside me. I need to feel him in the depths of my belly.

"Make yourself come," he orders. His cock swells and jerks inside me.

"Do it," he growls.

I arch my back, press into him, and grind myself against his pubic bone until I feel a knot forming in my stomach. Just as I am about to climax, he slips his hands under me, lifts me up and begins to slam into me. All his frustrations, his fear, his anxiety about losing me is in those raging thrusts. I welcome it and he goes wild, fucking me like a feral beast until even the veins in his temples bulge.

The burn inside me turns into raging flames.

"Rocco," I cry lustily, my whole body jerking under his.

I claw at the sheets. It feels as if my body is shattering into a million pieces, but every little piece is waiting. Then it happens... the waiting is over.

His hot cum spills deep inside me, and my body clenches as if it wants to keep and give life to everyone of those precious seeds.

I feel as if I am the luckiest girl alive. I watch his face, contorted with desire, his eyes like frozen lakes of blue. Little by little I will discover what lives in those frozen lakes.

I have sixty-three years to do so.

CHAPTER 70

AUTUMN

Two days later
The Parallel
https://www.youtube.com/watch?v=YkgkThdzX-8
-Imagine-

"Remember, Autumn, that not everyone will take up the offer to leave the Parallel."

"Why not?"

"Because, my love, some people value safety more than freedom."

"I think you're wrong. Everyone in the parallel is going to want to come to the surface. Why wouldn't they? They have been stuck underground for all their miserable lives."

Together we walk to the town square. All the residents are already gathered there to hear what the announcement is going to be. Rocco goes up on the makeshift stage and tells them about the surface of the earth. He tells them they are free to choose to live here underground or to go up to the surface and try to make their own way in life. It will be difficult, he warns them, but it will be worth it. There is so much to see and do.

When he finishes speaking, a hush falls over the crowd. "Who wants to come up with us to the surface?" he asks.

For a few seconds, no one moves. I stare at them astonished. I had thought there would be a stampede of people wanting to go up to the surface. There isn't. Then the redhead, April, starts moving to the front.

"I'll go to the surface," she says.

Slowly, in twos and threes other people join her, but the majority decide to remain where they are. The thought of the surface scares them. They didn't want change. They just wanted life to go on as it had been yesterday and the day before.

As Rocco had guessed they valued their safety more than freedom.

I look at the group of about twenty people. They look a little afraid, as if it might be a trick. I smile at them. They are my first handful of sand. I will teach them what the beings taught me. I will teach them to love themselves and each other so much that even the idea of filling their bodies with nanobots connecting to a global super brain will be an unthinkable aberrance. The beach will be moved.

EPILOGUE

AUTUMN

https://www.youtube.com/watch?v=YrLk4vdY28Q
-Hallelujah-

There are many things I find out about him. He knew the great Michelangelo Buonarroti and he was actually friends with my idol, Leonardo Da Vinci. He taught me about the many hidden messages in Leonardo's work. Secret images that you could only see in the mirror. Images of beings.

I find out that when he is really happy his cheeks become pink. They became pink when I told him I was pregnant, and they remained pink and flushed all through our wedding day.

Ah, our wedding.

I'd always thought I'd wear a simple white dress (I hate the meringue look) on a bright summer day. I'd never imagined I'd wear the most fabulous dusky-gold, custom made dress with a train so long it needed April to walk behind and keep adjusting it and get married in the middle of the night.

I thought since I didn't have any close family to speak of, it would just be a few old friends from school, and work, I never thought the entire church would be packed with people neither Rocco nor I knew. They were beings with the same spiritual mission as me who had turned up to witness our union.

"Who are all these people?" Larry whispered in my ear.

"I don't know," I whispered back, mystified.

But I felt their love radiating into me as Larry walked me down the aisle. Rocco was turned towards me. I looked into Rocco's breath-taking eyes and I felt as if I must be in the most fantastic dream. How could I be so lucky?

"Do you Autumn Delaney take this man to be your lawfully wedded husband?"

"I do." Of course, I do. Do you not see what a spectacular man he is?

The beings who filled the church pews filed out silently afterwards. There was no need for words.

We flew to Paris for our honeymoon. I loved Paris by night. If you don't count the dreadful abduction episode, I'd never been outside the States and it was such an adventure. I didn't think much of French men, they were not Marlboro men, that for sure, but the women had a style all of their own. Even when they wore jeans they wore them with red lipstick and a flair that I never saw back home.

Rocco could speak French. Actually, he could speak Italian, Latin, Dutch, Finnish, Spanish, Persian, Aramaic, quite a few

German dialects, and even languages that have since been lost to time.

Rocco's personal assistant, Gabriel had arranged for me to shop at some exclusive boutiques at night. I needed two new suitcases to pack my new wardrobe. Birkin bags and spectacular silk scarves from Hermes, classy houndstooth patterned suits from Chanel, sexy leather pants from Versace, and knee-length boots from Louis Vuitton. I felt so incredibly spoilt I actually felt guilty.

"Don't," he said. "How can you begrudge me the pleasure of spending money on you."

Gabriel had also arranged, and paid a great deal of money, for the Louvre to be opened just for us to have a night tour of it. Alone, we wandered around the rooms. He knew so much. I listened to his hypnotic voice tell about the different artists, he knew so many of them and I felt so much love for him I felt as if I was floating on air.

"Mmmm…" I couldn't help uttering, when the delicious smell of crepes cooking filled my nostrils. Vanilla, eggs, and chocolate. It was coming from a stall across the street. A man in a striped t-shirt and jaunty cap was making them.

"Would you like one?" he asked.

I immediately shook my head. I knew he could not eat them. They were poison to him.

"Why not?"

"Not hungry," I said with a big smile.

"Liar," he teased. "You're dying to have some."

"For your information, I'm not dying to have it. I just commented on the smell," I denied haughtily.

"Let's get this straight," he said. "Never deny yourself anything because I can't have it. That would break my heart. I want you to have everything you want."

"I don't want the crepe," I said softly.

"Okay then. I *want* you to have it. Are you going to deny me the pleasure of seeing you eat one?"

So it came about that he bought me a crepe filled with bananas and chocolate sauce, and we sat on a bench so I could eat it.

"I feel really bad about this," I said chewing my bottom lip.

He gazed into my eyes with amazement. "Do you really think I give any importance to eating a street crepe? It is nothing to me. I have you and everything else is superfluous. If I have it, I have it, if I don't, I don't. Now will you please eat the damn thing before it becomes cold."

In our room later, I lay next to him, satiated and asked him. "Rocco, what will happen when I start to age and you don't?"

He turned to look at me. "Then I'll fall utterly and completely in love with your wrinkles."

"I'm being serious here," I mock scolding.

"Close your eyes," he whispered. "Imagine you are me. You are going to live forever, but the only thing you love in the world is going to be taken away from you in sixty-three years and there is not a thing you can do about it."

My eyes popped open and I stared at him with pity.

He nodded. "Do you get it now?"

I nodded silently.

"I have enjoyed every precious second of our time together and I'm going to keep doing that."

"Okay," I whispered and wrapped my arms around him. At that moment I loved him, more than I had thought was possible. But I was wrong, because as the years went by, I loved him even more.

And my great love was never ending. It just kept on growing and growing.

SIXTY-THREE YEARS LATER

ROCCO

https://www.youtube.com/watch?v=fCZVL_8D048
Jerusalema ikhaya lami(Jerusalem is my home)
Ngilondoloze(Guard me),
Uhambe nami(Walk with me)
Ndawo yami ayikho lana(My place is not here)
Mbuso wami awukho lana(My kingdom is not here)

I didn't attend her funeral. It was held in the day, but our children and grandchildren did. Now that the sun has set I stand by her grave and lay flowers on the fresh dirt. She didn't suffer. She wasn't sick. She simply said, "My darling, it's nearly time."

We never slept that whole night. I didn't want to miss her passing. At four in the morning she turned towards the door, and smiled. "You have come."

I didn't have to look towards the door to know there was no one there. She turned her gaze back to me.

"I have to go," she whispered.

She saw the tears in my eyes, and she whispered. "I'll wait for you."

I nodded, I couldn't speak. I held her hand tightly as if I could stop her slipping away. I couldn't. She slipped away. I lay my head on her silent chest until it was morning. Then I made arrangements for her funeral.

Some small animal scurries in the dark behind me. No point standing here. She is not here under the dirt. Slowly, I turn away and begin to walk towards my car. The air is scented with night flowers. I breathe in their sweet scent and feel no pleasure. I get into my car and drive to my home.

We have moved homes every twenty years. It was hard to stop people from being curious about the man who never ages and the couple who never go out in the day. I put the window down and drive fast, very fast. The wind rushes into my face and that gives me no pleasure either.

I get home, and there are lights in some of the rooms. Some of the staff must have stayed. William died ten years ago. Sometimes I miss him. I go to the bar and pour myself a whisky. It gives me no pleasure.

"Can I get you something to eat?" Miriam, my housekeeper asks.

"No, thank you."

"Goodnight, my Lord," she says and withdraws quietly.

The phone rings, it is my youngest daughter, Virginia. "Hello Dad. How are you?"

"Fine. I'm fine. Are you all right?"

"I was thinking of coming and staying with you tonight," she says.

"What about the kids?"

"They'll be fine with their dad for one night."

"Don't do that sweetheart. I'm fine."

"I think you shouldn't be alone tonight."

"I want to be alone. I want to think of your mother."

"Oh Dad," she whispers brokenly.

"Hey, we knew, remember. We knew she was on loan from the angels. We always knew we had to give her back and exactly how much time we had left."

She sniffs. "I know, but…"

"I'll be fine. You go and snuggle up with your husband. Every moment is precious."

"Okay, Daddy. I'll call you tomorrow."

"I love you, sweetheart."

"I love you too, Daddy."

I put the phone down and almost immediately it rings again. It is my second son. He is the most caring of my sons.

"I'm coming over, Dad," he announces.

"Why?"

"Because we can get drunk together and talk about Mom."

"Maybe we do that another time. I'm tired today."

"I'm coming over anyway."

"Don't do that, Christof. It would be pointless, I'm just about to go upstairs now."

"Dad,"

"Yeah."

"It's going to be okay. We'll work through this together as a family."

"Of course, it's going to be okay. Give the babies a kiss from me."

"I love you, Dad."

"I love you too."

I leave the phone off the hook and go upstairs. I run a hot bath, then I put the envelope addressed to all my children with the letter I wrote many years ago on the pillow. I went to the cupboard to get the silver dagger I'd used to kill my family all those years ago.

It will stop my body's ability to instantly heal wounds for long enough for me to achieve my ends. I put it on the edge of the bathtub and get into the steaming water. I close my eyes and lean back in the hot water.

Suddenly, my eyes snap open and I see her sitting on the edge of the bath next to the dagger. She looks exactly like the girl I met sixty-three years ago. So utterly beautiful. Oh, how I love you, my Autumn.

She sighs softly. "You saved the dagger?"

"Yes. I always knew I would need it again."

"Are you sure you want to do this?" she asks, her voice is loving and soft.

"Yes."

"What about the children?"

I shrug. "They have their own lives now."

"Don't you want to travel? I used to hold you back with my frail body. Now you can go back to climbing mountains."

"I have lived for thousands and thousands of years, my darling. There is nothing I have not seen or done. Nowhere I have not been. I told you the time they came and snatched you away, I do not want to carry on without you. You didn't believe me then. Well, I was telling the truth. I lived only for you and our children when they were small and needed me. There is nothing for me here anymore. I don't want to outlive them. I can think of nothing worse. I want to join you."

She tilts her head. "But it would be such a waste. You are so beautiful and you are the last vampire on earth."

"And the loneliest."

"Oh, Rocco. You might regret it."

"No, my darling. I won't. Never. Forever without you by my side? No, I don't want to live a single day without you."

"You have so much to give the world," she says.

"Just wait for me, please. I won't be long." I cut into the veins of both wrists and submerge them into water. As the lifeblood seeps out of me, I smile at her. It doesn't take very long and then I see a flash of tall reeds waving in the wind. I hear water rushing by. Then I am standing next to her. How amazing. The bloodlust is gone. I am completely free of it. Finally, finally, the torture has ended. I turn to look at the pale body resting in the bloody water, his eyes are closed, and his expression is wonderfully peaceful. No, no regret. No regrets at all.

She smiles at me. "Ready?"

I smile back. My heart feels happy again. We will never be parted ever again. We'll be together for eternity.

Our fingers link and my beauty takes me to another new adventure.

The End

Thank you so much for reading my book

This story is close to my heart so I really hope you enjoyed it. Whatever you felt when you discovered Rocco's identify, whether it was surprise, horror, delight, or just the satisfaction of knowing you had guessed it right all along, please do not rob another reader of that experience by leaving a spoiler review. Thank you kindly for your consideration.

Please leave your precious review here:
The Other Side Of Midnight

COMING SOON...

The Russian Billionaire

CHAPTER 1

CONSTANTIN

My cellphone vibrates gently on my office desk. Stephan Priory. What does he want? I reach for the phone, and the girl under the desk stops sucking my cock and stares at me with her thickly lashed baby blue eyes.

"Carry on," I instruct, as I hit the accept option.

Obediently, she continues bobbing her head up and down, her voluptuous red lips making little wet sounds. I have a thing for girls with naturally fat lips, and as it happens she was good choice as she's actually very good at this. Years of experience no doubt.

"Stephan," I say crisply into the phone.

"Good evening, Mr. Tsarnov. Sorry to disturb you, but I just wanted to give you heads up on a developing situation. Um… we're going to have a slight PR problem when the Anton scandal breaks next month."

I frown. "Why? What does that fool have to do with me?"

"Well, you know what the... er...political climate is these days if you're a Russian billionaire. Pure paranoia and guilt by association."

"I met him *once* at a party," I say, irritated.

"I know, I know, but unfortunately, there's photo circulating online of you and him at that party."

I rake my fingers through the girl's long silky hair and she moans softly. "So?"

"The problem is I've been informed by my contact at Washington Post that they're planning to run with a center page spread story of the situation, and they're going to use that photo, but cropped to seem as if you were entertaining him alone on your yacht."

The girl starts to bob faster, as I watch my glistening cock slide in and out of her mouth, I weigh my options. Take the trouble to kill the story. Nah, those self-righteous pricks at the Washington Post can go and fuck themselves. "Let them run their lies. I have survived worse. Anything else?"

"Yeah." He clears his throat. "I'm afraid, there'll be pics of you and Putin looking very chummy too."

"For fucks sake," I explode.

The girl stops and looks at me questioningly.

"Carry on," I rasp at her.

"Sorry," Stephan says.

"I wasn't talking to you," I mutter.

"Oh!" He pauses, then continues. "We need to do something about this. The Hansom Cross contract is up for grabs in two months, and they won't want to be tarnished by this scandal.

At least not if it is going to be the way the Daily Mail are planning to present it."

I close my eyes and luxuriate in the hot, wet mouth of the girl. "You obviously have a suggestion. Spit it out."

"Yes, as a matter of fact I do. We should do our own PR offensive before that. You should do something big and flashy. Something that gets you in the media and makes you get noticed for all the right reasons."

"Mmmm…"

"I was thinking about the Huntingdon Children's Hospital Charity dinner. You're going to it on the 25th of this month. One of the things they'll be auctioning off is dinner dates. I suggest you blow a million on one of the girls at the auction. It'll be a great tax free, but glamorous way to cement your philanthropist status, and it's sexy enough to make it into lots of the newspapers, maybe even the evening news. I can almost see the headlines. Billionaire Russian spends a million on one dinner date for charity."

The girl feels my dick grow larger and starts sucking harder.

"Who are these girls?" I ask, watching her cheek hallow.

"I'm not hundred percent sure, but I think they're agency girls."

"Prostitutes?"

"Of course not," Stephan cries, alarmed as only an Englishman can be. "The girls at these events are usually either society ladies, or girls supplied by an agency, usually by out of work actresses or girls wanting to earn a bit of extra money. In this case, I believe the hospital is using an agency. They'll all be really good looking though. Just pick the girl you think will bore you the least. It'll only be a couple hours of your time, but the resulting free publicity will be worth it."

"Okay," I reply, cut the line, and toss my phone back on the desk.

I inhale deeply. Fuck, this girl is good. Then I grab her glossy head, thrust my cock deep into her throat, and fill her stomach with my seed.

She did look like she could do with a good meal.

CHAPTER 2

RAINE

"Oh Raine, I'm so sorry to hear that. That's terrible. What are you going to do?" Lois, my best friend asks, her forehead creased in a deep frown.

I drop my head in my hands. "I don't know. I feel so damn helpless. Ever since dad died, things have just been going from bad to worse. Mom's working three jobs, I'm working two, and still there's nothing ever left to put aside for Madison. If we don't get her the treatment soon... something bad is going to happen."

"Look, I have some money put aside. Take it for her."

"You have a $120,000 put aside?" I joke, but it comes out sounding miserable. My heart is filled with a great bitterness, which keeps me angry and confused inside. More and more I see the world as an unfair place where undeserving fat cats in suits are given government handouts of trillions that they then immediately use to gamble on the stock markets, while ordinary, hardworking people like Mom and me are taxed so heavily we can hardly even survive.

"God," Lois breathes. "A $120,000."

"And that's just for the operation," I mutter.

"There's got to be something we can do."

I lift my head and look at her. "There is. I'm thinking of working in a strip club."

Her eyes bulge with shock. "What?"

"I know I'm not beautiful in the classic sense of the word, my mouth is too big, but a lot of guys tell me I have a sexy body and that's the important thing in those dark places, isn't it?"

"You're kidding, right?" Lois erupts incredulously.

"Drastic situations call for drastic measures. Anyway, it'll be just for a while. Just until we have saved up enough for Madison's operation and paid off our old debts."

"No, that is a crazy idea. Do you know how dangerous those strip clubs are? That's where serial killers pick off their prey. And there's drugs there, and the men who—"

"Lois," someone calls from inside the kitchen.

"Coming," Lois shouts over her shoulder, then turns back to me. "I've got to go, but don't do anything stupid. We have to talk about this. Let me see if I can get a loan from the bank or something. We'll find a way out of this problem, okay?"

I sigh. There is no bank in the world who is going to give Lois the kind of money I need. I force a smile. "Okay, let's talk about this another time. I should go home now, anyway. I've got a ton of washing and ironing to do."

Lois's boss pops her head around the back door where Lois and I are standing. "Lois," she says, then stops, when she sees me. "Hey, it's Raine, right?"

I nod. "Yeah."

She jerks her head towards the interior of the Lake club. "Go on in, Lois. I want to have a word with Raine."

Lois widens her eyes at me, then scampers through the kitchen door and disappears.

"What are you doing tonight?" her boss asks me.

"This is my night off, so I'm going home to do some housework."

"You've done bar work before, haven't you?"

"Yeah."

"Good. I think one of my bartenders has let me down. Want to work the bar for me? I'll give you twenty dollars an hour since its such short notice. It'll be about five hours work. Cash in hand."

Cash in hand. What's there to even think about it? I nod quickly. "Yeah, twenty an hour would be fine."

"Come in then. Let's see if we can find you a white shirt and vest. You can keep the black slacks you have on."

Ten minutes later, I'm standing behind the bar, in a crisp white shirt and a maroon vest, watching the great and good come pouring into the party.

"Two dirty martinis, one without an olive, please," a man drawls from one end of the bar.

"Coming up," I say and get to work.

An hour passes quickly. Then the guests sit down to dinner and a lull settles around the bar. A woman in a black dress comes to sit at one of the barstools. She must be in her mid-forties. Her hair is colored bright red and she is wearing very fashionable white rimmed glasses. She smiles at me.

"Why's a girl like you looking so sad."

"I'm not sad," I deny immediately.

"Honey, I know sadness when I see it."

"I'm not sad," I repeat, with a tense smile. A man comes to the bar and orders a beer. I put his beer on a paper coaster in front of him and turn back to the red-head.

"Fine you're not sad, but let me guess. You have money problems?"

"Who doesn't I say lightly?"

"I can help you earn some serious money, up to $50,000 and more if it goes well," she says, as she licks the thin slice of lemon that come with her drink like a cat.

CHAPTER 3

RAINE

I keep my face expressionless. "Doing what?"

"There is a gala dinner with a charity auction for the Huntington Hospital on the 25th of this month. One fun part of the auction is for the single male guests. There will be five bachelors that night so there will be five girls up for auction. The men will be bidding for the privilege of buying dinner for the girl of their choice. It's all in good fun, and both the girls and the boys are at the end of day helping to raise a lot of money for charity." She pauses to take a delicate sip of her drink. "You can be one of those five girls."

I stare at her suspiciously, incredulously. "$50,000 for going on a dinner date?"

"The fifty grand is actually for showing up and taking part. However, if your highest bidder turns to be the Russian billionaire, Konstantin Tsarnov, who is one of the five bachelor guests, then your ability to earn money grows exponentially."

My jaw drops. Is this woman serious? She sounds like a total fantasist, but she doesn't look like one. She looks very polished and her eyes glitter with intelligence and cunning. Tempted and curious, I decide to play along for a bit.

"Why? What happens if he picks me?"

"Konstantin Tsarnov has something that doesn't belong to him. He stole it from his competitor, who is my client, and my client wants his property back. So, your job will be to seduce him into taking you to his house. Once there you will simply follow the map you will be given, find the thing and exchange it for a... replacement. You don't even have to sleep with him. Invent a believable excuse and leave."

I blink. "I think you want James Bond for your job, not me."

She smiles. "James Bond wouldn't work. He likes girls." Her gaze unconsciously drops to my mouth before coming to back to my eyes. "Girls like you. The job is actually much easier than you think. By the time they realize, if they ever realize, the original is gone, you will be long gone."

I touch my mouth self-consciously. "What makes you think he will pick me?"

"To be honest I don't know if he will pick you."

"So what happens if he picks one of the other girls?"

She smiles confidently. "All the other girls have the same deal as you, so it doesn't matter which girl he picks. As far as you're concerned, you'll have dinner at a fancy restaurant with the man who picks you and as soon as you text to tell us it's done, your money will be released from escrow and sent directly into your bank account, making you $50,000 richer."

"What is this thing I am supposed to steal?"

"You wouldn't be stealing. You would be returning something to its rightful owner. It's a tiny painting of a little boy on a beach. Five inches by six inches, it's small enough to put into your purse, and if you're wondering, its value is purely sentimental. As soon as he chooses you for his dinner companion another one $150,000 will be put into escrow. Once you hand the painting over to us, the money will be released to you and you will never hear from us again."

I take a deep breath. I know she is telling the truth and to be honest I am tempted. She makes it sound like such easy money and we are so desperate for some, but another part of me, tells me there is more, much more, that she is not telling me about this job. Five girls at $50,000 each plus another $150,000 makes it $400,000 for a painting that has no value beyond sentimental. I'm not buying it. Hell, I could even end up in prison if I get caught. Even the thought sends a shiver through my body.

"So what do you say?"

"Thank you, but no. If your boss wants his property back he should really find a less underhand way of getting back."

The woman smiles, and pushes her card towards me. "Call me if you change your mind before the 25th of this month. I have a strong feeling he will go for you and you can solve our problem and all your problems in one fell swoop. I might even be open to negotiating the final price."

Then stands and leaves.

Lois's boss is approaching me so I quickly stuff the card into my pocket and get on with cleaning some glasses.

The hours pass quickly and by the time I put the key into the door of our apartment, its late. I take my shoes off and tip toe into the house. Tonight is the only night my mom doesn't have to work late so I do not want to disturb her if she has fallen asleep in front of the TV. She is not asleep on the sofa. As I pass the bathroom I hear sobbing. Fear grips my heart.

"Mom," I call.

Immediately, the sobbing stops. I turn the door handle and go into the bathroom. My mom is slumped on the floor in the dark.

"Don't switch on the light," she whispers.

I sit on the floor next to her and take her hand in mine. Her hand is like ice. "What's wrong Mom?" I ask. My heart is thumping with fear.

"The doctor called. They're going to have to bring her surgery forward. She's not doing so good, Raine. She's struggling. My baby is struggling to live."

"We'll figure it out, Mom."

"No, we won't. I didn't tell you, but I lost my shifts at the grocery store last week. They're cutting back. Not that it matters. Those shifts hardly paid for our weekly food bill."

"Mom, I think I've got a way to pay for Madison's operation," I whisper in the dark.

End of sample.

Please pre-order here:
The Russian Billionaire

ABOUT THE AUTHOR

Please click on this link to receive news of my latest releases
and great giveaways.
http://bit.ly/10e9WdE

and remember
I **LOVE** hearing from readers so by all means come and say
hello here:

ALSO BY GEORGIA LE CARRE

Owned

42 Days

Besotted

Seduce Me

Love's Sacrifice

Masquerade

Pretty Wicked (novella)

Disfigured Love

Hypnotized

Crystal Jake 1,2&3

Sexy Beast

Wounded Beast

Beautiful Beast

Dirty Aristocrat

You Don't Own Me 1 & 2

You Don't Know Me

Blind Reader Wanted

Redemption

The Heir

Blackmailed By The Beast

Submitting To The Billionaire

The Bad Boy Wants Me

Nanny & The Beast

His Frozen Heart

The Man In The Mirror